The
BROWN FAIRY BOOK

"You will have to make me your wife" said the Elf-maiden

[*This illustration is reproduced in color between pages 74 and 75.*]

The
BROWN FAIRY
BOOK

Edited by Andrew Lang

With Numerous Illustrations by H. J. Ford

DOVER PUBLICATIONS, INC.
NEW YORK

Published in Canada by General Publishing Company, Ltd., 30 Lesmill Road, Don Mills, Toronto, Ontario.

Published in the United Kingdom by Constable and Company, Ltd., 10 Orange Street, London W. C. 2.

This Dover edition, first published in 1965, is an unabridged and unaltered republication of the work first published by Longmans, Green, and Co. in 1904.

International Standard Book Number: 0-486-21438-9

Library of Congress Catalog Card Number 65-25708

Manufactured in the United States of America

Dover Publications, Inc.
180 Varick Street
New York, N. Y. 10014

DEDICATED

TO

DIANA SCOTT LANG

PREFACE

THE stories in this Fairy Book come from all quarters of the world. For example, the adventures of 'Ball-Carrier and the Bad One' are told by Red Indian grandmothers to Red Indian children who never go to school, nor see pen and ink. 'The Bunyip' is known to even more uneducated little ones, running about with no clothes at all in the bush, in Australia. You may see photographs of these merry little black fellows before their troubles begin, in 'Northern Races of Central Australia,' by Messrs. Spencer and Gillen. They have no lessons except in tracking and catching birds, beasts, fishes, lizards, and snakes, all of which they eat. But when they grow up to be big boys and girls, they are cruelly cut about with stone knives and frightened with sham bogies—'all for their good' their parents say—and I think they would rather go to school, if they had their choice, and take their chance of being birched and bullied. However, many boys might think it better fun to begin to learn hunting as soon as they can walk. Other stories, like 'The Sacred Milk of Koumongoé,' come from the Kaffirs in Africa, whose dear papas are not so poor as those in Australia, but have plenty of cattle and milk, and good mealies to eat, and live in houses like very big bee-hives, and wear clothes of a sort, though not very like our own. 'Pivi and Kabo' is a tale from the brown people in the island of New Caledonia, where a boy is never allowed to speak to or even look at his own sisters; nobody knows why, so curious are the manners of this remote island. The story shows the advantages of good manners and pleasant behaviour ; and the natives do not now cook and eat each other, but live on fish, vegetables, pork, and chickens, and dwell in houses. ' What the Rose did to the Cypress,' is a story from Persia, where the people, of course, are civilised, and much like those of whom you read in ' The Arabian Nights.' Then there are tales like ' The Fox and the Lapp ' from the very north of Europe, where it is dark for half the year and day-light for the other half. The Lapps are a people not fond of soap and water, and very much given to art magic. Then there are tales from India, told to Major Campbell, who wrote them out, by Hindoos; these stories are ' Wali Dâd the Simple-hearted,' and ' The King who would be Stronger than Fate,' but was not so clever as his daughter. From Brazil, in South America, comes ' The Tortoise and the Mischievous Monkey,' with the adventures of other animals. Other tales are told in various parts of Europe, and in many languages ; but all people, black, white, brown, red, and yellow, are like each other when they tell stories ; for these are meant for children, who like the same sort of thing, whether they go to school and wear clothes, or, on the other hand, wear skins of beasts, or even nothing at all, and live on grubs and lizards and hawks and crows and serpents, like the little Australian blacks.

The tale of ' What the Rose did to the Cypress,' is translated out of a Persian manuscript by Mrs. Beveridge. ' Pivi and Kabo ' is translated by the Editor from a French version ; ' Asmund and Signy ' by Miss Blackley ; the Indian stories by Major Campbell, and all the rest are told by Mrs. Lang, who does not give them exactly as they are told by all sorts of outlandish natives, but makes them up in the hope white people will like them, skipping the pieces which they will not like. That is how this Fairy Book was made up for your entertainment.

CONTENTS

ILLUSTRATIONS

HALFTONE PLATES

[These illustrations are reproduced in full color following page 74.]

FULL-PAGE PLATES

IN TEXT

The
BROWN FAIRY BOOK

WHAT THE ROSE DID TO THE CYPRESS [1]

ONCE upon a time a great king of the East, named Saman-lālpōsh,[2] had three brave and clever sons—Tahmāsp, Qamās, and Almās-ruh-baksh.[3]   One day, when the king was sitting in his hall of audience, his eldest son, Prince Tahmāsp, came before him, and after greeting his father with due respect, said : ' O my royal father! I am tired of the town ; if you will give me leave, I will take my servants to-morrow and will go into the country and hunt on the hill-skirts; and when I have taken some game I will come back, at evening-prayer time.'   His father consented, and sent with him some of his own trusted servants, and also hawks, and falcons, hunting dogs, cheetahs and leopards.

At the place where the prince intended to hunt he saw a most beautiful deer.   He ordered that it should not be killed, but trapped or captured with a noose.   The deer looked about for a place where he might escape from the ring of the beaters, and spied one unwatched close to the prince himself.   It bounded high and leaped right over his head, got out of the ring, and tore like the eastern wind into the waste.   The prince put spurs to his horse and pursued it ; and was soon lost to the sight of his followers.

---

[1] Translated from two Persian MSS. in the possession of the British Museum and the India Office, and adapted, with some reservations, by Annette S. Beveridge.

[2] Jessamine, ruby-decked.   [3] Life-giving diamond.

Until the world-lighting sun stood above his head in the zenith he did not take his eyes off the deer; suddenly it disappeared behind some rising ground, and with all his search he could not find any further trace of it. He was now drenched in sweat, and he breathed with pain; and his horse's tongue hung from its mouth with thirst. He dismounted and toiled on, with bridle on arm, praying and casting himself on the mercy of heaven. Then his horse fell and surrendered its life to God. On and on he went across the sandy waste, weeping and with burning breast, till at length a hill rose into sight. He mustered his strength and climbed to the top, and there he found a giant tree whose foot kept firm the wrinkled earth, and whose crest touched the very heaven. Its branches had put forth a glory of leaves, and there were grass and a spring underneath it, and flowers of many colours.

Gladdened by this sight, he dragged himself to the water's edge, drank his fill, and returned thanks for his deliverance from thirst.

He looked about him and, to his amazement, saw close by a royal seat. While he was pondering what could have brought this into the merciless desert, a man drew near who was dressed like a faqīr, and had bare head and feet, but walked with the free carriage of a person of rank. His face was kind, and wise and thoughtful, and he came on and spoke to the prince.

'O good youth! how did you come here? Who are you? Where do you come from?'

The prince told everything just as it had happened to him, and then respectfully added: 'I have made known my own circumstances to you, and now I venture to beg you to tell me your own. Who are you? How did you come to make your dwelling in this wilderness?'

To this the faqīr replied: 'O youth! it would be best for you to have nothing to do with me and to know nothing of my fortunes, for my story is fit neither for telling nor for hearing.' The prince, however, pleaded so

THE DEER ELUDES PRINCE TAHMASP

hard to be told, that at last there was nothing to be done but to let him hear.

'Learn and know, O young man! that I am King Janāngīr[1] of Babylon, and that once I had army and servants, family and treasure; untold wealth and belongings. The Most High God gave me seven sons who grew up well versed in all princely arts. My eldest son heard from travellers that in Turkīstān, on the Chinese frontier, there is a king named Quimūs, the son of Tīmūs, and that he has an only child, a daughter named Mihr-afrūz,[2] who, under all the azure heaven, is unrivalled for beauty. Princes come from all quarters to ask her hand, and on one and all she imposes a condition. She says to them: "I know a riddle; and I will marry anyone who answers it, and will bestow on him all my possessions. But if a suitor cannot answer my question I cut off his head and hang it on the battlements of the citadel." The riddle she asks is, "What did the rose do to the cypress?"

'Now, when my son heard this tale, he fell in love with that unseen girl, and he came to me lamenting and bewailing himself. Nothing that I could say had the slightest effect on him. I said: "Oh my son! if there must be fruit of this fancy of yours, I will lead forth a great army against King Quimūs. If he will give you his daughter freely, well and good; and if not, I will ravage his kingdom and bring her away by force." This plan did not please him; he said: "It is not right to lay a kingdom waste and to destroy a palace so that I may attain my desire. I will go alone; I will answer the riddle, and win her in this way." At last, out of pity for him, I let him go. He reached the city of King Quimūs. He was asked the riddle and could not give the true answer; and his head was cut off and hung upon the battlements. Then I mourned him in black raiment for forty days.

'After this another and another of my sons were seized

---

[1] World-gripper.   [2] Love-enkindler.

by the same desire, and in the end all my seven sons went, and all were killed. In grief for their death I have abandoned my throne, and I abide here in this desert, withholding my hand from all State business and wearing myself away in sorrow.'

Prince Tahmāsp listened to this tale, and then the arrow of love for that unseen girl struck his heart also. Just at this moment of his ill-fate his people came up, and gathered round him like moths round a light. They brought him a horse, fleet as the breeze of the dawn ; he set his willing foot in the stirrup of safety and rode off. As the days went by the thorn of love rankled in his heart, and he became the very example of lovers, and grew faint and feeble. At last his confidants searched his heart and lifted the veil from the face of his love, and then set the matter before his father, King Saman-lāl-pōsh. ' Your son, Prince Tahmāsp, loves distractedly the Princess Mihr-afrūz, daughter of King Quimūs, son of Tīmūs.' Then they told the king all about her and her doings. A mist of sadness clouded the king's mind, and he said to his son : ' If this thing is so, I will in the first place send a courier with friendly letters to King Quimūs, and will ask the hand of his daughter for you. I will send an abundance of gifts, and a string of camels laden with flashing stones and rubies of Badakhshān. In this way I will bring her and her suite, and I will give her to you to be your solace. But if King Quimūs is unwilling to give her to you, I will pour a whirlwind of soldiers upon him, and I will bring to you, in this way, that most consequential of girls.' But the prince said that this plan would not be right, and that he would go himself, and would answer the riddle. Then the king's wise men said : ' This is a very weighty matter; it would be best to allow the prince to set out accompanied by some persons in whom you have confidence. Maybe he will repent and come back.' So King Saman ordered all preparations for the journey to be made, and then Prince

Tahmāsp took his leave and set out, accompanied by some of the courtiers, and taking with him a string of two-humped and raven-eyed camels laden with jewels, and gold, and costly stuffs.

By stage after stage, and after many days' journeying, he arrived at the city of King Quimūs. What did he see? A towering citadel whose foot kept firm the wrinkled earth, and whose battlements touched the blue heaven. He saw hanging from its battlements many heads, but it had not the least effect upon him that these were heads of men of rank; he listened to no advice about laying aside his fancy, but rode up to the gate and on into the heart of the city. The place was so splendid that the eyes of the ages have never seen its like, and there, in an open square, he found a tent of crimson satin set up, and beneath it two jewelled drums with jewelled sticks. These drums were put there so that the suitors of the princess might announce their arrival by beating on them, after which some one would come and take them to the king's presence. The sight of the drums stirred the fire of Prince Tahmāsp's love. He dismounted, and moved towards them; but his companions hurried after and begged him first to let them go and announce him to the king, and said that then, when they had put their posses-sions in a place of security, they would enter into the all-important matter of the princess. The prince, however, replied that he was there for one thing only; that his first duty was to beat the drums and announce himself as a suitor, when he would be taken, as such, to the king, who would then give him proper lodgment. So he struck upon the drums, and at once summoned an officer who took him to King Quimūs.

When the king saw how very young the prince looked, and that he was still drinking of the fountain of wonder, he said: 'O youth! leave aside this fancy which my daughter has conceived in the pride of her beauty. No one can answer her riddle, and she has done to death many men who had had no pleasure in life nor tasted its charms. God forbid that your spring also should be ravaged by the autumn winds of martyrdom.' All his urgency, however, had no effect in making the prince withdraw. At length it was settled between them that three days should be given to pleasant hospitality and that then should follow what had to be said and done. Then the prince went to his own quarters and was treated as became his station.

King Quimūs now sent for his daughter and for her mother, Gulrukh,[1] and talked to them. He said to Mihr-afrūz: 'Listen to me, you cruel flirt! Why do you persist in this folly? Now there has come to ask your hand a prince of the east, so handsome that the very sun grows modest before the splendour of his face; he is rich, and he has brought gold and jewels, all for you, if you will marry him. A better husband you will not find.'

But all the arguments of father and mother were wasted, for her only answer was : ' O my father ! I have sworn to myself that I will not marry, even if a thousand years go by, unless someone answers my riddle, and that I will give myself to that man only who does answer it.'

The three days passed ; then the riddle was asked : ' What did the rose do to the cypress ? ' The prince had an eloquent tongue, which could split a hair, and without hesitation he replied to her with a verse : 'Only the Omnipotent has knowledge of secrets; if any man says, "I know" do not believe him.'

Then a servant fetched in the polluted, blue-eyed headsman, who asked : ' Whose sun of life has come near its setting ? ' took the prince by the arm, placed him upon the cloth of execution, and then, all merciless and stony-hearted, cut his head from his body and hung it on the battlements.

The news of the death of Prince Tahmāsp plunged his father into despair and stupefaction. He mourned for

---

[1] Rose-cheek.

MIHR-AFRUZ & PRINCE TAHMASP

him in black raiment for forty days ; and then, a few days later, his second son, Prince Qamās, extracted from him leave to go too ; and he, also, was put to death. One son only now remained, the brave, eloquent, happy-natured Prince Almās-ruh-bakhsh. One day, when his father sat brooding over his lost children, Almās came before him and said : ' O father mine ! the daughter of King Quimūs has done my two brothers to death ; I wish to avenge them upon her.' These words brought his father to tears. ' O light of your father ! ' he cried, ' I have no one left but you, and now you ask me to let you go to your death.'

' Dear father ! ' pleaded the prince, ' until I have lowered the pride of that beauty, and have set her here before you, I cannot settle down or indeed sit down off my feet.'

In the end he, too, got leave to go ; but he went without a following and alone. Like his brothers, he made the long journey to the city of Quimūs the son of Tīmūs ; like them he saw the citadel, but he saw there the heads of Tahmāsp and Qamās. He went about in the city, saw the tent and the drums, and then went out again to a village not far off. Here he found out a very old man who had a wife 120 years old, or rather more. Their lives were coming to their end, but they had never beheld face of child of their own. They were glad when the prince came to their house, and they dealt with him as with a son. He put all his belongings into their charge, and fastened his horse in their out-house. Then he asked them not to speak of him to anyone, and to keep his affairs secret. He exchanged his royal dress for another, and next morning, just as the sun looked forth from its eastern oratory, he went again into the city. He turned over in his mind without ceasing how he was to find out the meaning of the riddle, and to give them a right answer, and who could help him, and how to avenge his brothers. He wandered about the city, but heard nothing of service, for there was no one in all that land who understood the riddle of Princess Mihr-afrūz.

One day he thought he would go to her own palace and see if he could learn anything there, so he went out to her garden-house. It was a very splendid place, with a wonderful gateway, and walls like Alexander's ramparts. Many gate-keepers were on guard, and there was no chance of passing them. His heart was full of bitterness, but he said to himself : ' All will be well ! it is here I shall get what I want.' He went round outside the garden wall hoping to find a gap, and he made supplication in the Court of Supplications and prayed, ' O Holder of the hand of the helpless ! show me my way.'

While he prayed he bethought himself that he could get into the garden with a stream of inflowing water. He looked carefully round, fearing to be seen, stripped, slid into the stream and was carried within the great walls. There he hid himself till his loin cloth was dry. The garden was a very Eden, with running water amongst its lawns, with flowers and the lament of doves and the jug-jug of nightingales. It was a place to steal the senses from the brain, and he wandered about and saw the house, but there seemed to be no one there. In the fore-court was a royal seat of polished jasper, and in the middle of the platform was a basin of purest water that flashed like a mirror. He pleased himself with these sights for a while, and then went back to the garden and hid himself from the gardeners and passed the night. Next morning he put on the appearance of a madman and wandered about till he came to a lawn where several peri-faced girls were amusing themselves. On a throne, jewelled and overspread with silken stuffs, sat a girl the splendour of whose beauty lighted up the place, and whose ambergris and attar perfumed the whole air. ' That must be Mihr-afrūz,' he thought, ' she is indeed lovely.' Just then one of the attendants came to the water's edge to fill a cup, and though the prince was in hiding, his face was reflected in the water. When she saw this image she was frightened, and let her cup fall into the stream, and thought, 'Is it an angel, or a peri, or a man?' Fear and trembling took hold of her, and she screamed as women scream. Then some of the other girls came and took her to the princess who asked: 'What is the matter, pretty one?'

'O princess! I went for water, and I saw an image, and I was afraid.' So another girl went to the water and saw the same thing, and came back with the same story. The princess wished to see for herself; she rose and paced to the spot with the march of a prancing peacock. When she saw the image she said to her nurse: 'Find out who is reflected in the water, and where he lives.' Her words reached the prince's ear, he lifted up his head; she saw him and beheld beauty such as she had never seen before. She lost a hundred hearts to him, and signed to her nurse to bring him to her presence. The prince let himself be persuaded to go with the nurse, but when the princess questioned him as to who he was and how he had got into her garden, he behaved like a man out of his mind—sometimes smiling, sometimes crying, and saying: 'I am hungry,' or words misplaced and random, civil mixed with the rude.

'What a pity!' said the princess, 'he is mad!' As she liked him she said: 'He is my mad man; let no one hurt him.' She took him to her house and told him not to go away, for that she would provide for all his wants. The prince thought, 'It would be excellent if here, in her very house, I could get the answer to her riddle; but I must be silent, on pain of death.'

Now in the princess's household there was a girl called Dil-arām [1]; she it was who had first seen the image of the prince. She came to love him very much, and she spent day and night thinking how she could make her affection known to him. One day she escaped from the

[1] Heartsease.

princess's notice and went to the prince, and laid her head on his feet and said : ' Heaven has bestowed on you beauty and charm. Tell me your secret ; who are you, and how did you come here ? I love you very much, and if you would like to leave this place I will go with you. I have wealth equal to the treasure of the miserly Qarūn.' But the prince only made answer like a man distraught, and told her nothing. He said to himself, ' God forbid that the veil should be taken in vain from my secret ; that would indeed disgrace me.' So, with streaming eyes and burning breast, Dil-arām arose and went to her house and lamented and fretted.

Now whenever the princess commanded the prince's attendance, Dil-arām, of all the girls, paid him attention and waited on him best. The princess noticed this, and said : ' O Dil-arām ! you must take my madman into your charge and give him whatever he wants.' This was the very thing Dil-arām had prayed for. A little later she took the prince into a private place and she made him take an oath of secrecy, and she herself took one and swore, ' By Heaven ! I will not tell your secret. Tell me all about yourself so that I may help you to get what you want.' The prince now recognised in her words the per-fume of true love, and he made compact with her. ' O lovely girl ! I want to know what the rose did to the cypress. Your mistress cuts off men's heads because of this riddle ; what is at the bottom of it, and why does she do it ? ' Then Dil-arām answered : ' If you will promise to marry me and to keep me always amongst those you favour, I will tell you all I know, and I will keep watch about the riddle.'

' O lovely girl,' rejoined he, ' if I accomplish my pur-pose, so that I need no longer strive for it, I will keep my compact with you. When I have this woman in my power and have avenged my brothers, I will make you my solace.'

' O wealth of my life and source of my joy !' responded

The Shadow in the Stream

Dil-arām, ' I do not know what the rose did to the cypress; but so much I know that the person who told Mihr-afrūz about it is a negro whom she hides under her throne. He fled here from Wāq of the Caucasus—it is there you must make inquiry ; there is no other way of getting at the truth.' On hearing these words, the prince said to his heart, ' O my heart ! your task will yet wear away much of your life.'

He fell into long and far thought, and Dil-arām looked at him and said : ' O my life and my soul ! do not be sad. If you would like this woman killed, I will put poison into her cup so that she will never lift her head from her drugged sleep again.'

' O Dil-arām ! such a vengeance is not manly. I shall not rest till I have gone to Wāq of the Caucasus and have cleared up the matter.' Then they repeated the agreement about their marriage, and bade one another good-bye.

The prince now went back to the village, and told the old man that he was setting out on a long journey, and begged him not to be anxious, and to keep safe the goods which had been entrusted to him.

The prince had not the least knowledge of the way to Wāq of the Caucasus, and was cast down by the sense of his helplessness. He was walking along by his horse's side when there appeared before him an old man of serene countenance, dressed in green and carrying a staff, who resembled Khizr.[1] The prince thanked heaven, laid the hands of reverence on his breast and salaamed. The old man returned the greeting graciously, and asked : ' How fare you? Whither are you bound? You look like a traveller.'

' O revered saint ! I am in this difficulty : I do not know the way to Wāq of the Caucasus.' The old man of good counsel looked at the young prince and said : 'Turn back from this dangerous undertaking. Do not go ;

---

[1] Elias.

choose some other task ! If you had a hundred lives you would not bring one out safe from this journey.' But his words had no effect on the prince's resolve. ' What object have you,' the old man asked, ' in thus consuming your life ? '

' I have an important piece of business to do, and only this journey makes it possible. I must go; I pray you, in God's name, tell me the way.'

When the saint saw that the prince was not to be moved, he said : ' Learn and know, O youth ! that Wāq of Qāf is in the Caucasus and is a dependency of it. In it there are jins, demons, and peris. You must go on along this road till it forks into three ; take neither the right hand nor the left, but the middle path. Follow this for a day and a night. Then you will come to a column on which is a marble slab inscribed with Cufic characters. Do what is written there ; beware of disobedience.' Then he gave his good wishes for the journey and his blessing, and the prince kissed his feet, said good-bye, and, with thanks to the Causer of Causes, took the road.

After a day and a night he saw the column rise in silent beauty to the heavens. Everything was as the wise old man had said it would be, and the prince, who was skilled in all tongues, read the following Cufic inscription: ' O travellers ! be it known to you that this column has been set up with its tablet to give true directions about these roads. If a man would pass his life in ease and pleasantness, let him take the right-hand path. If he take the left, he will have some trouble, but he will reach his goal without much delay. Woe to him who chooses the middle path ! if he had a thousand lives he would not save one ; it is very hazardous; it leads to the Caucasus, and is an endless road. Beware of it ! '

The prince read and bared his head and lifted his hands in supplication to Him who has no needs, and prayed, ' O Friend of the traveller ! I, Thy servant, come

to Thee for succour. My purpose lies in the land of Qāf
and my road is full of peril. Lead me by it.' Then he
took a handful of earth and cast it on his collar, and said:
' O earth ! be thou my grave ; and O vest ! be thou my
winding-sheet ! ' Then he took the middle road and went
along it, day after day, with many a silent prayer, till he
saw trees rise from the weary waste of sand. They grew
in a garden, and he went up to the gate and found it a
slab of beautifully worked marble, and that near it there
lay sleeping, with his head on a stone, a negro whose
face was so black that it made darkness round him. His
upper lip, arched like an eyebrow, curved upwards to his
nostrils and his lower hung down like a camel's. Four
millstones formed his shield, and on a box-tree close by
hung his giant sword. His loin-cloth was fashioned of
twelve skins of beasts, and was bound round his waist
by a chain of which each link was as big as an elephant's
thigh.

The prince approached and tied up his horse near
the negro's head. Then he let fall the Bismillāh from his
lips, entered the garden and walked through it till he
came to the private part, delighting in the great trees, the
lovely verdure, and the flowery borders. In the inner
garden there were very many deer. These signed to him
with eye and foot to go back, for that this was enchanted
ground ; but he did not understand them, and thought their
pretty gestures were a welcome. After a while he reached
a palace which had a porch more splendid than Cæsar's,
and was built of gold and silver bricks. In its midst
was a high seat, overlaid with fine carpets, and into it
opened eight doors, each having opposite to it a marble
basin.

Banishing care, Prince Almās walked on through the
garden, when suddenly a window opened and a girl, who
was lovely enough to make the moon writhe with jealousy,
put out her head. She lost her heart to the good looks
of the prince, and sent her nurse to fetch him so that

she might learn where he came from and how he had got into her private garden where even lions and wolves did not venture. The nurse went, and was struck with amazement at the sun-like radiance of his face; she salaamed and said : 'O youth! welcome! the lady of the garden calls you; come!' He went with her and into a palace which was like a house in Paradise, and saw seated on the royal carpets of the throne a girl whose brilliance shamed the shining sun. He salaamed; she rose, took him by the hand and placed him near her. 'O young man! who are you? where do you come from? How did you get into this garden?' He told her his story from beginning to end, and Lady Latīfa [1] replied : 'This is folly! It will make you a vagabond of the earth, and lead you to destruction. Come, cease such talk! No one can go to the Caucasus. Stay with me and be thankful, for here is a throne which you can share with me, and in my society you can enjoy my wealth. I will do whatever you wish ; I will bring here King Quimūs and his daughter, and you can deal with them as you will.'

'O Lady Latīfa,' he said, 'I have made a compact with heaven not to sit down off my feet till I have been to Wāq of Qāf and have cleared up this matter, and have taken Mihr-afrūz from her father, as brave men take, and have put her in prison. When I have done all this I will come back to you in state and with a great following, and I will marry you according to the law.' Lady Latīfa arguèd and urged her wishes, but in vain ; the prince was not to be moved. Then she called to the cupbearers for new wine, for she thought that when his head was hot with it he might consent to stay. The pure, clear wine was brought; she filled a cup and gave to him. He said : 'O most enchanting sweetheart! it is the rule for the host to drink first and then the guest.' So to make him lose his head, she drained the cup; then filled it again and gave him. He drank it off, and she took a lute from one

[1] Pleasure.

PRINCE ALMAS TRANSFORMED

H. FORD

[*This illustration is reproduced in color between pages 74 and 75.*]

of the singers and played upon it with skill which witched away the sense of all who heard. But it was all in vain; three days passed in such festivities, and on the fourth the prince said : ' O joy of my eyes ! I beg now that you will bid me farewell, for my way is long and the fire of your love darts flame into the harvest of my heart. By heaven's grace I may accomplish my purpose, and, if so, I will come back to you.'

Now she saw that she could not in any way change his resolve, she told her nurse to bring a certain casket which contained, she said, something exhilarating which would help the prince on his journey. The box was brought, and she divided off a portion of what was within and gave it to the prince to eat. Then, and while he was all unaware, she put forth her hand to a stick fashioned like a snake ; she said some words over it and struck him so sharply on the shoulder that he cried out ; then he made a pirouette and found that he was a deer.

When he knew what had been done to him he thought, ' All the threads of affliction are gathered to- gether ; I have lost my last chance ! ' He tried to escape, but the magician sent for her goldsmith, who, coming, overlaid the deer-horns with gold and jewels. The kerchief which that day she had had in her hand was then tied round its neck, and this freed it from her attentions.

The prince-deer now bounded into the garden and at once sought some way of escape. It found none, and it joined the other deer, which soon made it their leader. Now, although the prince had been transformed into the form of a deer, he kept his man's heart and mind. He said to himself, ' Thank heaven that the Lady Latīfa has changed me into this shape, for at least deer are beautiful.' He remained for some time living as a deer amongst the rest, but at length resolved that an end to such a life must be put in some way. He looked again for some place by which he could get out of the magic garden.

Following round the wall he reached a lower part ; he remembered the Divine Names and flung himself over, saying, ' Whatever happens is by the will of God.' When he looked about he found that he was in the very same place he had jumped from ; there was the palace, there the garden and the deer ! Eight times he leaped over the wall and eight times found himself where he had started from ; but after the ninth leap there was a change, there was a palace and there was a garden, but the deer were gone.

Presently a girl of such moon-like beauty opened a window that the prince lost to her a hundred hearts. She was delighted with the beautiful deer, and cried to her nurse : ' Catch it ! if you will I will give you this necklace, every pearl of which is worth a kingdom.' The nurse coveted the pearls, but as she was three hundred years old she did not know how she could catch a deer. However, she went down into the garden and held out some grass, but when she went near the creature ran away. The girl watched with great excitement from the palace window, and called : ' O nurse, if you don't catch it, I will kill you ! ' ' I am killing myself,' shouted back the old woman. The girl saw that nurse tottering along and went down to help, marching with the gait of a prancing peacock. When she saw the gilded horns and the ker-chief she said: ' It must be accustomed to the hand, and be some royal pet ! ' The prince had it in mind that this might be another magician who could give him some other shape, but still it seemed best to allow himself to be caught. So he played about the girl and let her catch him by the neck. A leash was brought, fruits were given, and it was caressed with delight. It was taken to the palace and tied at the foot of the Lady Jamīla's raised seat, but she ordered a longer cord to be brought so that it might be able to jump up beside her.

When the nurse went to fix the cord she saw tears falling from its eyes, and that it was dejected and sorrowful. 'O Lady Jamīla! this is a wonderful deer, it is crying; I never saw a deer cry before.' Jamīla darted down like a flash of lightning, and saw that it was so. It rubbed its head on her feet and then shook it so sadly that the girl cried for sympathy. She patted it and said: 'Why are you sad, my heart? Why do you cry, my soul? Is it because I have caught you? I love you better than my own life.' But, spite of her comforting, it cried the more. Then Jamīla said: 'Unless I am mistaken, this is the work of my wicked sister Latīfa, who by magic art turns servants of God into beasts of the field.' At these words the deer uttered sounds, and laid its head on her feet. Then Jamīla was sure it was a man, and said: 'Be comforted, I will restore you to your own shape.' She bathed herself and ordered the deer to be bathed, put on clean raiment, called for a box which stood in an alcove, opened it and gave a portion of what was in it to the deer to eat. Then she slipped her hand under her carpet and produced a stick to which she said something. She struck the deer hard, it pirouetted and became Prince Almās.

The broidered kerchief and the jewels lay upon the ground. The prince prostrated himself in thanks to heaven and Jamīla, and said: 'O delicious person! O Chinese Venus! how shall I excuse myself for giving you so much trouble? With what words can I thank you?' Then she called for a clothes-wallet and chose out a royal dress of honour. Her attendants dressed him in it, and brought him again before the tender-hearted lady. She turned to him a hundred hearts, took his hand and seated him beside her, and said: 'O youth! tell me truly who you are and where you come from, and how you fell into the power of my sister.'

Even when he was a deer the prince had much admired Jamīla; now he thought her a thousand times more lovely than before. He judged that in truth alone was safety, and so told her his whole story. Then she

asked : ' O Prince Almās-ruh-bakhsh, do you still wish so
much to make this journey to Wāq of Qāf ? What hope is
there in it ? The road is dangerous even near here, and
this is not yet the borderland of the Caucasus. Come,
give it up ! It is a great risk, and to go is not wise. It
would be a pity for a man like you to fall into the hands of
jins and demons. Stay with me, and I will do whatever
you wish.'

' O most delicious person ! ' he answered, ' you are
very generous, and the choice of my life lies in truth in
your hands ; but I beg one favour of you. If you love me,
so do I too love you. If you really love me, do not forbid
me to make this journey, but help me as far as you can.
Then it may be that I shall succeed, and if I return with
my purpose fulfilled I will marry you according to the
law, and take you to my own country, and we will spend
the rest of our lives together in pleasure and good com-
panionship. Help me, if you can, and give me your
counsel.'

' O very stuff of my life,' replied Jamīla, ' I will give
you things that are not in kings' treasuries, and which will
be of the greatest use to you. First, there are the bow
and arrows of his Reverence the Prophet Salih. Secondly,
there is the Scorpion of Solomon (on whom be peace),
which is a sword such as no king has ; steel and stone are
one to it ; if you bring it down on a rock it will not be
injured, and it will cleave whatever you strike. Thirdly,
there is the dagger which the sage Tīmūs himself made ; this
is most useful, and the man who wears it would not bend
under seven camels' loads. What you have to do first is
to get to the home of the Sīmurgh,[1] and to make friends
with him. If he favours you, he will take you to Wāq of
Qāf ; if not, you will never get there, for seven seas are
on the way, and they are such seas that if all the kings
of the earth, and all their vazīrs, and all their wise men

---

[1] Thirty-birds.

considered for a thousand years, they would not be able to cross them.'

'O most delicious person! where is the Sīmurgh's home? How shall I get there?'

'O new fruit of life! you must just do what I tell you, and you must use your eyes and your brains, for if you don't you will find yourself at the place of the negroes, who are a bloodthirsty set; and God forbid they should lay hands on your precious person.'

Then she took the bow and quiver of arrows, the sword, and the dagger out of a box, and the prince let fall a *Bismillāh*, and girt them all on. Then Jamīla of the houri-face, produced two saddle-bags of ruby-red silk, one filled with roasted fowl and little cakes, and the other with stones of price. Next she gave him a horse as swift as the breeze of the morning, and she said : 'Accept all these things from me; ride till you come to a rising ground, at no great distance from here, where there is a spring. It is called the Place of Gifts, and you must stay there one night. There you will see many wild beasts—lions, tigers, leopards, apes, and so on. Before you get there you must capture some game. On the long road beyond there dwells a lion-king, and if other beasts did not fear him they would ravage the whole country and let no one pass. The lion is a red transgressor, so when he comes rise and do him reverence ; take a cloth and rub the dust and earth from his face, then set the game you have taken before him, well cleansed, and lay the hands of respect on your breast. When he wishes to eat, take your knife and cut pieces of the meat and set them before him with a bow. In this way you will enfold that lion-king in perfect friendship, and he will be most useful to you, and you will be safe from molestation by the negroes. When you go on from the Place of Gifts, be sure you do not take the right-hand road ; take the left, for the other leads by the negro castle, which is known as the Place of Clashing Swords, and where there are forty negro captains each over three

thousand or four thousand more. Their chief is Taram-
tāq.[1] Further on than this is the home of the Sīmurgh.'

Having stored these things in the prince's memory,
she said : ' You will see everything happen just as I have
said.' Then she escorted him a little way ; they parted,
and she went home to mourn his absence.

Prince Almās, relying on the Causer of Causes, rode
on to the Place of Gifts and dismounted at the platform.
Everything happened just as Jamīla had foretold ; when
one or two watches of the night had passed, he saw that
the open ground around him was full of such stately and
splendid animals as he had never seen before. By-and-
by, they made way for a wonderfully big lion, which was
eighty yards from nose to tail-tip, and was a magnificent
creature. The prince advanced and saluted it ; it proudly
drooped its head and forelocks and paced to the platform.
Seventy or eighty others were with it, and now encircled
it at a little distance. It laid its right paw over its left,
and the prince took the kerchief Jamīla had given him
for the purpose, and rubbed the dust and earth from its
face ; then brought forward the game he had prepared,
and crossing his hands respectfully on his breast stood
waiting before it. When it wished for food he cut off
pieces of the meat and put them in its mouth. The
serving lions also came near and the prince would have
stayed his hand, but the king-lion signed to him to feed
them too. This he did, laying the meat on the platform.
Then the king-lion beckoned the prince to come near and
said : ' Sleep at ease ; my guards will watch.' So, surrounded by the lion-guard, he slept till dawn, when the king-
lion said good-bye, and gave him a few of his own hairs
and said : ' When you are in any difficulty, burn one of
these and I will be there.' Then it went off into the jungle.

Prince Almās immediately started ; he rode till he
came to the parting of the ways. He remembered quite
well that the right-hand way was short and dangerous,

[1] Pomp and Pride.

but he bethought himself too that whatever was written
on his forehead would happen, and took the forbidden

PRINCE ALMAS BRINGS
GAME TO THE KING LION

road. By and by he saw a castle, and knew from what
Jamīla had told him that it was the Place of Clashing

Swords. He would have liked to go back by the way he had come, but courage forbade, and he said, 'What has been preordained from eternity will happen to me,' and went on towards the castle. He was thinking of tying his horse to a tree which grew near the gate when a negro came out and spied him. 'Ha!' said the wretch to himself, 'this is good; Taram-tāq has not eaten man-meat for a long time, and is craving for some. I will take this creature to him.' He took hold of the prince's reins, and said: 'Dismount, man-child! Come to my master. He has wanted to eat man-meat this long time back.' 'What nonsense are you saying?' said the prince, and other such words. When the negro understood that he was being abused, he cried: 'Come along! I will put you into such a state that the birds of the air will weep for you.' Then the prince drew the Scorpion of Solomon and struck him—struck him on the leathern belt and shore him through so that the sword came out on the other side. He stood upright for a little while, muttered some words, put out his hand to seize the prince, then fell in two and surrendered his life.

There was water close at hand, and the prince made his ablution, and then said: 'O my heart! a wonderful task lies upon you.' A second negro came out of the fort, and seeing what had been done, went back and told his chief. Others wished to be doubled, and went out, and of every one the Scorpion of Solomon made two. Then Taram-tāq sent for a giant negro named Chil-māq, who in the day of battle was worth three hundred, and said to him: 'I shall thank you to fetch me that man.'

Chil-māq went out, tall as a tower, and bearing a shield of eight millstones, and as he walked he shouted: 'Ho! blunder-head! by what right do you come to our country and kill our people? Come! make two of me.' As the prince was despicable in his eyes, he tossed aside his club and rushed to grip him with his hands. He caught him by the collar, tucked him under his arm and set off with

Chil-maq carries off Almas

him to Taram-tāq. But the prince drew the dagger of Tīmūs and thrust it upwards through the giant's armpit, for its full length. This made Chil-māq drop him and try to pick up his club; but when he stooped the mighty sword shore him through at the waist.

When news of his champion's death reached Taram-tāq he put himself at the head of an army of his negroes and led them forth. Many fell before the magic sword, and the prince laboured on in spite of weakness and fatigue till he was almost worn out. In a moment of respite from attack he struck his fire-steel and burned a hair of the king-lion; and he had just succeeded in this when the negroes charged again and all but took him prisoner. Suddenly from behind the distant veil of the desert appeared an army of lions led by their king. ' What brings these scourges of heaven here?' cried the negroes. They came roaring up, and put fresh life into the prince. He fought on, and when he struck on a belt the wearer fell in two, and when on a head he cleft to the waist. Then the ten thousand mighty lions joined the fray and tore in pieces man and horse.

Taram-tāq was left alone; he would have retired into his fort, but the prince shouted : ' Whither away, accursed one ? Are you fleeing before me?' At these defiant words the chief shouted back, ' Welcome, man ! Come here and I will soften you to wax beneath my club.' Then he hurled his club at the prince's head, but it fell harmless because the prince had quickly spurred his horse forward. The chief, believing he had hit him, was looking down for him, when all at once he came up behind and cleft him to the waist and sent him straight to hell.

The king-lion greatly praised the dashing courage of Prince Almās. They went together into the Castle of Clashing Swords and found it adorned and fitted in princely fashion. In it was a daughter of Taram-tāq, still a child. She sent a message to Prince Almās saying,

'O king of the world! choose this slave to be your handmaid. Keep her with you ; where you go, there she will
go!' He sent for her and she kissed his feet and received
the Mussulman faith at his hands. He told her he was
going a long journey on important business, and that
when he came back he would take her and her possessions
to his own country, but that for the present she must stay
in the castle. Then he made over the fort and all that
was in it to the care of the lion, saying: 'Guard them,
brother! let no one lay a hand on them.' He said good-
bye, chose a fresh horse from the chief's stable and once
again took the road.

After travelling many stages and for many days, he
reached a plain of marvellous beauty and refreshment.
It was carpeted with flowers—roses, tulips, and clover ;
it had lovely lawns, and amongst them running water.
This choicest place of earth filled him with wonder.
There was a tree such as he had never seen before ; its
branches were alike, but it bore flowers and fruit of a
thousand kinds. Near it a reservoir had been fashioned
of four sorts of stone—touchstone, pure stone, marble,
and loadstone. In and out of it flowed water like attar.
The prince felt sure this must be the place of the Sīmurgh ;
he dismounted, turned his horse loose to graze, ate some
of the food Jamīla had given him, drank of the stream
and lay down to sleep.

He was still dozing when he was aroused by the
neighing and pawing of his horse. When he could see
clearly he made out a mountain-like dragon whose heavy
breast crushed the stones beneath it into putty. He
remembered the Thousand Names of God and took the
bow of Salih from its case and three arrows from their
quiver. He bound the dagger of Tīmus firmly to his
waist and hung the scorpion of Solomon round his neck.
Then he set an arrow on the string and released it with
such force that it went in at the monster's eye right up
to the notch. The dragon writhed on itself, and belched

forth an evil vapour, and beat the ground with its head till the earth quaked. Then the prince took a second arrow and shot into its throat. It drew in its breath and would have sucked the prince into its maw, but when he was within striking distance he drew his sword and, having committed himself to God, struck a mighty blow which cut the creature's neck down to the gullet. The foul vapour of the beast and horror at its strangeness now overcame the prince, and he fainted. When he came to himself he found that he was drenched in the gore of the dead monster. He rose and thanked God for his deliverance.

The nest of the Sīmurgh was in the wonderful tree above him, and in it were young birds; the parents were away searching for food. They always told the children, before they left them, not to put their heads out of the nest; but, to-day, at the noise of the fight below, they looked down and so saw the whole affair. By the time the dragon had been killed they were very hungry and set up a clamour for food. The prince therefore cut up the dragon and fed them with it, bit by bit, till they had eaten the whole. He then washed himself and lay down to rest, and he was still asleep when the Sīmurgh came home. As a rule, the young birds raised a clamour of welcome when their parents came near, but on this day they were so full of dragon-meat that they had no choice, they had to go to sleep.

As they flew nearer, the old birds saw the prince lying under the tree and no sign of life in the nest. They thought that the misfortune which for so many earlier years had befallen them had again happened and that their nestlings had disappeared. They had never been able to find out the murderer, and now suspected the prince. 'He has eaten our children and sleeps after it; he must die,' said the father-bird, and flew back to the hills and clawed up a huge stone which he meant to let fall on the prince's head. But his mate said, 'Let us look into the nest first for to kill an innocent person would condemn us at the Day of Resurrection.' They flew nearer, and presently the young birds woke and cried, ' Mother, what have you brought for us ? ' and they told the whole story of the fight, and of how they were alive only by the favour of the young man under the tree, and of his cutting up the dragon and of their eating it. The mother-bird then remarked, ' Truly, father ! you were about to do a strange thing, and a terrible sin has been averted from you.' Then the Sīmurgh flew off to a distance with the great stone and dropped it. It sank down to the very middle of the earth.

Coming back, the Sīmurgh saw that a little sunshine fell upon the prince through the leaves, and it spread its wings and shaded him till he woke. When he got up he salaamed to it, who returned his greeting with joy and gratitude, and caressed him and said : ' O youth, tell me true ! who are you, and where are you going ? And how did you cross that pitiless desert where never yet foot of man had trod ? ' The prince told his story from beginning to end, and finished by saying : ' Now it is my heart's wish that you should help me to get to Wāq of the Caucasus. Perhaps, by your favour, I shall accomplish my task and avenge my brothers.' In reply the Sīmurgh first blessed the deliverer of his children, and then went on : ' What you have done no child of man has ever done before ; you assuredly have a claim on all my help, for every year up till now that dragon has come here and has destroyed my nestlings, and I have never been able to find who was the murderer and to avenge myself. By God's grace you have removed my children's powerful foe. I regard you as a child of my own. Stay with me ; I will give you everything you desire, and I will establish a city here for you, and will furnish it with every requisite ; I will give you the land of the Caucasus, and will make its princes subject to you. Give up the journey to Wāq, it is full of risk, and the jins there will certainly kill you.' But

nothing could move the prince, and seeing this the bird
went on : ' Well, so be it ! When you wish to set forth
you must go into the plain and take seven head of deer,
and must make water-tight bags of their hides and keep
their flesh in seven portions. Seven seas lie on our way—
I will carry you over them ; but if I have not food and
drink we shall fall into the sea and be drowned. When
I ask for it you must put food and water into my mouth.
So we shall make the journey safely.'

The prince did all as he was told, then they took
flight ; they crossed the seven seas, and at each one the
prince fed the Sīmurgh. When they alighted on the
shore of the last sea, it said : ' O my son ! there lies your
road ; follow it to the city. Take thee three feathers of
mine, and, if you are in a difficulty, burn one and I will be
with you in the twinkling of an eye.'

The prince walked on in solitude till he reached the
city. He went in and wandered about through all
quarters, and through bazaars and lanes and squares,
in the least knowing from whom he could ask in-
formation about the riddle of Mihr-afrūz. He spent
seven days thinking it over in silence. From the first
day of his coming he had made friends with a young
cloth-merchant, and a great liking had sprung up between
them. One day he said abruptly to his companion : ' O
dear friend ! I wish you would tell me what the rose did
to the cypress, and what the sense of the riddle is.' The
merchant started, and exclaimed : ' If there were not
brotherly affection between us, I would cut off your head
for asking me this ! ' ' If you meant to kill me,' retorted
the prince, ' you would still have first to tell me what I
want to know.' When the merchant saw that the prince
was in deadly earnest, he said : ' If you wish to hear the
truth of the matter you must wait upon our king. There
is no other way ; no one else will tell you. I have a
well-wisher at the Court, named Farrūkh-fāl,[1] and will

[1] Of happy omen.

introduce you to him.' 'That would be excellent,' cried
the prince. A meeting was arranged between Farrūkh-
fāl and Almās, and then the amīr took him to the king's
presence and introduced him as a stranger and traveller
who had come from afar to sit in the shadow of King
Sinaubar.

Now the Sīmurgh had given the prince a diamond
weighing thirty misqāls, and he offered this to the king,
who at once recognised its value, and asked where it had
been obtained. 'I, your slave, once had riches and state
and power; there are many such stones in my country.
On my way here I was plundered at the Castle of Clashing Swords, and I saved this one thing only, hidden in my
bathing-cloth.' In return for the diamond, King Sinaubar
showered gifts of much greater value, for he remembered
that it was the last possession of the prince. He showed
the utmost kindness and hospitality, and gave his vazīr
orders to instal the prince in the royal guest-house. He
took much pleasure in his visitor's society; they were
together every day and spent the time most pleasantly.
Several times the king said : 'Ask me for something, that
I may give it you.' One day he so pressed to know what
would pleasure the prince, that the latter said: 'I have
only one wish, and that I will name to you in private.'
The king at once commanded every one to withdraw, and
then Prince Almās said : 'The desire of my life is to know
what the rose did to the cypress, and what meaning there
is in the words.' The king was astounded. 'In God's
name ! if anyone else had said that to me I should have
cut off his head instantly.' The prince heard this in
silence, and presently so beguiled the king with pleasant
talk that to kill him was impossible.

Time flew by, the king again and again begged the
prince to ask some gift of him, and always received this
same reply : 'I wish for your Majesty's welfare, what more
can I desire ? ' One night there was a banquet, and cupbearers carried round gold and silver cups of sparkling

The Punishment of the Rose

[*This illustration is reproduced in color between pages 74 and 75.*]

wine, and singers with sweetest voices contended for the prize. The prince drank from the king's own cup, and when his head was hot with wine he took a lute from one of the musicians and placed himself on the carpet-border and sang and sang till he witched away the sense of all who listened. Applause and compliments rang from every side. The king filled his cup and called the prince and gave it him and said : 'Name your wish ! it is yours.' The prince drained off the wine and answered: 'O king of the world! learn and know that I have only one aim in life, and this is to know what the rose did to the cypress.'

'Never yet,' replied the king, 'has any man come out from that question alive. If this is your only wish, so be it ; I will tell you. But I will do this on one condition only, namely, that when you have heard you will submit yourself to death.' To this the prince agreed, and said : 'I set my foot firmly on this compact.'

The king then gave an order to an attendant ; a costly carpet overlaid with European velvet was placed near him, and a dog was led in by a golden and jewelled chain and set upon the splendid stuffs. A band of fair girls came in and stood round it in waiting.

Then, with ill words, twelve negroes dragged in a lovely woman, fettered on hands and feet and meanly dressed, and they set her down on the bare floor. She was extraordinarily beautiful, and shamed the glorious sun. The king ordered a hundred stripes to be laid on her tender body ; she sighed a long sigh. Food was called for and table-cloths were spread. Delicate meats were set before the dog, and water given it in a royal cup of Chinese crystal. When it had eaten its fill, its leavings were placed before the lovely woman and she was made to eat of them. She wept and her tears were pearls ; she smiled and her lips shed roses. Pearls and flowers were gathered up and taken to the treasury.

'Now,' said the king, 'you have seen these things and

your purpose is fulfilled.' 'Truly,' said the prince, 'I have seen things which I have not understood ; what do they mean, and what is the story of them ? Tell me and kill me.'

Then said the king : ' The woman you see there in chains is my wife ; she is called Gul, the Rose, and I am Sinaubar, the Cypress. One day I was hunting and became very thirsty. After great search I discovered a well in a place so secret that neither bird nor beast nor man could find it without labour. I was alone, I took my turban for a rope and my cap for a bucket. There was a good deal of water, but when I let down my rope, some- thing caught it, and I could not in any way draw it back. I shouted down into the well : " O ! servant of God ! who- ever you are, why do you deal unfairly with me ? I am dying of thirst, let go ! in God's name." A cry came up in answer, " O servant of God ! we have been in the well a long time ; in God's name get us out ! " After trying a thousand schemes, I drew up two blind women. They said they were perīs, and that their king had blinded them in his anger and had left them in the well alone.

' " Now," they said, " if you will get us the cure for our blindness we will devote ourselves to your service, and will do whatever you wish."

' " What is the cure for your blindness ? "

' " Not far from this place," they said, " a cow comes up from the great sea to graze ; a little of her dung would cure us. We should be eternally your debtors. Do not let the cow see you, or she will assuredly kill you."

' With renewed strength and spirit I went to the shore. There I watched the cow come up from the sea, graze, and go back. Then I came out of my hiding, took a little of her dung and conveyed it to the perīs. They rubbed it on their eyes, and by the Divine might saw again.

' They thanked heaven and me, and then considered what they could do to show their gratitude to me. " Our perī-king," they said, "has a daughter whom he keeps under his own eye and thinks the most lovely girl on earth. In good sooth, she has not her equal! Now we will get you into her house and you must win her heart, and if she has an inclination for another, you must drive it out and win her for yourself. Her mother loves her so dearly that she has no ease but in her presence, and

The DOG & his attendants

she will give her to no one in marriage. Teach her to love you so that she cannot exist without you. But if the matter becomes known to her mother she will have you burned in the fire. Then you must beg, as a last favour, that your body may be anointed with oil so that you may burn the more quickly and be spared torture. If the perī-king allows this favour, we two will manage to be your anointers, and we will put an oil on you such that if you were a thousand years in the fire not a trace of burning would remain."

' In the end the two perīs took me to the girl's house. I saw her sleeping daintily. She was most lovely, and I was so amazed at the perfection of her beauty that I stood with senses lost, and did not know if she were real or a dream. When at last I saw that she was a real girl, I returned thanks that I, the runner, had come to my goal, and that I, the seeker, had found my treasure.

' When the perī opened her eyes she asked in affright : " Who are you ? Have you come to steal ? How did you get here ? Be quick ! save yourself from this whirlpool of destruction, for the demons and perīs who guard me will wake and seize you."

' But love's arrow had struck me deep, and the girl, too, looked kindly on me. I could not go away. For some months I remained hidden in her house. We did not dare to let her mother know of our love. Sometimes the girl was very sad and fearful lest her mother should come to know. One day her father said to her : " Sweetheart, for some time I have noticed that your beauty is not what it was. How is this ? Has sickness touched you ? Tell me that I may seek a cure." Alas ! there was now no way of concealing the mingled delight and anguish of our love ; from secret it became known. I was put in prison and the world grew dark to my rose, bereft of her lover.

' The perī-king ordered me to be burnt, and said : " Why have you, a man, done this perfidious thing in my house ? " His demons and perīs collected ambar-wood and made a pile, and would have set me on it, when I remembered the word of life which the two perīs I had rescued had breathed into my ear, and I asked that my body might be rubbed with oil to release me the sooner from torture. This was allowed, and those two contrived to be the anointers. I was put into the fire and it was

kept up for seven days and nights. By the will of the
Great King it left no trace upon me. At the end of a
week the perī-king ordered the ashes to be cast upon the
dust-heap, and I was found alive and unharmed.

‘Perīs who had seen Gul consumed by her love for me
now interceded with the king, and said : “ It is clear that
your daughter’s fortunes are bound up with his, for the
fire has not hurt him. It is best to give him the girl, for
they love one another. He is King of Wāq of Qāf, and
you will find none better.”

‘To this the king agreed, and made formal marriage
between Gul and me. You now know the price I paid
for this faithless creature. O prince! remember our
compact.’

‘I remember,’ said the prince; ‘ but tell me what
brought Queen Gul to her present pass ? ’

‘One night,’ continued King Sinaubar, ‘ I was aroused
by feeling Gul’s hands and feet, deadly cold, against my
body. I asked her where she had been to get so cold, and
she said she had had to go out. Next morning, when I
went to my stable I saw that two of my horses, Windfoot and Tiger, were thin and worn out. I reprimanded
the groom and beat him. He asked where his fault lay,
and said that every night my wife took one or other of these
horses and rode away, and came back only just before
dawn. A flame kindled in my heart, and I asked myself
where she could go and what she could do. I told the
groom to be silent, and when next Gul took a horse from
the stable to saddle another quickly and bring it to me.
That day I did not hunt, but stayed at home to follow the
matter up. I lay down as usual at night and pretended
to fall asleep. When I seemed safely off, Gul got up and
went to the stable as her custom was. That night it was
Tiger’s turn. She rode off on him, and I took Windfoot
and followed. With me went that dog you see, a faithful
friend who never left me.

‘When I came to the foot of those hills which lie

outside the city I saw Gul dismount and go towards a house which some negroes have built there. Over against the door was a high seat, and on it lay a giant negro, before whom she salaamed. He got up and beat her till she was marked with weals, but she uttered no complaint. I was dumfounded, for once when I had struck her with a rose-stalk she had complained and fretted for three days! Then the negro said to her: "How now, ugly one and shaven head! Why are you so late, and why are you not wearing wedding garments?" She answered him: "That person did not go to sleep quickly, and he stayed at home all day, so that I was not able to adorn myself. I came as soon as I could." In a little while he called her to sit beside him; but this was more than I could bear. I lost control of myself and rushed upon him. He clutched my collar and we grappled in a death struggle. Suddenly she came behind me, caught my feet and threw me. While he held me on the ground, she drew out my own knife and gave it to him. I should have been killed but for that faithful dog which seized his throat and pulled him down and pinned him to the ground. Then I got up and despatched the wretch. There were four other negroes at the place; three I killed and the fourth got away, and has taken refuge beneath the throne of Mihr-afrūz, daughter of King Quimūs. I took Gul back to my palace, and from that time till now I have treated her as a dog is treated, and I have cared for my dog as though it were my wife. Now you know what the rose did to the cypress; and now you must keep compact with me.'

'I shall keep my word,' said the prince; 'but may a little water be taken to the roof so that I may make my last ablution?'

To this request the king consented. The prince mounted to the roof, and, getting into a corner, struck his fire-steel and burned one of the Sīmurgh's feathers in the flame. Straightway it appeared, and by the majesty of its

presence made the city quake. It took the prince on its
back and soared away to the zenith.

After a time King Sinaubar said : 'That young man is
a long time on the roof; go and bring him here.' But
there was no sign of the prince upon the roof; only, far
away in the sky, the Sīmurgh was seen carrying him off.
When the king heard of his escape he thanked heaven
that his hands were clean of this blood.

Up and up flew the Sīmurgh, till earth looked like an
egg resting on an ocean. At length it dropped straight
down to its own place, where the kind prince was
welcomed by the young birds and most hospitably enter-
tained. He told the whole story of the rose and the
cypress, and then, laden with gifts which the Sīmurgh had
gathered from cities far and near, he set his face for the
Castle of Clashing Swords. The king-lion came out to
meet him ; he took the negro chief's daughter—whose
name was also Gul—in lawful marriage, and then marched
with her and her possessions and her attendants to the
Place of Gifts. Here they halted for a night, and at dawn
said good-bye to the king-lion and set out for Jamīla's
country.

When the Lady Jamīla heard that Prince Almās was
near, she went out, with many a fair handmaid, to give
him loving reception. Their meeting was joyful, and they
went together to the garden-palace. Jamīla summoned all
her notables, and in their presence her marriage with the
prince was solemnised. A few days later she entrusted
her affairs to her vazīr, and made preparation to go with
the prince to his own country. Before she started she
restored all the men whom her sister, Latīfa, had bewitched, to their own forms, and received their blessings,
and set them forward to their homes. The wicked Latīfa
herself she left quite alone in her garden-house. When all
was ready they set out with all her servants and slaves, all
her treasure and goods, and journeyed at ease to the city
of King Quimūs.

When King Quimūs heard of the approach of such a great company, he sent out his vazīr to give the prince honourable meeting, and to ask what had procured him the favour of the visit. The prince sent back word that he had no thought of war, but he wrote : ' Learn and know, King Quimūs, that I am here to end the crimes of your insolent daughter who has tyrannously done to death many kings and kings' sons, and has hung their heads on your citadel. I am here to give her the answer to her riddle.' Later on he entered the city, beat boldly on the drums, and was conducted to the presence.

The king entreated him to have nothing to do with the riddle, for that no man had come out of it alive. ' O king ! ' replied the prince, ' it is to answer it that I am here ; I will not withdraw.'

Mihr-afrūz was told that one man more had staked his head on her question, and that this was one who said he knew the answer. At the request of the prince, all the officers and notables of the land were summoned to hear his reply to the princess. All assembled, and the king and his queen Gul-rukh, and the girl and the prince were there.

The prince addressed Mihr-afrūz : ' What is the question you ask ? '

' What did the rose do to the cypress ? ' she rejoined.

The prince smiled, and turned and addressed the assembly.

' You who are experienced men and versed in affairs, did you ever know or hear and see anything of this matter ? '

' No ! ' they answered, ' no one has ever known or heard or seen aught about it ; it is an empty fancy.'

' From whom, then, did the princess hear of it ? This empty fancy it is that has done many a servant of God to death ! '

All saw the good sense of his words and showed their approval. Then he turned to the princess : ' Tell us the truth, princess ; who told you of this thing ? I know it hair by hair, and in and out ; but if I tell you what I know, who is there that can say I speak the truth ? You must produce the person who can confirm my words.'

Her heart sank, for she feared that her long-kept secret was now to be noised abroad. But she said merely : ' Explain yourself.'

' I shall explain myself fully when you bring here the negro whom you hide beneath your throne.'

Here the king shouted in wonderment : ' Explain yourself, young man ! What negro does my daughter hide beneath her throne ? '

' That,' said the prince, ' you will see if you order to be brought here the negro who will be found beneath the throne of the princess.'

Messengers were forthwith despatched to the garden-house, and after awhile they returned bringing a negro whom they had discovered in a secret chamber under-neath the throne of Mihr-afrūz, dressed in a dress of honour, and surrounded with luxury. The king was overwhelmed with astonishment, but the girl had taken heart again. She had had time to think that perhaps the prince had heard of the presence of the negro, and knew no more. So she said haughtily : ' Prince ! you have not answered my riddle.'

' O most amazingly impudent person,' cried he, ' do you not yet repent ? '

Then he turned to the people, and told them the whole story of the rose and the cypress, of King Sinaubar and Queen Gul. When he came to the killing of the negroes, he said to the one who stood before them : ' You, too, were present.'

' That is so ; all happened as you have told it ! '

There was great rejoicing in the court and all through the country over the solving of the riddle, and because now no more kings and princes would be killed. King Quimūs made over his daughter to Prince Almās, but the latter refused to marry her, and took her as his captive. He then asked that the heads should be removed from the battlements and given decent burial. This was done. He received from the king everything that belonged to Mihr-afrūz; her treasure of gold and silver; her costly stuffs and carpets; her household plenishing; her horses and camels; her servants and slaves.

Then he returned to his camp and sent for Dil-arām, who came bringing her goods and chattels, her gold and her jewels. When all was ready, Prince Almās set out for home, taking with him Jamīla, and Dil-arām and Gul, daughter of Taram-tāq, and the wicked Mihr-afrūz, and all the belongings of the four, packed on horses and camels, and in carts without number.

As he approached the borders of his father's country word of his coming went before him, and all the city came forth to give him welcome. King Saman-lāl-pōsh—Jessamine, wearer of rubies—had so bewept the loss of his sons that he was now blind. When the prince had kissed his feet and received his blessing, he took from a casket a little collyrium of Solomon, which the Sīmurgh had given him, and which reveals the hidden things of earth, and rubbed it on his father's eyes. Light came, and the king saw his son.

Mihr-afrūz was brought before the king, and the prince said : ' This is the murderer of your sons; do with her as you will.' The king fancied that the prince might care for the girl's beauty, and replied : ' You have humbled her ; do with her as you will.'

Upon this the prince sent for four swift and strong horses, and had the negro bound to each one of them ; then each was driven to one of the four quarters, and he tore in pieces like muslin.

This frightened Mihr-afrūz horribly, for she thought the same thing might be done to herself. She cried out to the prince : ' O Prince Almās ! what is hardest to get is most valued. Up till now I have been subject to no

man, and no man had had my love. The many kings
and kings' sons who have died at my hands have died
because it was their fate to die like this. In this matter
I have not sinned. That was their fate from eternity ;
and from the beginning it was predestined that my fate
should be bound up with yours.'

The prince gave ear to the argument from pre-ordain-
ment, and as she was a very lovely maiden he took her
too in lawful marriage. She and Jamīla set up house
together, and Dil-arām and Gul set up theirs ; and the
prince passed the rest of his life with the four in perfect
happiness, and in pleasant and sociable entertainment.

Now has been told what the rose did to the cypress.

Finished, finished, finished !

BALL-CARRIER AND THE BAD ONE

FAR, far in the forest there were two little huts, and in each of them lived a man who was a famous hunter, his wife, and three or four children. Now the children were forbidden to play more than a short distance from the door, as it was known that, away on the other side of the wood near the great river, there dwelt a witch who had a magic ball that she used as a means of stealing children.

Her plan was a very simple one, and had never yet failed. When she wanted a child she just flung her ball in the direction of the child's home, and however far off it might be, the ball was sure to reach it. Then, as soon as the child saw it, the ball would begin rolling slowly back to the witch, just keeping a little ahead of the child, so that he always thought that he could catch it the next minute. But he never did, and, what was more, his parents never saw him again.

Of course you must not suppose that all the fathers and mothers who had lost children made no attempts to find them, but the forest was so large, and the witch was so cunning in knowing exactly where they were going to search, that it was very easy for her to keep out of the way. Besides, there was always the chance that the children might have been eaten by wolves, of which large herds roamed about in winter.

One day the old witch happened to want a little boy, so she threw her ball in the direction of the hunters' huts. A child was standing outside, shooting at a mark with his bow and arrows, but the moment he saw the ball, which was made of glass whose blues and greens and

THE BOY IN THE WITCH'S HUT.

whites, all frosted over, kept changing one into the other, he flung down his bow, and stooped to pick the ball up.

But as he did so it began to roll very gently downhill. The boy could not let it roll away, when it was so close to him, so he gave chase. The ball seemed always within his grasp, yet he could never catch it; it went quicker and quicker, and the boy grew more and more excited. That time he almost touched it—no, he missed it by a hair's breadth! Now, surely, if he gave a spring he could get in front of it! He sprang forward, tripped and fell, and found himself in the witch's house!

'Welcome! welcome! grandson!' said she; 'get up and rest yourself, for you have had a long walk, and I am sure you must be tired!' So the boy sat down, and ate some food which she gave him in a bowl. It was quite different from anything he had tasted before, and he thought it was delicious. When he had eaten up every bit, the witch asked him if he had ever fasted.

'No,' replied the boy, 'at least I have been obliged to sometimes, but never if there was any food to be had.'

'You will have to fast if you want the spirits to make you strong and wise, and the sooner you begin the better.'

'Very well,' said the boy, 'what do I do first?'

'Lie down on those buffalo skins by the door of the hut,' answered she; and the boy lay down, and the squirrels and little bears and the birds came and talked to him.

At the end of ten days the old woman came to him with a bowl of the same food that he had eaten before.

'Get up, my grandson, you have fasted long enough. Have the good spirits visited you, and granted you the strength and wisdom that you desire?'

'Some of them have come, and have given me a portion of both,' answered the boy, 'but many have stayed away from me.'

'Then,' said she, 'you must fast ten days more.'

So the boy lay down again on the buffalo skins, and fasted for ten days, and at the end of that time he turned

his face to the wall, and fasted for twenty days longer.
At length the witch called to him, and said :

'Come and eat something, my grandson.' At the
sound of her voice the boy got up and ate the food she
gave him. When he had finished every scrap she spoke as
before : 'Tell me, my grandson, have not the good spirits
visited you all these many days that you have fasted ? '

' Not all, grandmother,' answered he ; 'there are still
some who keep away from me and say that I have not
fasted long enough.'

' Then you must fast again,' replied the old woman,
'and go on fasting till you receive the gifts of *all* the good
spirits. Not one must be missing.'

The boy said nothing, but lay down for the third time
on the buffalo skins, and fasted for twenty days more.
And at the end of that time the witch thought he was
dead, his face was so white and his body so still. But
when she had fed him out of the bowl he grew stronger,
and soon was able to sit up.

' You have fasted a long time,' said she, ' longer than
anyone ever fasted before. Surely the good spirits must
be satisfied *now* ? '

' Yes, grandmother,' answered the boy, ' they have all
come, and have given me their gifts.'

This pleased the old woman so much that she brought
him another basin of food, and while he was eating it
she talked to him, and this is what she said : ' Far away,
on the other side of the great river, is the home of the
Bad One. In his house is much gold, and what is more
precious even than the gold, a little bridge, which
lengthens out when the Bad One waves his hand, so that
there is no river or sea that he cannot cross. Now I want
that bridge and some of the gold for myself, and that is
the reason that I have stolen so many boys by means of my
ball. I have tried to teach them how to gain the gifts of
the good spirits, but none of them would fast long enough,
and at last I had to send them away to perform simple,

easy little tasks. But you have been strong and faithful, and you can do this thing if you listen to what I tell you ! When you reach the river tie this ball to your foot, and it will take you across—you cannot manage it in any other way. But do not be afraid; trust to the ball, and you will be quite safe ! '

The boy took the ball and put it in a bag. Then he made himself a club and a bow, and some arrows which would fly further than anyone else's arrows, because of the strength the good spirits had given him. They had also bestowed on him the power of changing his shape, and had increased the quickness of his eyes and ears so that nothing escaped him. And in some way or other they made him understand that if he needed more help they would give it to him.

When all these things were ready the boy bade fare-well to the witch and set out. He walked through the forest for several days without seeing anyone but his friends the squirrels and the bears and the birds, but though he stopped and spoke to them all, he was careful not to let them know where he was going.

At last, after many days, he came to the river, and beyond it he noticed a small hut standing on a hill which he guessed to be the home of the Bad One. But the stream flowed so quickly that he could not see how he was ever to cross it, and in order to test how swift the current really was, he broke a branch from a tree and threw it in. It seemed hardly to touch the water before it was carried away, and even his magic sight could not follow it. He could not help feeling frightened, but he hated giving up anything that he had once undertaken, and, fastening the ball on his right foot, he ventured on the river. To his surprise he was able to stand up ; then a panic seized him, and he scrambled up the bank again. In a minute or two he plucked up courage to go a little further into the river, but again its width frightened him, and a second time he turned back. However, he felt rather ashamed of his cowardice, as it was quite clear that his ball *could* support him, and on his third trial he got safely to the other side.

Once there he replaced the ball in the bag, and looked carefully round him. The door of the Bad One's hut was open, and he saw that the ceiling was supported by great wooden beams, from which hung the bags of gold and the little bridge. He saw, too, the Bad One sitting in the midst of his treasures eating his dinner, and drinking something out of a horn. It was plain to the boy that he must invent some plan of getting the Bad One out of the way, or else he would never be able to steal the gold or the bridge.

What should he do ? Give horrible shrieks as if he were in pain ? But the Bad One would not care whether he were murdered or not ! Call him by his name ? But the Bad One was very cunning, and would suspect some trick. He must try something better than that ! Then suddenly an idea came to him, and he gave a little jump of joy. ' Oh, how stupid of me not to think of that before ! ' said he, and he wished with all his might that the Bad One should become very hungry—so hungry that he could not wait a moment for fresh food to be brought to him. And sure enough at that instant the Bad One called out to his servant, ' You did not bring food that would satisfy a sparrow. Fetch some more at once, for I am perfectly starving.' Then, without giving the woman time to go to the larder, he got up from his chair, and rolled, staggering from hunger, towards the kitchen.

Directly the door had closed on the Bad One the boy ran in, pulled down a bag of gold from the beam, and tucked it under his left arm. Next he unhooked the little bridge and put it under his right. He did not try to escape, as most boys of his age would have done, for the wisdom put into his mind by the good spirits taught him that before he could reach the river and make use of the bridge the Bad One would have tracked him by his footsteps and been upon him. So, making himself very small and thin, he hid himself behind a pile of buffalo skins in the corner, first tearing a slit through one of them, so that he could see what was going on.

He had hardly settled himself when the servant entered the room, and, as she did so, the last bag of gold on the beam fell to the ground—for they had begun to fall directly the boy had taken the first one. She cried to her master that someone had stolen both the bag and the bridge, and the Bad One rushed in, mad with anger, and bade her go and seek for footsteps outside, that they might find out where the thief had gone. In a few minutes she returned, saying that he must be in the house, as she could not see any footsteps leading to the river, and began to move all the furniture in the room, without discovering Ball-Carrier.

'But he *must* be here somewhere,' she said to herself, examining for the second time the pile of buffalo skins ; and Ball-Carrier, knowing that he could not possibly escape now, hastily wished that the Bad One should be unable to eat any more food at present.

'Ah, there is a slit in this one,' cried the servant, shaking the skin ; 'and here he is.' And she pulled out Ball-Carrier, looking so lean and small that he would hardly have made a mouthful for a sparrow.

'Was it you who took my gold and bridge ?' asked the Bad One.

'Yes,' answered Ball-Carrier, 'it was I who took them.'

The Bad One made a sign to the woman, who inquired where he had hidden them. He lifted his left arm where the gold was, and she picked up a knife and scraped his skin so that no gold should be left sticking to it.

'What have you done with the bridge ?' said she. And he lifted his right arm, from which she took the bridge, while the Bad One looked on, well pleased. 'Be sure that he does not run away,' chuckled he. 'Boil some

THE DEATH OF THE BAD ONE

water, and get him ready for cooking, while I go and invite my friends the water-demons to the feast.'

The woman seized Ball-Carrier between her finger and thumb, and was going to carry him to the kitchen, when the boy spoke :

' I am very lean and small now,' he said, ' hardly worth the trouble of cooking ; but if you were to keep me two days, and gave me plenty of food, I should get big and fat. As it is, your friends the water-demons would think you meant to laugh at them, when they found that *I* was the feast.'

' Well, perhaps you are right,' answered the Bad One ; ' I will keep you for two days.' And he went out to visit the water-demons.

Meanwhile the servant, whose name was Lung-Woman, led him into a little shed, and chained him up to a ring in the wall. But food was given him every hour, and at the end of two days he was as fat and big as a Christmas turkey, and could hardly move his head from one side to the other.

' He will do now,' said the Bad One, who came constantly to see how he was getting on. ' I shall go and tell the water-demons that we expect them to dinner to-night. Put the kettle on the fire, but be sure on no account to taste the broth.'

Lung-Woman lost no time in obeying her orders. She built up the fire, which had got very low, filled the kettle with water, and passing a rope which hung from the ceiling through the handle, swung it over the flames. Then she brought in Ball-Carrier, who, seeing all these preparations, wished that as long as *he* was in the kettle the water might not really boil, though it would hiss and bubble, and also, that the spirits would turn the water into fat.

The kettle soon began to sing and bubble, and Ball-Carrier was lifted in. Very soon the fat which was to make the sauce rose to the surface, and Ball-Carrier, who

was bobbing about from one side to the other, called out
that Lung-Woman had better taste the broth, as he thought
that some salt should be added to it.   The servant knew
quite well that her master had forbidden her to do anything of the kind, but when once the idea was put into
her head, she found the smell from the kettle so delicious
that she unhooked a long ladle from the wall and plunged
it into the kettle.

'You will spill it all, if you. stand so far off,' said the
boy; 'why don't you come a little nearer?' And as she
did so he cried to the spirits to give him back his usual
size and strength and to make the water scalding hot.
Then he gave the kettle a kick, which upset all the boiling
water upon her, and jumping over her body he seized
once more the gold and the bridge, picked up his club
and bow and arrows, and after setting fire to the Bad
One's hut, ran down to the river, which he crossed safely
by the help of the bridge.

The hut, which was made of wood, was burned to the
ground before the Bad One came back with a large crowd
of water-demons.   There was not a sign of anyone or
anything, so he started for the river, where he saw Ball-
Carrier sitting quietly on the other side.   Then the Bad
One knew what had happened, and after telling the water-
demons that there would be no feast after all, he called
to Ball-Carrier, who was eating an apple.

'I know your name now,' he said, 'and as you have
ruined me, and I am not rich any more, will you take me
as your servant?'

'Yes, I will, though you have tried to kill me,' answered
Ball-Carrier, throwing the bridge across the water as he
spoke.   But when the Bad One was in the midst of the
stream, the boy wished it to become small ; and the Bad
One fell into the water and was drowned, and the world
was rid of him.

[*U.S. Bureau of Ethnology.*]

HOW BALL-CARRIER FINISHED HIS TASK

AFTER Ball-Carrier had managed to drown the Bad One so that he could not do any more mischief, he forgot the way to his grandmother's house, and could not find it again, though he searched everywhere. During this time he wandered into many strange places, and had many adventures; and one day he came to a hut where a young girl lived. He was tired and hungry and begged her to let him in and rest, and he stayed a long while, and the girl became his wife. One morning he saw two children playing in front of the hut, and went out to speak to them. But as soon as they saw him they set up cries of horror and ran away. 'They are the children of my sister who has been on a long journey,' replied his wife, ' and now that she knows you are my husband she wants to kill you.'

'Oh, well, let her try,' replied Ball-Carrier. 'It is not the first time people have wished to do that. And here I am still, you see ! '

' Be careful,' said the wife, ' she is very cunning.' But at this moment the sister-in-law came up.

' How do you do, brother-in-law ? I have heard of you so often that I am very glad to meet you. I am told that you are more powerful than any man on earth, and as I am powerful too, let us try which is the strongest.'

' That will be delightful,' answered he. ' Suppose we begin with a short race, and then we will go on to other things.'

' That will suit me very well,' replied the woman, who

was a witch. 'And let us agree that the one who wins shall have the right to kill the other.'

'Oh, certainly,' said Ball-Carrier; 'and I don't think we shall find a flatter course than the prairie itself—no one knows how many miles it stretches. We will run to the end and back again.'

This being settled they both made ready for the race, and Ball-Carrier silently begged the good spirits to help him, and not to let him fall into the hands of this wicked witch.

'When the sun touches the trunk of that tree we will start,' said she, as they both stood side by side. But with the first step Ball-Carrier changed himself into a wolf and for a long way kept ahead. Then gradually he heard her creeping up behind him, and soon she was in front. So Ball-Carrier took the shape of a pigeon and flew rapidly past her, but in a little while she was in front again, and the end of the prairie was in sight. 'A crow can fly faster than a pigeon,' thought he, and as a crow he managed to pass her and held his ground so long that he fancied she was quite beaten. The witch began to be afraid of it too, and putting out all her strength slipped past him. Next he put on the shape of a hawk, and in this form he reached the bounds of the prairie, he and the witch turning homewards at the moment.

Bird after bird he tried, but every time the witch gained on him and took the lead. At length the goal was in sight, and Ball-Carrier knew that unless he could get ahead now he would be killed before his own door, under the eyes of his wife. His eyes had grown dim from fatigue, his wings flapped wearily and hardly bore him along, while the witch seemed as fresh as ever. What bird was there whose flight was swifter than his? Would not the good spirits tell him? Ah, of course he knew; why had he not thought of it at first and spared himself all that fatigue? And the next instant a humming bird, dressed in green and blue, flashed past the woman

THE WITCH OUTSTRIPS THE WOLF

and entered the house. The witch came panting up, furious at having lost the race which she felt certain of winning ; and Ball-Carrier, who had by this time changed back into his own shape, struck her on the head and killed her.

For a long while Ball-Carrier was content to stay quietly at home with his wife and children, for he was tired of adventures, and only did enough hunting to supply the house with food. But one day he happened to eat some poisonous berries that he had found in the forest, and grew so ill that he felt he was going to die.

' When I am dead do not bury me in the earth,' he said, ' but put me over there, among that clump of trees.' So his wife and her three children watched by him as long as he was alive, and after he was dead they took him up and laid the body on a platform of stakes which they had prepared in the grove. And as they returned weeping to the hut they caught a glimpse of the ball rolling away down the path back to the old grandmother. One of the sons sprang forward to stop it, for Ball-Carrier had often told them the tale of how it had helped him to cross the river, but it was too quick for him, and they had to content themselves with the war club and bow and arrows, which were put carefully away.

By-and-by some travellers came past, and the chief among them asked leave to marry Ball-Carrier's daughter. The mother said she must have a little time to think over it, as her daughter was still very young ; so it was settled that the man should go away for a month with his friends, and then come back to see if the girl was willing.

Now ever since Ball-Carrier's death the family had been very poor, and often could not get enough to eat. One morning the girl, who had had no supper and no breakfast, wandered off to look for cranberries, and though she was quite near home was astonished at noticing a large hut, which certainly had not been there

when last she had come that way. No one was about, so
she ventured to peep in, and her surprise was increased at
seeing, heaped up in one corner, a quantity of food of all
sorts, while a little robin redbreast stood perched on a
beam looking down upon her.

'It is my father, I am sure,' she cried; and the bird
piped in answer.

From that day, whenever they wanted food they went
to the hut, and though the robin could not speak, he
would hop on their shoulders and let them feed him with
the food they knew he liked best.

When the man came back he found the girl looking
so much prettier and fatter than when he had left her,
that he insisted that they should be married on the spot.
And the mother, who did not know how to get rid of him,
gave in.

The husband spent all his time in hunting, and the
family had never had so much meat before; but the man,
who had seen for himself how poor they were, noticed
with amazement that they did not seem to care about it,
or to be hungry. 'They must get food from somewhere,'
he thought, and one morning, when he pretended to be
going out to hunt, he hid in a thicket to watch. Very
soon they all left the house together, and walked to the
other hut, which the girl's husband saw for the first time,
as it was hid in a hollow. He followed, and noticed that
each one went up to the redbreast, and shook him by the
claw; and he then entered boldly and shook the bird's
claw too. The whole party afterwards sat down to dinner,
after which they all returned to their own hut.

The next day the husband declared that he was very ill,
and could not eat anything; but this was only a pretence
so that he might get what he wanted. The family were
all much distressed, and begged him to tell them what
food he fancied.

'Oh! I could not eat any food,' he answered every
time, and at each answer his voice grew fainter and

WAKE UP MY GRANDSON
IT IS TIME TO GO HOME

fainter, till they thought he would die from weakness
before their eyes.

'There must be *some* thing you could take, if you
would only say what it is,' implored his wife.

' No, nothing, nothing ; except, perhaps—but of course
that is impossible ! '

' No, I am sure it is not,' replied she ; ' you shall have
it, I promise—only tell me what it is.'

' I think—but I could not ask you to do such a thing.
Leave me alone, and let me die quietly.'

' You shall *not* die,' cried the girl, who was very fond
of her husband, for he did not beat her as most girls'
husbands did. ' Whatever it is, I will manage to get it
for you.'

' Well, then, I *think*, if I had that—redbreast, nicely
roasted, I could eat a little bit of his wing ! '

The wife started back in horror at such a request ; but
the man turned his face to the wall, and took no notice,
as he thought it was better to leave her to herself for a
little.

Weeping and wringing her hands, the girl went down
to her mother. The brothers were very angry when they
heard the story, and declared that, if any one were to die,
it certainly should not be the robin. But all that night
the man seemed getting weaker and weaker, and at last,
quite early, the wife crept out, and stealing to the hut,
killed the bird, and brought him home to her husband.

Just as she was going to cook it her two brothers came
in. They cried out in horror at the sight, and, rushing out
of the hut, declared they would never see her any more.
And the poor girl, with a heavy heart, took the body of the
redbreast up to her husband.

But directly she entered the room the man told her
that he felt a great deal better, and that he would rather
have a piece of bear's flesh, well boiled, than any bird,
however tender. His wife felt very miserable to think

that their beloved redbreast had been sacrificed for nothing, and begged him to try a little bit.

'You felt so sure that it would do you good before,' said she, 'that I can't help thinking it would quite cure you now.' But the man only flew into a rage, and flung the bird out of the window. Then he got up and went out.

Now all this while the ball had been rolling, rolling, rolling to the old grandmother's hut on the other side of the world, and directly it rolled into her hut she knew that her grandson must be dead. Without wasting any time she took a fox skin and tied it round her forehead, and fastened another round her waist, as witches always do when they leave their own homes. When she was ready she said to the ball : 'Go back the way you came, and lead me to my grandson.' And the ball started with the old woman following.

It was a long journey, even for a witch, but, like other things, it ended at last ; and the old woman stood before the platform of stakes, where the body of Ball-Carrier lay.

'Wake up, my grandson, it is time to go home,' the witch said. And Ball-Carrier stepped down off the platform, and brought his club and bow and arrows out of the hut, and set out, for the other side of the world, behind the old woman.

When they reached the hut where Ball-Carrier had fasted so many years ago, the old woman spoke for the first time since they had started on their way.

'My grandson, did you ever manage to get that gold from the Bad One ? '

'Yes, grandmother, I got it.'

'Where is it ? ' she asked.

'Here, in my left arm-pit,' answered he.

So she picked up a knife and scraped away all the gold which had stuck to his skin, and which had been sticking there ever since he first stole it. After she had finished she asked again :

' My grandson, did you manage to get that bridge from the Bad One ? '

' Yes, grandmother, I got that too,' answered he.

' Where is it ? ' she asked, and Ball-Carrier lifted his right arm, and pointed to his arm-pit.

' Here is the bridge, grandmother,' said he.

Then the witch did something that nobody in the world could have guessed that she would do. First, she took the gold and said to Ball-carrier :

' My grandson, this gold must be hidden in the earth, for if people think they can get it when they choose, they will become lazy and stupid. But if we take it and bury it in different parts of the world they will have to work for it if they want it, and then will only find a little at a time.' And as she spoke, she pulled up one of the poles of the hut, and Ball-Carrier saw that underneath was a deep, deep hole, which seemed to have no bottom. Down this hole she poured all the gold, and when it was out of sight it ran about all over the world, where people that dig hard sometimes find it. And after that was done she put the pole back again.

Next she lifted down a spade from a high shelf, where it had grown quite rusty, and dug a very small hole on the opposite side of the hut—very small, but very deep.

' Give me the bridge,' said she, ' for I am going to bury it here. If anyone was to get hold of it, and find that they could cross rivers and seas without any trouble, they would never discover how to cross them for themselves. I am a witch, and if I had chosen I could easily have cast my spells over the Bad One, and have made him deliver them to you the first day you came into my hut. But then you would never have fasted, and never have planned how to get what you wanted, and never have known the good spirits, and would have been fat and idle to the end of your days. And now go ; in that hut, which you can just see far away, live your father and mother, who are old people now, and need a son to hunt for them. You have done what you were set to do, and I need you no more.'

Then Ball-Carrier remembered his parents and went back to them.

[From *Bureau of Ethnology.* 'Indian Folklore.']

THE BUNYIP

Long, long ago, far, far away on the other side of the world, some young men left the camp where they lived to get some food for their wives and children. The sun was hot, but they liked heat, and as they went they ran races and tried who could hurl his spear the farthest, or was cleverest in throwing a strange weapon called a boomerang, which always returns to the thrower. They did not get on very fast at this rate, but presently they reached a flat place that in time of flood was full of water, but was now, in the height of summer, only a set of pools, each surrounded with a fringe of plants, with bulrushes standing in the inside of all. In that country the people are fond of the roots of bulrushes, which they think as good as onions, and one of the young men said that they had better collect some of the roots and carry them back to the camp. It did not take them long to weave the tops of the willows into a basket, and they were just going to wade into the water and pull up the bulrush roots when a youth suddenly called out: 'After all, why should we waste our time in doing work that is only fit for women and children? Let them come and get the roots for themselves; but we will fish for eels and anything else we can get.'

This delighted the rest of the party, and they all began to arrange their fishing lines, made from the bark of the yellow mimosa, and to search for bait for their hooks. Most of them used worms, but one, who had put a piece of raw meat for dinner into his skin wallet, cut off a little bit and baited his line with it, unseen by his companions.

For a long time they cast patiently, without receiving a single bite; the sun had grown low in the sky, and it seemed as if they would have to go home empty-handed, not even with a basket of roots to show; when the youth, who had baited his hook with raw meat, suddenly saw his line disappear under the water. Something, a very heavy fish he supposed, was pulling so hard that he could hardly keep his feet, and for a few minutes it seemed either as if he must let go or be dragged into the pool. He cried to his friends to help him, and at last, trembling with fright at what they were going to see, they managed between them to land on the bank a creature that was neither a calf nor a seal, but something of both, with a long, broad tail. They looked at each other with horror, cold shivers running down their spines; for though they had never beheld it, there was not a man amongst them who did not know what it was— the cub of the awful Bunyip!

All of a sudden the silence was broken by a low wail, answered by another from the other side of the pool, as the mother rose up from her den and came towards them, rage flashing from her horrible yellow eyes. ' Let it go ! let it go !' whispered the young men to each other; but the captor declared that he had caught it, and was going to keep it. ' He had promised his sweetheart,' he said, ' that he would bring back enough meat for her father's house to feast on for three days, and though they could not eat the little Bunyip, her brothers and sisters should have it to play with.' So, flinging his spear at the mother to keep her back, he threw the little Bunyip on to his shoulders, and set out for the camp, never heeding the poor mother's cries of distress.

By this time it was getting near sunset, and the plain was in shadow, though the tops of the mountains were still quite bright. The youths had all ceased to be afraid,

The Bunyip

PRINCE ALMAS TRANSFORMED

From "What the Rose did to the Cypress." See p. 20.

The Punishment of the Rose

From "What the Rose did to the Cypress." See p. 37.

"Oh do stop for a minute" said HELGA HÁBOGI'S HORSES BUT HÁBOGI WOULD NOT STOP OR LISTEN

From "Hábogi." See p. 129.

· LISTEN · LISTEN · SAID · THE · MERMAID · TO · THE · PRINCE ·

From "The Mermaid and the Boy." See p. 178.

"You will have to make me your wife" said the Elf-maiden.

From "The Elf Maiden." See p. 193.

The PRINCESS and the SNAKE

From "The Prince and the Three Fates." See p. 239.

RUBEZAHL AND THE PRINCESS

From "Rübezahl." See p. 290.

THE DRAGON AND THE MIRROR

From "The Knights of the Fish." See p. 346.

when they were startled by a low rushing sound behind
them, and, looking round, saw that the pool was slowly
rising, and the spot where they had landed the Bunyip
was quite covered. 'What could it be?' they asked
one of another; 'there was not a cloud in the sky,
yet the water had risen higher already than they had
ever known it do before.' For an instant they stood
watching as if they were frozen, then they turned and
ran with all their might, the man with the Bunyip running faster than all. When he reached a high peak over-
looking all the plain he stopped to take breath, and
turned to see if he was safe yet. Safe! why only the
tops of the trees remained above that sea of water, and
these were fast disappearing. They must run fast indeed
if they were to escape. So on they flew, scarcely feeling
the ground as they went, till they flung themselves on
the ground before the holes scooped out of the earth
where they had all been born. The old men were sitting
in front, the children were playing, and the women
chattering together, when the little Bunyip fell into their
midst, and there was scarcely a child among them who
did not know that something terrible was upon them.
'The water! the water!' gasped one of the young men;
and there it was, slowly but steadily mounting the ridge
itself. Parents and children clung together, as if by that
means they could drive back the advancing flood; and the
youth who had caused all this terrible catastrophe, seized
his sweetheart, and cried: 'I will climb with you to the top
of that tree, and there no waters can reach us.' But, as he
spoke, something cold touched him, and quickly he glanced
down at his feet. Then with a shudder he saw that they
were feet no longer, but bird's claws. He looked at the
girl he was clasping, and beheld a great black bird
standing at his side; he turned to his friends, but a
flock of great awkward flapping creatures stood in their
place. He put up his hands to cover his face, but they
were no more hands, only the ends of wings; and when

he tried to speak, a noise such as he had never heard before seemed to come from his throat, which had suddenly become narrow and slender. Already the water had risen to his waist, and he found himself sitting easily upon it, while its surface reflected back the image of a black swan, one of many.

Never again did the swans become men; but they are still different from other swans, for in the night-time those who listen can hear them talk in a language that is certainly not swan's language; and there are even sounds of laughing and talking, unlike any noise made by the swans whom we know.

The little Bunyip was carried home by its mother, and after that the waters sank back to their own channels. The side of the pool where she lives is always shunned by everyone, as nobody knows when she may suddenly put out her head and draw him into her mighty jaws. But people say that underneath the black waters of the pool she has a house filled with beautiful things, such as mortals who dwell on the earth have no idea of. Though how they know I cannot tell you, as nobody has ever seen it.

[From *Journal of Anthropological Institute.*]

FATHER GRUMBLER

ONCE upon a time there lived a man who had nearly as many children as there were sparrows in the garden. He had to work very hard all day to get them enough to eat, and was often tired and cross, and abused everything and everybody, so that people called him 'Father Grumbler.'

By-and-by he grew weary of always working, and on Sundays he lay a long while in bed, instead of going to church. Then after a time he found it dull to sit so many hours by himself, thinking of nothing but how to pay the rent that was owing, and as the tavern across the road looked bright and cheerful, he walked in one day and sat down with his friends. 'It was just to chase away Care,' he said; but when he came out, hours and hours after, Care came out with him.

Father Grumbler entered his house feeling more dismal than when he left it, for he knew that he had wasted both his time and money.

'I will go and see the Holy Man in the cave near the well,' he said to himself, 'and perhaps he can tell me why all the luck is for other people, and only misfortunes happen to me.' And he set out at once for the cave.

It was a long way off, and the road led over mountains and through valleys; but at last he reached the cave where the Holy Man dwelt, and knocked at the door.

'Who is there?' asked a voice from within.

'It is I, Holy Man, Father Grumbler, you know, who has as many children as sparrows in the garden.'

'Well, and what is it that you want?'

'I want to know why other people have all the luck, and only misfortunes happen to me!'

The Holy Man did not answer, but went into an inner cave, from which he came out bearing something in his hand. 'Do you see this basket?' said he. 'It is a magical basket, and if you are hungry you have only got to say: "Little basket, little basket, do your duty," and you will eat the best dinner you ever had in your life. But when you have had enough, be sure you don't forget to cry out: "That will do for to-day." Oh!—and one thing more—you need not show it to everybody and declare that I have given it to you. Do you understand?'

Father Grumbler was always accustomed to think of himself as so unlucky that he did not know whether the Holy Man was not playing a trick upon him; but he took the basket without being polite enough to say either 'Thank you,' or 'Good-morning,' and went away. However, he only waited till he was out of sight of the cave before he stooped down and whispered: 'Little basket, little basket, do your duty.'

Now the basket had a lid, so that he could not see what was inside, but he heard quite clearly strange noises, as if a sort of scuffling was going on. Then the lid burst open, and a quantity of delicious little white rolls came tumbling out one after the other, followed by a stream of small fishes all ready cooked. What a quantity there were to be sure! The whole road was covered with them, and the banks on each side were beginning to disappear. Father Grumbler felt quite frightened at the torrent, but at last he remembered what the Holy Man had told him, and cried at the top of his voice: 'Enough! enough! That will do for to-day!' And the lid of the basket closed with a snap.

Father Grumbler sighed with relief and happiness as he looked around him, and sitting down on a heap of stones, he ate till he could eat no more. Trout, salmon, turbot, soles, and a hundred other fishes whose names he

did not know, lay boiled, fried, and grilled within reach of
his hands. As the Holy Man had said, he had never
eaten such a dinner ; still, when he had done, he shook his
head, and grumbled ; ' Yes, there is plenty to eat, of course,

but it only makes me thirsty, and there is not a drop to
drink anywhere.'

Yet, somehow, he could never tell why, he looked up
and saw the tavern in front of him, which he thought was
miles, and miles, and miles away.

'Bring the best wine you have got, and two glasses, good mother,' he said as he entered, 'and if you are fond of fish there is enough here to feed the house. Only there is no need to chatter about it all over the place. You understand? Eh?' And without waiting for an answer he whispered to the basket: 'Little basket, little basket, do your duty.' The innkeeper and his wife thought that their customer had gone suddenly mad, and watched him closely, ready to spring on him if he became violent; but both instinctively jumped backwards, nearly into the fire, as rolls and fishes of every kind came tumbling out of the basket, covering the tables and chairs and the floor, and even overflowing into the street.

'Be quick, be quick, and pick them up,' cried the man. 'And if these are not enough, there are plenty more to be had for the asking.'

The innkeeper and his wife did not need telling twice. Down they went on their knees and gathered up everything they could lay hands on. But busy though they seemed, they found time to whisper to each other:

'If we can only get hold of that basket it will make our fortune!'

So they began by inviting Father Grumbler to sit down to the table, and brought out the best wine in the cellar, hoping it might loosen his tongue. But Father Grumbler was wiser than they gave him credit for, and though they tried in all manner of ways to find out who had given him the basket, he put them off, and kept his secret to himself. Unluckily, though he did not *speak*, he did drink, and it was not long before he fell fast asleep. Then the woman fetched from her kitchen a basket, so like the magic one that no one, without looking very closely, could tell the difference, and placed it in Father Grumbler's hand, while she hid the other carefully away.

It was dinner time when the man awoke, and, jumping up hastily, he set out for home, where he found all the children gathered round a basin of thin soup, and pushing their wooden bowls forward, hoping to have the first spoonful. Their father burst into the midst of them, bearing his basket, and crying :

' Don't spoil your appetites, children, with that stuff. Do you see this basket ? Well, I have only got to say, " Little basket, little basket, do your duty," and you will see what will happen. Now you shall say it instead of me, for a treat.'

The children, wondering and delighted, repeated the words, but nothing happened. Again and again they tried, but the basket was only a basket, with a few scales of fish sticking to the bottom, for the innkeeper's wife had taken it to market the day before.

' What is the matter with the thing ? ' cried the father at last, snatching the basket from them, and turning it all over, grumbling and swearing while he did so, under the eyes of his astonished wife and children, who did not know whether to cry or to laugh.

' It certainly smells of fish,' he said, and then he stopped, for a sudden thought had come to him.

' Suppose it is not mine at all ; supposing—— Ah, the scoundrels ! '

And without listening to his wife and children, who were frightened at his strange conduct and begged him to stay at home, he ran across to the tavern and burst open the door.

' Can I do anything for you, Father Grumbler ? ' asked the innkeeper's wife in her softest voice.

' I have taken the wrong basket—by mistake, of course,' said he. ' Here is yours, will you give me back my own ? '

' Why, what are you talking about ? ' answered she. ' You can see for yourself that there is no basket here.'

And though Father Grumbler *did* look, it was quite true that none was to be seen.

' Come, take a glass to warm you this cold day,' said the woman, who was anxious to keep him in a good temper, and as this was an invitation Father Grumbler never refused, he tossed it off and left the house.

He took the road that led to the Holy Man's cave, and made such haste that it was not long before he reached it.

'Who is there?' said a voice in answer to his knock.

'It is me, it is me, Holy Man. You know quite well. Father Grumbler, who has as many children as sparrows in the garden.'

'But, my good man, it was only yesterday that I gave you a handsome present.'

'Yes, Holy Man, and here it is. But something has happened, I don't know what, and it won't work any more.'

'Well, put it down. I will go and see if I can find anything for you.'

In a few minutes the Holy Man returned with a cock under his arm.

'Listen to me,' he said, 'whenever you want money, you have only to say: "Show me what you can do, cock," and you will see some wonderful things. But, remember, it is not necessary to let all the world into the secret.'

'Oh no, Holy Man, I am not so foolish as that.'

'Nor to tell everybody that I gave it to you,' went on the Holy Man. 'I have not got these treasures by the dozen.'

And without waiting for an answer he shut the door.

As before, the distance seemed to have wonderfully shortened, and in a moment the tavern rose up in front of Father Grumbler. Without stopping to think, he went straight in, and found the innkeeper's wife in the kitchen making a cake.

'Where have you come from, with that fine red cock in your basket,' asked she, for the bird was so big that the lid would not shut down properly.

'Oh, I come from a place where they don't keep these

things by the dozen,' he replied, sitting down in front of the table.

The woman said no more, but set before him a bottle of his favourite wine, and soon he began to wish to display his prize.

'Show me what you can do, cock,' cried he. And the cock stood up and flapped his wings three times, crowing

'COQUERICO'

The Wonderful Cock

'coquerico' with a voice like a trumpet, and at each crow there fell from his beak golden drops, and diamonds as large as peas.

This time Father Grumbler did not invite the innkeeper's wife to pick up his treasures, but put his own hat under the cock's beak, so as to catch everything he let fall; and he did not see the husband and wife exchanging glances with each other which said, 'That would be a splendid cock to put with our basket.'

'Have another glass of wine?' suggested the inn-keeper, when they had finished admiring the beauty of the cock, for they pretended not to have seen the gold or the diamonds. And Father Grumbler, nothing loth, drank one glass after another, till his head fell forward on the table, and once more he was sound asleep. Then the woman gently coaxed the cock from the basket and carried it off to her own poultry yard, from which she brought one exactly like it, and popped it in its place.

Night was falling when the man awoke, and throwing proudly some grains of gold on the table to pay for the wine he had drunk, he tucked the cock comfortably into his basket and set out for home.

His wife and all the children were waiting for him at the door, and as soon as she caught sight of him she broke out:

'You are a nice man to go wasting your time and your money drinking in that tavern, and leaving us to starve! Aren't you ashamed of yourself?'

'You don't know what you are talking of,' he answered. 'Money? Why, I have gold and diamonds now, as much as I want. Do you see that cock? Well, you have only to say to him, "Show what you can do, cock," and some-thing splendid will happen.'

Neither wife nor children were inclined to put much faith in him after their last experience; however, they thought it was worth trying, and did as he told them. The cock flew round the room like a mad thing, and crowed till their heads nearly split with the noise; but no gold or diamonds dropped on the brick floor—not the tiniest grain of either.

Father Grumbler stared in silence for an instant, and then he began to swear so loudly that even his family,

accustomed as they were to his language, wondered at
him.

At last he grew a little quieter, but remained as
puzzled as ever.

'Can I have forgotten the words? But I *know* that
was what he said! And I saw the diamonds with my

The Holy Man gives the bag
to Father Grumbler

own eyes!' Then suddenly he seized the cock, shut it
into the basket, and rushed out of the house.

His heavy wooden shoes clattered as he ran along the
road, and he made such haste that the stars were only
just beginning to come out when he reached the cave of
the Holy Man.

'Who is that knocking?' asked a voice from within.

' It is me !   It is me !   Holy Man ! you know ! Father——'

' But, my good fellow, you really should give some one else a chance.   This is the third time you have been—and at such an hour, too ! '

' Oh, yes, Holy Man, I know it is very late, but you will forgive me ! It is your cock—there is something the matter.   It is like the basket.   Look ! '

' *That* my cock ? *That* my basket ? Somebody has played you a trick, my good man ! '

' A trick ? ' repeated Father Grumbler, who began to understand what had happened. ' Then it must have been those two—— '

' I warned you not to show them to anybody,' said the Holy Man. ' You deserve—— but I will give you one more chance.'   And, turning, he unhooked something from the wall.

' When you wish to dust your own jacket or those of your friends,' he said, ' you have only got to say, " Flack, flick, switch, be quick," and you will see what happens. That is all I have to tell you.'   And, smiling to himself, the Holy Man pushed Father Grumbler out of the cave.

' Ah, I understand now,' muttered the good man, as he took the road home ; ' but I think I have got you two rascals ! ' and he hurried on to the tavern with his basket under his arm, and the cock and the switch both inside.

' Good evening, friends ! ' he said, as he entered the inn. ' I am very hungry, and should be glad if you would roast this cock for me as soon as possible. *This* cock and no other—mind what I say,' he went on. ' Oh, and another thing ! You can light the fire with this basket. When you have done that I will show you something I have in my bag,' and, as he spoke, he tried to imitate the smile that the Holy Man had given *him.*

These directions made the innkeeper's wife very uneasy.   However, she said nothing, and began to roast the cock, while her husband did his best to make the man sleepy with wine, but all in vain.

After dinner, which he did not eat without grumbling, for the cock was very tough, the man struck his hand on the table, and said : 'Now listen to me. Go and fetch my cock and my basket, at once. Do you hear?'

'Your cock, and your basket, Father Grumbler? But you have just——'

'*My* cock and *my* basket!' interrupted he. 'And, if you are too deaf and too stupid to understand what that means, I have got something which may help to teach you.' And opening the bag, he cried : 'Flack! flick! switch, be quick.'

And flack! flick! like lightning a white switch sprang out of the bag, and gave such hearty blows to the inn-keeper and his wife, and to Father Grumbler into the bargain, that they all jumped as high as feathers when a mattress is shaken.

'Stop! stop! make it stop, and you shall have back your cock and basket,' cried the man and his wife. And Father Grumbler, who had no wish to go on, called out between his hops : 'Stop then, can't you? That is enough for to-day!'

But the switch paid no attention, and dealt out its blows as before, and *might* have been dealing them to this day, if the Holy Man had not heard their cries and come to the rescue. 'Into the bag, quick!' said he, and the switch obeyed.

'Now go and fetch me the cock and the basket,' and the woman went without a word, and placed them on the table.

'You have all got what you deserved,' continued the Holy Man, 'and I have no pity for any of you. I shall take my treasures home, and perhaps some day I may find a man who knows how to make the best of the chances that are given him. But that will never be *you*,' he added, turning to Father Grumbler.

[From *Contes Populaires.*]

Down in the south, where the sun shines so hotly that everything and everybody sleeps all day, and even the great forests seem silent, except early in the morning and late in the evening—down in this country there once lived a young man and a maiden. The girl had been born in the town, and had scarcely ever left it ; but the young man was a native of another country, and had only come to the city near the great river because he could find no work to do where he was.

A few months after his arrival, when the days were cooler, and the people did not sleep so much as usual, a great feast was held a little way out of the town, and to this feast everyone flocked from thirty miles and more. Some walked and some rode, some came in beautiful golden coaches ; but all had on splendid dresses of red or blue, while wreaths of flowers rested on their hair.

It was the first time that the youth had been present on such an occasion, and he stood silently aside watching the graceful dances and the pretty games played by the young people. And as he watched, he noticed one girl, dressed in white with scarlet pomegranates in her hair, who seemed to him lovelier than all the rest.

When the feast was over, and the young man returned home, his manner was so strange that it drew the attention of all his friends.

Through his work next day the youth continued to see the girl's face, throwing the ball to her companions, or

threading her way between them as she danced. At
night sleep fled from him, and after tossing for hours on
his bed, he would get up and plunge into a deep pool that
lay a little way in the forest.

This state of things went on for some weeks, then at
last chance favoured him. One evening, as he was passing
near the house where she lived, he saw her standing with
her back to the wall, trying to beat off with her fan the
attacks of a savage dog that was leaping at her throat.
Alonzo, for such was his name, sprang forward, and with
one blow of his fist stretched the creature dead upon the
road. He then helped the frightened and half-fainting
girl into the large cool verandah where her parents were
sitting, and from that hour he was a welcome guest in
the house, and it was not long before he was the promised
husband of Julia.

Every day, when his work was done, he used to go up
to the house, half hidden among flowering plants and
brilliant creepers, where humming-birds darted from bush
to bush, and parrots of all colours, red and green and grey,
shrieked in chorus. There he would find the maiden
waiting for him, and they would spend an hour or two
under the stars, which looked so large and bright that
you felt as if you could almost touch them.

' What did you do last night after you went home? '
suddenly asked the girl one evening.

' Just the same as I always do,' answered he. ' It was
too hot to sleep, so it was no use going to bed, and I
walked straight off to the forest and bathed in one of
those deep dark pools at the edge of the river. I have
been there constantly for several months, but last night
a strange thing happened. I was taking my last plunge,
when I heard—sometimes from one side, and sometimes
from another—the sound of a voice singing more sweetly
than any nightingale, though I could not catch any words.
I left the pool, and, dressing myself as fast as I could,
I searched every bush and tree round the water, as I

fancied that perhaps it was my friend who was playing a trick on me, but there was not a creature to be seen ; and when I reached home I found my friend fast asleep.'

As Julia listened her face grew deadly white, and her whole body shivered as if with cold. From her childhood she had heard stories of the terrible beings that lived in the forests and were hidden under the banks of the rivers, and could only be kept off by powerful charms. Could the voice which had bewitched Alonzo have come from one of these ? Perhaps, who knows, it might be the voice of the dreaded Yara herself, who sought young men on the eve of their marriage as her prey.

For a moment the girl sat choked with fear, as these thoughts rushed through her; then she said : ' Alonzo, will you promise me something ? '

' What is that ? ' asked he.

' It is something that has to do with our future happiness.'

' Oh ! it is serious, then ? Well, of course I promise. Now tell me ! '

' I want you to promise,' she answered, lowering her voice to a whisper, ' never to bathe in those pools again.'

' But why not, queen of my soul; have I not gone there always, and nothing has harmed me, flower of my heart ? '

' No ; but perhaps something will. If you will not promise I shall go mad with fright. Promise me.'

' Why, what is the matter ? You look so pale ! Tell me why you are so frightened ? '

' Did you not hear the song ? ' she asked, trembling.

' Suppose I did, how could that hurt me ? It was the loveliest song I ever heard ! '

' Yes, and after the song will come the apparition ; and after that—after that——'

' I don't understand. Well—after that ? '

' After that—death.'

Alonzo stared at her. Had she really gone mad ?

Such talk was very unlike Julia; but before he could collect his senses the girl spoke again :

' That is the reason why I implore you never to go there again ; at any rate till after we are married.'

' And what difference will our marriage make ? '

' Oh, there will be no danger then ; you can go to bathe as often as you like ! '

' But tell me why you are so afraid ? '

' Because the voice you heard—I know you will laugh, but it is quite true—it was the voice of the Yara.'

At these words Alonzo burst into a shout of laughter ; but it sounded so harsh and loud that Julia shrank away shuddering. It seemed as if he could not stop himself, and the more he laughed the paler the poor girl became, murmuring to herself as she watched him :

' Oh, heaven ! you have seen her ! you have seen her ! what shall I do ? '

Faint as was her whisper, it reached the ears of Alonzo, who, though he still could not speak for laughing, shook his head.

' You may not know it, but it is true. Nobody who has not seen the Yara laughs like that.' And Julia flung herself on the ground weeping bitterly.

At this sight Alonzo became suddenly grave, and kneeling by her side, gently raised her up.

' Do not cry so, my angel,' he said, 'I will promise anything you please. Only let me see you smile again.'

With a great effort Julia checked her sobs, and rose to her feet.

' Thank you,' she answered. ' My heart grows lighter as you say that ! I know you will try to keep your word and to stay away from the forest. But—the power of the Yara is very strong, and the sound of her voice is apt to make men forget everything else in the world. Oh, I have seen it, and more than one betrothed maiden lives alone, broken-hearted. If ever you should return to the pool where you first heard the voice, promise me that you

will at least take this with you.' And opening a curiously
carved box, she took out a sea-shell shot with many

Julia sings her song into the shell

colours, and sang a song softly into it. 'The moment
you hear the Yara's voice,' said she, 'put this to your

ear, and you will hear my song instead. Perhaps—I do
not know for certain—but perhaps, I may be stronger
than the Yara.'

It was late that night when Alonzo returned home.
The moon was shining on the distant river, which looked
cool and inviting, and the trees of the forest seemed to
stretch out their arms and beckon him near. But the
young man steadily turned his face in the other direction,
and went home to bed.

The struggle had been hard, but Alonzo had his reward
next day in the joy and relief with which Julia greeted
him. He assured her that having overcome the tempta-
tion once the danger was now over ; but she, knowing
better than he did the magic of the Yara's face and voice,
did not fail to make him repeat his promise when he
went away.

For three nights Alonzo kept his word, not because he
believed in the Yara, for he thought that the tales about
her were all nonsense, but because he could not bear the
tears with which he knew that Julia would greet him, if he
confessed that he had returned to the forest. But, in spite
of this, the song rang in his ears, and daily grew louder.

On the fourth night the attraction of the forest grew
so strong that neither the thought of Julia nor the pro-
mises he had made her could hold him back. At eleven
o'clock he plunged into the cool darkness of the trees, and
took the path that led straight to the river. Yet, for the
first time, he found that Julia's warnings, though he
had laughed at her at the moment, had remained in his
memory, and he glanced at the bushes with a certain
sense of fear which was quite new to him.

When he reached the river he paused and looked
round for a moment to make sure that the strange feeling
of some one watching him was fancy, and he was really
alone. But the moon shone brightly on every tree, and
nothing was to be seen but his own shadow ; nothing was
to be heard but the sound of the rippling stream.

He threw off his clothes, and was just about to dive in headlong, when something—he did not know what—suddenly caused him to look round.   At the same instant the moon passed from behind a cloud, and its rays fell on a beautiful golden-haired woman standing half hidden by the ferns.

With one bound he caught up his mantle, and rushed headlong down the path he had come, fearing at each step to feel a hand laid on his shoulder.   It was not till he had left the last trees behind him, and was standing in the open plain, that he dared to look round, and then he thought a figure in white was still standing there waving her arms to and fro.   This was enough ; he ran along the road harder than ever, and never paused till he was safe in his own room.

With the earliest rays of dawn he went back to the forest to see whether he could find any traces of the Yara, but though he searched every clump of bushes, and looked up every tree, everything was empty, and the only voices he heard were those of parrots, which are so ugly that they only drive people away.

' I think I must be mad,' he said to himself, ' and have dreamt all that folly ' ; and going back to the city he began his daily work.   But either that was harder than usual, or he must be ill, for he could not fix his mind upon it, and everybody he came across during the day inquired if anything had happened to give him that white, frightened look.

' I must be feverish,' he said to himself; ' after all, it is rather dangerous to take a cold bath when one is feeling so hot.'   Yet he knew, while he said it, that he was counting the hours for night to come, that he might return to the forest.

In the evening he went as usual to the creeper-covered house.   But he had better have stayed away, as his face was so pale and his manner so strange, that the poor girl saw that something terrible had occurred.   Alonzo,

THE YARA DEFEATED

however, refused to answer any of her questions, and all she could get was a promise to hear everything next day.

On pretence of a violent headache, he left Julia much earlier than usual and hurried quickly home. Taking down a pistol, he loaded it and put it in his belt, and a little before midnight he stole out on the tips of his toes, so as to disturb nobody. Once outside he hastened down the road which led to the forest.

He did not stop till he had reached the river pool, when, holding the pistol in his hand, he looked about him. At every little noise—the falling of a leaf, the rustle of an animal in the bushes, the cry of a night-bird—he sprang up and cocked his pistol in the direction of the sound. But though the moon still shone he saw nothing, and by and by a kind of dreamy state seemed to steal over him as he leant against a tree.

How long he remained in this condition he could not have told, but suddenly he awoke with a start, on hearing his name uttered softly.

' Who is that ? ' he cried, standing upright instantly ; but only an echo answered him. Then his eyes grew fascinated with the dark waters of the pool close to his feet, and he looked at it as if he could never look away.

He gazed steadily into the depths for some minutes, when he became aware that down in the darkness was a bright spark, which got rapidly bigger and brighter. Again that feeling of awful fear took possession of him, and he tried to turn his eyes from the pool. But it was no use ; something stronger than himself compelled him to keep them there.

At last the waters parted softly, and floating on the surface he saw the beautiful woman whom he had fled from only a few nights before. He turned to run, but his feet were glued to the spot.

She smiled at him and held out her arms, but as she did so there came over him the remembrance of Julia, as he had seen her a few hours earlier, and her warnings and fears for the very danger in which he now found himself.

Meanwhile the figure was always drawing nearer, nearer; but, with a violent effort, Alonzo shook off his stupor, and taking aim at her shoulder he pulled the trigger. The report awoke the sleeping echoes, and was repeated all through the forest, but the figure smiled still, and went on advancing. Again Alonzo fired, and a second time the bullet whistled through the air, and the figure advanced nearer. A moment more, and she would be at his side.

Then, his pistol being empty, he grasped the barrel with both hands, and stood ready to use it as a club should the Yara approach any closer. But now it seemed her turn to feel afraid, for she paused for an instant while he pressed forward, still holding the pistol above his head, prepared to strike.

In his excitement he had forgotten the river, and it was not till the cold water touched his feet that he stood still by instinct. The Yara saw that he was wavering, and suffering herself to sway gently backwards and forwards on the surface of the river, she began to sing. The song floated through the trees, now far and now near; no one could tell whence it came, the whole air seemed full of it. Alonzo felt his senses going and his will failing. His arms dropped heavily to his side, but in falling struck against the sea shell, which, as he had promised Julia, he had always carried in his coat.

His dimmed mind was just clear enough to remember what she had said, and with trembling fingers, that were almost powerless to grasp, he drew it out. As he did so the song grew sweeter and more tender than before, but he shut his ears to it and bent his head over the shell. Out of its depths arose the voice of Julia singing to him as she had sung when she gave him the shell, and though the notes sounded faint at first, they swelled louder and louder till the mist which had gathered about him was blown away.

Then he raised his head, feeling that he had been through strange places, where he could never wander any more ; and he held himself erect and strong, and looked about him. Nothing was to be seen but the shining of the river, and the dark shadows of the trees ; nothing was to be heard but the hum of the insects, as they darted through the night.

[Adapted from *Folklore Brésilien.*]

THE CUNNING HARE

In a very cold country, far across the seas, where ice and snow cover the ground for many months in the year, there lived a little hare, who, as his father and mother were both dead, was brought up by his grand-mother. As he was too young, and she was too old, to work, they were very poor, and often did not have enough to eat.

One day, when the little fellow was hungrier than usual, he asked his grandmother if he might not go down to the river and catch a fish for their breakfast, as the thaw had come and the water was flowing freely again. She laughed at him for thinking that any fish would let itself be caught by a hare, especially such a young one ; but as she had the rheumatism very badly, and could get no food herself, she let him go. 'If he does not catch a fish he may find something else,' she said to herself. So she told her grandson where to look for the net, and how he was to set it across the river ; but just as he was start-ing, feeling himself quite a man, she called him back.

'After all, I don't know what is the use of your going, my boy ! For even if you should catch a fish, I have no fire to cook it with.'

'Let me catch my fish, and I will soon make you a fire,' he answered gaily, for he was young, and knew nothing about the difficulties of fire-making.

It took him some time to haul the net through bushes and over fields, but at length he reached a pool in the river which he had often heard was swarming with fish,

The little Jrare is caught

and here he set the net, as his grandmother had directed him.

He was so excited that he hardly slept all night, and at the very first streak of dawn he ran as fast as ever he could down to the river. His heart beat as quickly as if he had had dogs behind him, and he hardly dared to look, lest he should be disappointed. Would there be even one fish? And at this thought the pangs of hunger made him feel quite sick with fear. But he need not have been afraid; in every mesh of the net was a fine fat fish, and of course the net itself was so heavy that he could only lift one corner. He threw some of the fish back into the water, and buried some more in a hole under a stone, where he would be sure to find them. Then he rolled up the net with the rest, put it on his back and carried it home. The weight of the load caused his back to ache, and he was thankful to drop it outside their hut, while he rushed in, full of joy, to tell his grandmother. ' Be quick and clean them!' he said,' and I will go to those people's tents on the other side of the water.'

The old woman stared at him in horror as she listened to his proposal. Other people had tried to steal fire before, and few indeed had come back with their lives; but as, contrary to all her expectations, he had managed to catch such a number of fish, she thought that perhaps there was some magic about him which she did not know of, and did not try to hinder him.

When the fish were all taken out, he fetched the net which he had laid out to dry, folded it up very small, and ran down to the river, hoping that he might find a place narrow enough for him to jump over; but he soon saw that it was too wide for even the best jumper in the world. For a few moments he stood there, wondering what was to be done, then there darted into his head some words of a spell which he had once heard a wizard use, while drinking from the river. He repeated them, as well as he could remember, and waited to see what

would happen. In five minutes such a grunting and
a puffing was heard, and columns of water rose into
the air, though he could not tell what had made them.
Then round the bend of the stream came fifteen huge
whales, which he ordered to place themselves heads to
tails, like stepping stones, so that he could jump from one
to the other till he landed on the opposite shore. Directly
he got there he told the whales that he did not need
them any more, and sat down in the sand to rest.

Unluckily some children who were playing about
caught sight of him, and one of them, stealing softly up
behind him, laid tight hold of his ears. The hare, who
had been watching the whales as they sailed down the
river, gave a violent start, and struggled to get away; but
the boy held on tight, and ran back home, as fast as he
could go.

'Throw it in the pot,' said the old woman, as soon as
he had told his story; 'put it in that basket, and as soon
as the water boils in the pot we will hang it over the
fire!'

'Better kill it first,' said the old man; and the hare
listened, horribly frightened, but still looking secretly to
see if there was no hole through which he could escape,
if he had a chance of doing so. Yes, there was one, right
in the top of the tent, so, shaking himself, as if with
fright, he let the end of his net unroll itself a little.

'I wish that a spark of fire would fall on my net,'
whispered he; and the next minute a great log fell forward
into the midst of the tent, causing every one to spring
backwards. The sparks were scattered in every direction,
and one fell on the net, making a little blaze. In an
instant the hare had leaped through the hole, and was
racing towards the river, with men, women, and children
after him. There was no time to call back the whales, so,
holding the net tight in his mouth, he wished himself
across the river. Then he jumped high into the air, and
landed safe on the other side, and after turning round to

be sure that there was no chance of anyone pursuing him, trotted happily home to his grandmother.

'Didn't I tell you I would bring you fire?' said he, holding up his net, which was now burning briskly.

'But how did you cross the water?' inquired the old woman.

'Oh, I just jumped!' said he. And his grandmother asked him no more questions, for she saw that he was wiser than she.

[' Indian Folk Tales.'   *Bureau of Ethnology.*]

THE TURTLE AND HIS BRIDE

THERE was once a turtle who lived among a great many people of different kinds, in a large camp near a big river which was born right up amongst the snows, and flowed straight away south till it reached a sea where the water was always hot.

There were many other turtles in the camp, and this turtle was kind and pleasant to them all, but he did not care for any of them very much, and felt rather lonely.

At last he built himself a hut, and filled it with skins for seats, and made it as comfortable as any hut for miles round; and when it was quite finished he looked about among the young women to see which of them he should ask to be his wife.

It took him some time to make up his mind, for no turtle likes being hurried, but at length he found one girl who seemed prettier and more industrious than the rest, and one day he entered her home, and said : 'Will you marry me?'

The young woman was so surprised at this question that she dropped the beaded slipper she was making, and stared at the turtle. She felt inclined to laugh—the idea was so absurd; but she was kind-hearted and polite, so she looked as grave as she could, and answered :

'But how are you going to provide for a family? Why, when the camp moves, you will not even be able to keep up with the rest!'

'I can keep up with the best of them,' replied the

turtle, tossing his head. But though he was very much offended he did not let the girl see it, and begged and, prayed her so hard to marry him that, at last, she consented, very unwillingly.

'You will have to wait till the spring, though,' she said; 'I must make a great many slippers and dresses for myself, as I shall not have much time afterwards.'

This did not please the turtle; but he knew it was no use talking, so all he answered was:

'I shall go to war and take some captives, and I shall be away several months. And when I return I shall expect you to be ready to marry me.'

So he went back to his hut, and at once set about his preparations. The first thing he did was to call all his relations together, and ask them if they would come with him and make war on the people of a neighbouring village. The turtles, who were tired of doing nothing, agreed at once, and next day the whole tribe left the camp. The girl was standing at the door of her hut as they passed, and laughed out loud—they moved so slowly. Her lover, who was marching at the head, grew very angry at this, and cried out:

'In four days from now you will be weeping instead of laughing, because there will be hundreds of miles between you and me.'

'In four days,' replied the girl—who had only promised to marry him in order to get rid of him—'in four days you will hardly be out of sight.'

'Oh, I did not mean four days, but four *years*,' answered the turtle, hastily; 'whatever happens I shall be back by then.'

The army marched on, till one day, when they felt as if they must have got half round the earth, though they were scarcely four miles from the camp, they found a large tree lying across their path. They looked at it with dismay, and the oldest among them put their heads together to see what was to be done.

'Can't we manage to get past by the top?' asked one.

THE GIRL LAUGHS AT THE ARMY OF TURTLES

'Why, it would take us *years*,' exclaimed another. 'Just look at all those tall green branches, spreading in every direction. If once we got entangled in *them*, we should never get out again !'

'Well then, let us go round by the bottom,' said a third.

'How are we to do that, when the roots have made a deep hole, and above that is a high bank?' replied a fourth. 'No; the only way *I* can think of, is to burn a large hole in the trunk.' And this they did, but the trunk was very thick, and would not burn through.

'It is no use, we must give it up,' they agreed at last. 'After all, nobody need ever know! We have been away such a long while that we might easily have had all sorts of adventures.' And so the whole company turned homewards again.

They took even longer to go back than they had to come, for they were tired and footsore with their journey. When they drew near the camp they plucked up their courage, and began to sing a war-song. At this the villagers came flocking to see what spoils the turtles had won, but, as they approached, each turtle seized some one by the wrist, exclaiming : 'You are our spoils ; you are our prisoners!'

'Now that I have got you I will keep you,' said the leader, who had happened to seize his betrothed.

Everybody was naturally very angry at this behaviour, and the girl most of all, and in her secret heart she determined to have her revenge. But, just at present, the turtles were too strong, so the prisoners had to put on their smartest slippers and their brightest clothes, and dance a war dance while the turtles sang. They danced so long that it seemed as if they would never stop, till the turtle who was leading the singing suddenly broke into a loud chant :

Whoever comes here, will die, will die!

At this all the dancers grew so frightened that they

burst through the ring of their captors, and ran back to the village, the turtles following—very slowly. On the way the chief turtle met a man, who said to him:

'That woman who was to have been your wife has married another man!'

'Is that true?' said the turtle. 'Then I must see him.'

But as soon as the villager was out of sight the turtle stopped, and taking a bundle containing fringes and ornaments from his back, he hung them about him, so that they rattled as he walked. When he was quite close to the hut where the woman lived, he cried out:

'Here I am to claim the woman who promised to be my wife.'

'Oh, here is the turtle,' whispered the husband hurriedly; 'what is to be done now?'

'Leave that to me; I will manage him,' replied the wife, and at that moment the turtle came in, and seized her by the wrist. 'Come with me,' he said sternly.

'You broke your promise,' answered she. 'You said you would be back soon, and it is more than a year since you went! How was I to know that you were alive?'

At her words the husband took courage, and spoke hastily:

'Yes, you promised you would go to war and bring back some prisoners, and you have not done it.'

'I *did* go, and made many prisoners,' retorted the turtle angrily, drawing out his knife. 'Look here, if she won't be *my* wife, she sha'n't be *yours*. I will cut her in two; and you shall have one half, and I the other.'

'But half a woman is no use to me,' answered the man. 'If you want her so much you had better take her.' And the turtle, followed by his relations, carried her off to his own hut.

Now the woman saw she would gain nothing by being sulky, so she pretended to be very glad to have got rid of her husband; but all the while she was trying to invent a

THE TURTLE OUTWITTED

plan to deliver herself from the turtle. At length she re-membered that one of her friends had a large iron pot, and when the turtle had gone to his room to put away his fringes, she ran over to her neighbour's and brought it back. Then she filled it with water and hung it over the fire to boil. It was just beginning to bubble and hiss when the turtle entered.

'What are you doing there?' asked he, for he was always afraid of things that he did not understand.

'Just warming some water,' she answered. 'Do you know how to swim?'

'Yes, of course I do. What a question! But what does it matter to you?' said the turtle, more suspicious than ever.

'Oh, I only thought that after your long journey you might like to wash. The roads are so muddy, after the winter's rains. I could rub your shell for you till it was bright and shining again.

'Well, I *am* rather muddy. If one is fighting, you know, one cannot stop to pick one's way. I should certainly be more comfortable if my back was washed.'

The woman did not wait for him to change his mind. She caught him up by his shell and popped him straight into the pot, where he sank to the bottom, and died instantly.

The other turtles, who were standing at the door, saw their leader disappear, and felt it was their duty as soldiers to follow him; and, springing into the pot, died too. All but one young turtle, who, frightened at not seeing any of his friends come out again, went as fast as he could to a clump of bushes, and from there made his way to the river. His only thought was to get away as far as possible from that dreadful hut; so he let the river carry him where it was going itself, and at last, one day, he found himself in the warm sea, where, if he is not dead, you may meet him still.

[*Bureau of Ethnology.*]

HOW GEIRALD THE COWARD WAS PUNISHED

ONCE upon a time there lived a poor knight who had a great many children, and found it very hard to get enough for them to eat. One day he sent his eldest son, Rosald, a brave and honest youth, to the neighbouring town to do some business, and here Rosald met a young man named Geirald, with whom he made friends.

Now Geirald was the son of a rich man, who was proud of the boy, and had all his life allowed him to do whatever he fancied, and, luckily for the father, he was prudent and sensible, and did not waste money, as many other rich young men might have done. For some time he had set his heart on travelling into foreign countries, and after he had been talking for a little while to Rosald, he asked if his new friend would be his companion on his journey.

'There is nothing I should like better,' answered Rosald, shaking his head sorrowfully; 'but my father is very poor, and he could never give me the money.'

'Oh, if that is your only difficulty, it is all right,' cried Geirald. 'My father has more money than he knows what to do with, and he will give me as much as I want for both of us ; only, there is one thing you must promise me, Rosald, that, supposing we have any adventures, you will let the honour and glory of them fall to me.'

'Yes, of course, that is only fair,' answered Rosald, who never cared about putting himself forward. 'But I cannot go without telling my parents. I am sure they will think me lucky to get such a chance.'

As soon as the business was finished, Rosald hastened home. His parents were delighted to hear of his good fortune, and his father gave him his own sword, which was growing rusty for want of use, while his mother saw that his leather jerkin was in order.

'Be sure you keep the promise you made to Geirald,' said she, as she bade him good-bye, 'and, come what may, see that you never betray him.'

Full of joy Rosald rode off, and the next day he and Geirald started off to seek adventures. To their disappointment their own land was so well governed that nothing out of the common was very likely to happen, but directly they crossed the border into another kingdom all seemed lawlessness and confusion.

They had not gone very far, when, riding across a mountain, they caught a glimpse of several armed men hiding amongst some trees in their path, and remembered suddenly some talk they had heard of a band of twelve robbers who lay in wait for rich travellers. The robbers were more like savage beasts than men, and lived somewhere at the top of the mountain in caves and holes in the ground. They were all called 'Hankur,' and were distinguished one from another by the name of a colour —blue, grey, red, and so on, except their chief, who was known as Hankur the Tall. All this and more rushed into the minds of the two young men as they saw the flash of their swords in the moonlight.

'It is impossible to fight them—they are twelve to two,' whispered Geirald, stopping his horse in the path. 'We had much better ride back and take the lower road. It would be stupid to throw away our lives like this.'

'Oh, we can't turn back,' answered Rosald, 'we should be ashamed to look anyone in the face again! And, besides, it is a grand opportunity to show what we are made of. Let us tie up our horses here, and climb up the rocks so that we can roll stones down on them.'

'Well, we might try that, and then we shall always

have our horses,' said Geirald.   So they went up the rocks silently and carefully.

The robbers were lying all ready, expecting every moment to see their victims coming round the corner a few yards away, when a shower of huge stones fell on their heads, killing half the band.   The others sprang up the rock, but as they reached the top the sword of Rosald swung round, and one man after another rolled down into the valley.   At last the chief managed to spring up, and, grasping Rosald by the waist, flung away his sword, and the two fought desperately, their bodies swaying always nearer the edge.   It seemed as if Rosald, being the smaller of the two, *must* fall over, when, with his left hand, he drew the robber's sword out of its sheath and plunged it into his heart.   Then he took from the dead man a beautiful ring set with a large stone, and put it on his own finger.

The fame of this wonderful deed soon spread through the country, and people would often stop Geirald's horse, and ask leave to see the robber's ring, which was said to have been stolen from the father of the reigning king. And Geirald showed them the ring with pride, and listened to their words of praise, and no one would ever have guessed anyone else had destroyed the robbers.

In a few days they left that kingdom and rode on to another, where they thought they would stop through the remainder of the winter, for Geirald liked to be comfortable, and did not care about travelling through ice and snow.   But the king would only grant them leave to stop on condition that, before the winter was ended, they should give him some fresh proof of the courage of which he had heard so much.   Rosald's heart was glad at the king's message, and as for Geirald, he felt that as long as Rosald was there all would go well.   So they both bowed low and replied that it was the king's place to command and theirs to obey.

'Well, then,' said his Majesty, 'this is what I want

you to do : In the north-east part of my kingdom there
dwells a giant, who has an iron staff twenty yards long,
and he is so quick in using it, that even fifty knights have
no chance against him. The bravest and strongest young
men of my court have fallen under the blows of that staff;
but, as you overcame the twelve robbers so easily, I feel
that I have reason to hope that you may be able to
conquer the giant. In three days from this you will
set out.'

'We will be ready, your Majesty,' answered Rosald;
but Geirald remained silent.

'How can we possibly fight against a giant that has
killed fifty knights?' cried Geirald, when they were outside
the castle. 'The king only wants to get rid of us! He
won't think about us for the next three days—that is
one comfort—so we shall have plenty of time to cross the
borders of the kingdom and be out of his reach.'

'We mayn't be able to kill the giant, but we certainly can't run away till we have tried,' answered Rosald.
'Besides, think how glorious it will be if we *do* manage to
kill him! I know what sort of weapon I shall use.
Come with me now, and I will see about it.' And, taking
his friend by the arm, he led him into a shop where he
bought a huge lump of solid iron, so big that they could
hardly lift it between them. However, they just managed
to carry it to a blacksmith's where Rosald directed that it
should be beaten into a thick club, with a sharp spike at
one end. When this was done to his liking he took it
home under his arm.

Very early on the third morning the two young men
started on their journey, and on the fourth day they
reached the giant's cave before he was out of bed.
Hearing the sound of footsteps, the giant got up and
went to the entrance to see who was coming, and Rosald,
expecting something of the sort, struck him such a blow

on the forehead that he fell to the ground. Then, before he could rise to his feet again, Rosald drew out his sword and cut off his head.

'It was not so difficult after all, you see,' he said, turning to Geirald. And placing the giant's head in a leathern wallet which was slung over his back, they began their journey to the castle.

As they drew near the gates, Rosald took the head from the wallet and handed it to Geirald, whom he followed into the king's presence.

'The giant will trouble you no more,' said Geirald, holding out the head. And the king fell on his neck and kissed him, and cried joyfully that he was the ' bravest knight in all the world, and that a feast should be made for him and Rosald, and that the great deed should be proclaimed throughout the kingdom. And Geirald's heart swelled with pride, and he almost forgot that it was Rosald and not he, who had slain the giant.

By-and-by a whisper went round that a beautiful lady who lived in the castle would be present at the feast, with twenty-four lovely maidens, her attendants. The lady was the queen of her own country, but as her father and mother had died when she was a little girl, she had been left in the care of this king who was her uncle.

She was now old enough to govern her own kingdom, but her subjects did not like being ruled by a woman, and said that she must find a husband to help her in managing her affairs. Prince after prince had offered himself, but the young queen would have nothing to say to any of them, and at last told her ministers that if she was to have a husband at all she must choose him for herself, as she would certainly not marry any of those whom they had selected for her. The ministers replied that in that case she had better manage her kingdom alone, and the queen, who knew nothing about business, got things into such a confusion that at last she threw them up altogether, and went off to her uncle.

Now when she heard how the two young men had
slain the giant, her heart was filled with admiration of

" THE GIANT WILL TROUBLE YOU NO MORE " said Geirald

their courage, and she declared that if a feast was held
she would certainly be present at it.

And so she was; and when the feast was over she

asked the king, her guardian, if he would allow the two heroes who had killed the robbers and slain the giant to fight a tourney the next day with one of her pages. The king gladly gave his consent, and ordered the lists to be made ready, never doubting that two great champions would be eager for such a chance of adding to their fame. Little did he guess that Geirald had done all he could to persuade Rosald to steal secretly out of the castle during the night, 'for,' said he, 'I don't believe they are pages at all, but well-proved knights, and how can we, so young and untried, stand up against them?'

'The honour will be all the higher if we gain the day,' answered Rosald; but Geirald would listen to nothing, and only declared that he did not care about honour, and would rather be alive than have every honour in the world heaped on him. Go he would, and as Rosald had sworn to give him his company, he must come with him.

Rosald was much grieved when he heard these words, but he knew that it was useless attempting to persuade Geirald, and turned his thoughts to forming some plan to prevent this disgraceful flight. Suddenly his face brightened. 'Let us change clothes,' he said, 'and *I* will do the fighting, while you shall get the glory. Nobody will ever know.' And to this Geirald readily consented.

Whether Geirald was right or not in thinking that the so-called page was really a well-proved knight, it is certain that Rosald's task was a very hard one. Three times they came together with a crash which made their horses reel; once Rosald knocked the helmet off his foe, and received in return such a blow that he staggered in his saddle. Shouts went up from the lookers-on, as first one and then the other seemed gaining the victory; but at length Rosald planted his spear in the armour which covered his adversary's breast and bore him steadily backward. 'Unhorsed! unhorsed!' cried the people; and Rosald then himself dismounted and helped his adversary to rise.

In the confusion that followed it was easy for Rosald

— GEIRALD CLAIMS HIS REWARD AND THE QVEEN DEMANDS ANOTHER TEST —

to slip away and return Geirald his proper clothes. And in these, torn and dusty with the fight, Geirald answered the king's summons to come before him.

'You have done what I expected you to do,' said he, 'and now, choose your reward.'

'Grant me, sire, the hand of the queen, your niece,' replied the young man, bowing low, 'and I will defend her kingdom against all her enemies.'

'She could choose no better husband,' said the king, 'and if she consents I do.' And he turned towards the queen, who had not been present during the fight, but had just slipped into a seat by his right hand. Now the queen's eyes were very sharp, and it seemed to her that the man who stood before her, tall and handsome though he might be, was different in many slight ways, and in one in particular, from the man who had fought the tourney. How there could be any trickery she could not understand, and why the real victor should be willing to give up his prize to another was still stranger; but something in her heart warned her to be careful. She answered: 'You may be satisfied, uncle, but *I* am not. One more proof I must have; let the two young men now fight against each other. The man *I* marry must be the man who killed the robbers and the giant, and overcame my page.' Geirald's face grew pale as he heard these words. He knew there was no escape for him now, though he did not doubt for one moment that Rosald would keep his compact loyally to the last. But how would it be possible that even Rosald should deceive the watchful eyes of the king and his court, and still more those of the young queen whom he felt uneasily had suspected him from the first?

The tourney was fought, and in spite of Geirald's fears Rosald managed to hang back to make attacks which were never meant to succeed, and to allow strokes which he could easily have parried to attain their end. At length, after a great show of resistance, he fell heavily to the ground. And as he fell he knew that it was not alone the glory that was his rightfully which he gave up, but the hand of the queen that was more precious still.

But Geirald did not even wait to see if he was wounded; he went straight to the wall where the royal banner waved and claimed the reward which was now his.

The crowd of watchers turned towards the queen, expecting to see her stoop and give some token to the victor. Instead, to the surprise of everyone, she merely smiled gracefully, and said that before she bestowed her hand one more test must be imposed, but this should be the last. The final tourney should be fought; Geirald and Rosald should meet singly two knights of the king's court, and he who could unhorse his foe should be master of herself and of her kingdom. The combat was fixed to take place at ten o'clock the following day.

All night long Geirald walked about his room, not daring to face the fight that lay in front of him, and trying with all his might to discover some means of escaping it. All night long he moved restlessly from door to window; and when the trumpets sounded, and the combatants rode into the field, he alone was missing. The king sent messengers to see what had become of him, and he was found, trembling with fear, hiding under his bed. After that there was no need of any further proof. The combat was declared unnecessary, and the queen pronounced herself quite satisfied, and ready to accept Rosald as her husband.

'You forgot one thing,' she said, when they were alone. 'I recognised my father's ring which Hankur the Tall had stolen, on the finger of your right hand, and I knew that it was you and not Geirald who had slain the robber band. *I* was the page who fought you, and again I saw the ring on your finger, though it was absent from his when he stood before me to claim the prize. That was why I ordered the combat between you, though your faith to your word prevented my plan being successful, and I had to try another. The man who keeps his promise at all costs to himself is the man I can trust, both for myself and for my people.'

So they were married, and returned to their own kingdom, which they ruled well and happily. And many years after a poor beggar knocked at the palace gates and asked for money, for the sake of days gone by—and this was Geirald.

[From *Neuislandischem Volksmärcher*.]

HÁBOGI

ONCE upon a time there lived two peasants who had three daughters, and, as generally happens, the youngest was the most beautiful and the best tempered, and when her sisters wanted to go out she was always ready to stay at home and do their work.

Years passed quickly with the whole family, and one day the parents suddenly perceived that all three girls were grown up, and that very soon they would be thinking of marriage.

'Have you decided what your husband's name is to be?' said the father, laughingly, to his eldest daughter, one evening when they were all sitting at the door of their cottage. 'You know that is a very important point!'

'Yes; I will never wed any man who is not called Sigmund,' answered she.

'Well, it is lucky for you that there are a great many Sigmunds in this part of the world,' replied her father, 'so that you can take your choice! And what do *you* say?' he added, turning to the second.

'Oh, *I* think that there is no name so beautiful as Sigurd,' cried she.

'Then you won't be an old maid either,' answered he. 'There are seven Sigurds in the next village alone! And you, Helga?'

Helga, who was still the prettiest of the three, looked up. She also had her favourite name, but, just as she was going to say it, she seemed to hear a voice whisper: 'Marry no one who is not called Hábogi.'

The girl had never heard of such a name, and did not like it, so she determined to pay no attention; but as she opened her mouth to tell her father that her husband must be called Njal, she found herself answering instead : 'If I do marry it will be to no one except Hábogi.'

'Who *is* Hábogi?' asked her father and sisters; 'We never heard of such a person.'

'All I can tell you is that he will be my husband, if ever I have one,' returned Helga; and that was all she would say.

Before very long the young men who lived in the neighbouring villages or on the sides of the mountains, had heard of this talk of the three girls, and Sigmunds and Sigurds in scores came to visit the little cottage. There were other young men too, who bore different names, though not one of them was called 'Hábogi,' and these thought that they might perhaps gain the heart of the youngest. But though there was more than one 'Njal' amongst them, Helga's eyes seemed always turned another way.

At length the two elder sisters made their choice from out of the Sigurds and the Sigmunds, and it was decided that both weddings should take place at the same time. Invitations were sent out to the friends and relations, and when, on the morning of the great day, they were all assembled, a rough, coarse old peasant left the crowd and came up to the brides' father.

'My name is Hábogi, and Helga must be my wife,' was all he said. And though Helga stood pale and trembling with surprise, she did not try to run away.

'I cannot talk of such things just now,' answered the father, who could not bear the thought of giving his favourite daughter to this horrible old man, and hoped, by putting it off, that something might happen. But the sisters, who had always been rather jealous of Helga, were secretly pleased that their bridegrooms should outshine hers.

When the feast was over, Hábogi led up a beautiful
horse from a field where he had left it to graze, and bade
Helga jump up on its splendid saddle, all embroidered in
scarlet and gold. ' You shall come b ck again,' said he;
' but now you must see the house that you are to live in.'
And though Helga was very unwilling to go, something
inside her forced her to obey.

The old man settled her comfortably, then sprang up
in front of her as easily as if he had been a boy, and,
shaking the reins, they were soon out of sight.

After some miles they rode through a meadow, with
grass so green that Helga's eyes felt quite dazzled; and
feeding on the grass were a quantity of large fat sheep,
with the curliest and whitest wool in the world.

' What lovely sheep ! whose are they ? ' cried Helga.

' Your Hábogi's,' answered he, ' all that you see
belongs to him ; but the finest sheep in the whole herd,
which has little golden bells hanging between its horns,
you shall have for yourself.'

This pleased Helga very much, for she had never had
anything of her own ; and she smiled quite happily as she
thanked Hábogi for his present.

They soon left the sheep behind them, and entered a
large field with a river running through it, where a
number of beautiful grey cows were standing by a gate
waiting for a milk-maid to come and milk them.

' Oh, what lovely cows ! ' cried Helga again ; ' I am
sure their milk must be sweeter than any other cows.'
How I should like to have some !   I wonder to whom
they belong ? '

' To your Hábogi,' replied he ; ' and some day you
shall have as much milk as you like, but we cannot stop
now.   Do you see that big grey one, with the silver
bells between her horns ?   That is to be yours, and you
can have her milked every morning the moment you
wake.'

And Helga's eyes shone, and though she did not say

"Oh do stop for a minute" said HELGA HABOGI'S HORSES But HABOGI would not stop or listen

[This illustration is reproduced in color between pages 74 and 75.]

anything, she thought that she would learn to milk the cow herself.

A mile further on they came to a wide common, with short, springy turf, where horses of all colours, with skins of satin, were kicking up their heels in play. The sight of them so delighted Helga that she nearly sprang from her saddle with a shriek of joy.

'Whose are they? Oh! whose are they?' she asked. 'How happy any man must be who is the master of such lovely creatures!'

'They are your Hábogi's,' replied he, 'and the one which you think the most beautiful of all you shall have for yourself, and learn to ride him.'

At this Helga quite forgot the sheep and the cow.

'A horse of my own!' said she. 'Oh, stop one moment, and let me see which I will choose. The white one? No. The chestnut? No. I think, after all, I like the coal-black one best, with the little white star on his forehead. Oh, do stop, just for a minute.'

But Hábogi would not stop or listen. 'When you are married you will have plenty of time to choose one,' was all he answered, and they rode on two or three miles further.

At length Hábogi drew rein before a small house, very ugly and mean-looking, and that seemed on the point of tumbling to pieces.

'This is my house, and is to be yours,' said Hábogi, as he jumped down and held out his arms to lift Helga from the horse. The girl's heart sank a little, as she thought that the man who possessed such wonderful sheep, and cows, and horses, might have built himself a prettier place to live in; but she did not say so. And, taking her arm, he led her up the steps.

But when she got inside, she stood quite bewildered at the beauty of all around her. None of her friends owned such things, not even the miller, who was the richest man she knew. There were carpets everywhere,

thick and soft, and of deep rich colours ; and the cushions
were of silk, and made you sleepy even to look at them ;
and curious little figures in china were scattered about.
Helga felt as if it would take her all her life to see everything properly, and it only seemed a second since she
had entered the house, when Hábogi came up to her.

'I must begin the preparations for our wedding at
once,' he said ; 'but my foster-brother will take you home,
as I promised.   In three days he will bring you back here,
with your parents and sisters, and any guests you may
invite, in your company.   By that time the feast will be
ready.'

Helga had so much to think about, that the ride
home appeared very short.   Her father and mother were
delighted to see her, as they did not feel sure that so
ugly and cross-looking a man as Hábogi might not have
played her some cruel trick.   And after they had given her
some supper they begged her to tell them all she had
done.   But Helga only told them that they should see
for themselves on the third day, when they would come
to her wedding.

It was very early in the morning when the party set
out, and Helga's two sisters grew green with envy as
they passed the flocks of sheep, and cows, and horses, and
heard that the best of each was given to Helga herself ;
but when they caught sight of the poor little house which
was to be her home their hearts grew light again.

'I should be ashamed of living in such a place,'
whispered each to the other ; and the eldest sister spoke
of the carved stone over *her* doorway, and the second
boasted of the number of rooms *she* had.   But the
moment they went inside they were struck dumb with
rage at the splendour of everything, and their faces grew
white and cold with fury when they saw the dress which
Hábogi had prepared for his bride—a dress that glittered
like sunbeams dancing upon ice.

'She *shall* not look so much finer than us,' they cried

The Jealous Sisters,
Spell-bound
in the Ashpit

passionately to each other as soon as they were alone; and when night came they stole out of their rooms, and taking out the wedding-dress, they laid it in the ash-pit, and heaped ashes upon it. But Hábogi, who knew a little magic, and had guessed what they would do, changed the ashes into roses, and cast a spell over the sisters, so that they could not leave the spot for a whole day, and every one who passed by mocked at them.

The next morning when they all awoke the ugly little tumble-down house had disappeared, and in its place stood a splendid palace. The guests' eyes sought in vain for the bridegroom, but could only see a handsome young man, with a coat of blue velvet and silver and a gold crown upon his head.

'Who is that?' they asked Helga.

'That is my Hábogi,' said she.

[*Neuisländischen Volksmärchen.*]

HOW THE LITTLE BROTHER SET FREE HIS BIG BROTHERS

In a small hut, right in the middle of the forest, lived a man, his wife, three sons and a daughter. For some reason, all the animals seemed to have left that part of the country, and food grew very scarce; so, one morning, after a night of snow, when the tracks of beasts might be easily seen, the three boys started off to hunt.

They kept together for some time, till they reached a place where the path they had been following split into two, and one of the brothers called his dog and went to the left, while the others took the trail to the right. These had not gone far when their dogs scented a bear, and drove him out from the thicket. The bear ran across a clearing, and the elder brother managed to place an arrow right in his head.

They both took up the bear, and carried it towards home, meeting the third at the spot where they had parted from him. When they reached home they threw the bear down on the floor of the hut saying,

'Father, here is a bear which we killed; now we can have some dinner.'

But the father, who was in a bad temper, only said:

'When I was a young man we used to get two bears in one day.'

The sons were rather disappointed at hearing this, and though there was plenty of meat to last for two or three days, they started off early in the morning down the same trail that they had followed before. As they drew near the fork a bear suddenly ran out from behind a tree, and took the path on the right. The two elder boys and their

EVERY TIME A BEAR WAS KILLED HIS SHADOW
RETURNED TO THE HOUSE OF THE GREAT BEAR-CHIEF

dogs pursued him, and soon the second son, who was also a good shot, killed him instantly with an arrow. At the fork of the trail, on their way home, they met the youngest, who had taken the left-hand road, and had shot a bear for himself. But when they threw the two bears triumphantly on the floor of the hut their father hardly looked at them, and only said :

'When *I* was a young man I used to get three bears in one day.'

The next day they were luckier than before, and brought back three bears, on which their father told them that *he* had always killed four. However, that did not prevent him from skinning the bears and cooking them in a way of his own, which he thought very good, and they all ate an excellent supper.

Now these bears were the servants of the great bear chief who lived in a high mountain a long way off. And every time a bear was killed his shadow returned to the house of the bear chief, with the marks of his wounds plainly to be seen by the rest.

The chief was furious at the number of bears the hunters had killed, and determined that he would find some way of destroying them. So he called another of his servants, and said to him :

'Go to the thicket near the fork, where the boys killed your brothers, and directly they or the dogs see you return here as fast as ever you can. The mountain will open to let you in, and the hunters will follow you. Then I shall have them in my power, and be able to revenge myself.'

The servant bowed low, and started at once for the fork, where he hid himself in the bushes.

By-and-by the boys came in sight, but this time there were only two of them, as the youngest had stayed at home. The air was warm and damp, and the snow soft and slushy, and the elder brother's bowstring hung loose, while the bow of the younger caught in a tree and snapped in half. At that moment the dogs began to bark loudly, and the bear rushed out of the thicket and set off in the direction of the mountain. Without thinking that they had nothing to defend themselves with, should the bear turn and attack them, the boys gave chase. The bear, who knew quite well that he could not be shot, sometimes slackened his pace and let the dogs get quite close; and in this way the elder son reached the mountain without observing it, while his brother, who had hurt his foot, was still far behind.

As he ran up, the mountain opened to admit the bear, and the boy, who was close on his heels, rushed in after him, and did not know where he was till he saw bears sitting on every side of him, holding a council. The animal he had been chasing sank panting in their midst, and the boy, very much frightened, stood still, letting his bow fall to the ground.

' Why are you trying to kill all my servants ? ' asked the chief. ' Look round and see their shades, with arrows sticking in them. It was I who told the bear to-day how he was to lure you into my power. I shall take care that you shall not hurt my people any more, because you will become a bear yourself.'

At this moment the second brother came up—for the mountain had been left open on purpose to tempt him also—and cried out breathlessly : ' Don't you see that the bear is lying close to you ? Why don't you shoot him ? ' And, without waiting for a reply, pressed forward to drive his arrow into the heart of the bear. But the elder one caught his raised arm, and whispered : ' Be quiet ! can't you tell where you are ? ' Then the boy looked up and saw the angry bears about him. On the one side were the servants of the chief, and on the other the servants of the chief's sister, who was sorry for the two youths, and begged that their lives might be spared. The chief answered that he would not kill them, but only cast a spell over them, by which their heads and bodies should remain as they were, but their arms and legs should change into those of a bear, so that they would go on all fours for the rest of their lives. And, stooping over a spring of water, he dipped a handful of moss in it and rubbed it over the arms and legs of the boys. In an instant the transformation took place, and two creatures, neither beast nor human, stood before the chief.

Now the bear chief of course knew that the boys' father would seek for his sons when they did not return

How the boys were half turned into BEARS

home, so he sent another of his servants to the hiding-place at the fork of the trail to see what would happen. He had not waited long, when the father came in sight, stooping as he went to look for his sons' tracks in the snow. When he saw the marks of snow-shoes along the path on the right he was filled with joy, not knowing that the servant had made some fresh tracks on purpose to mislead him; and he hastened forward so fast that he fell headlong into a pit, where the bear was sitting. Before he could pick himself up the bear had quietly broken his neck, and, hiding the body under the snow, sat down to see if anyone else would pass that way.

Meanwhile the mother at home was wondering what had become of her two sons, and as the hours went on, and their father never returned, she made up her mind to go and look for him. The youngest boy begged her to let him undertake the search, but she would not hear of it, and told him he must stay at home and take care of his sister. So, slipping on her snow-shoes, she started on her way.

As no fresh snow had fallen, the trail was quite easy to find, and she walked straight on, till it led her up to the pit where the bear was waiting for her. He grasped her as she fell and broke her neck, after which he laid her in the snow beside her husband, and went back to tell the bear chief.

Hour after hour dragged heavily by in the forest hut, and at last the brother and sister felt quite sure that in some way or other all the rest of the family had perished. Day after day the boy climbed to the top of a tall tree near the house, and sat there till he was almost frozen, looking on all sides through the forest openings, hoping that he might see someone coming along. Very soon all the food in the house was eaten, and he knew he would have to go out and hunt for more. Besides, he wished to seek for his parents.

The little girl did not like being left alone in the hut, and cried bitterly; but her brother told her that there was no use sitting down quietly to starve, and that whether he found any game or not he would certainly be back before the following night. Then he cut himself some arrows, each from a different tree, and winged with the feathers of four different birds. He then made himself a bow, very light and strong, and got down his snow-shoes. All this took some time, and he could not start that day, but early next morning he called his little dog Redmouth, whom he kept in a box, and set out.

After he had followed the trail for a great distance he grew very tired, and sat upon the branch of a tree to rest. But Redmouth barked so furiously that the boy thought that perhaps his parents might have been killed under its branches, and, stepping back, shot one of his arrows at the root of the tree. Whereupon a noise like thunder shook it from top to bottom, fire broke out, and in a few minutes a little heap of ashes lay in the place where it had stood.

Not knowing quite what to make of it all, the boy continued on the trail, and went down the right-hand fork till he came to the clump of bushes where the bears used to hide.

Now, as was plain by his being able to change the shape of the two brothers, the bear chief knew a good deal of magic, and he was quite aware that the little boy was following the trail, and he sent a very small but clever bear servant to wait for him in the bushes and to try to tempt him into the mountain. But somehow his spells could not have worked properly that day, as the bear chief did not know that Redmouth had gone with his master, or he would have been more careful. For the moment the dog ran round the bushes barking loudly, the little bear servant rushed out in a fright, and set out for the mountains as fast as he could.

The dog followed the bear, and the boy followed the dog, until the mountain, the house of the great bear chief, came in sight. But along the road the snow was so wet and heavy that the boy could hardly get along, and then the thong of his snow-shoes broke, and he had to stop and mend it, so that the bear and the dog got so far ahead that he could scarcely hear the barking. When the strap was firm again the boy spoke to his snow-shoes and said:

' Now you must go as fast as you can, or, if not, I shall lose the dog as well as the bear.' And the snow-shoes sang in answer that they would run like the wind.

As he came along, the bear chief's sister was looking out of the window, and took pity on this little brother, as she had on the two elder ones, and waited to see what the boy would do, when he found that the bear servant and the dog had already entered the mountain.

The little brother was certainly very much puzzled at not seeing anything of either of the animals, which had vanished suddenly out of his sight. He paused for an instant to think what he should do next, and while he did so he fancied he heard Redmouth's voice on the opposite side of the mountain. With great difficulty he scrambled over steep rocks, and forced a path through tangled thickets ; but when he reached the other side the sound appeared to start from the place from which he had come. Then he had to go all the way back again, and at the very top, where he stopped to rest, the barking was directly beneath him, and he knew in an instant where he was and what had happened.

' Let my dog out at once, bear chief ! ' cried he. ' If you do not, I shall destroy your palace.' But the bear chief only laughed, and said nothing. The boy was very angry at his silence, and aiming one of his arrows at the bottom of the mountain, shot straight through it.

As the arrow touched the ground a rumbling was heard, and with a roar a fire broke out which seemed to split the whole mountain into pieces. The bear chief and all his servants were burnt up in the flames, but his sister and all that belonged to her were spared because she had tried to save the two elder boys from punishment.

As soon as the fire had burnt itself out the little hunter entered what was left of the mountain, and the first thing he saw was his two brothers—half bear, half boy.

' Oh, help us ! help us ! ' cried they, standing on their

hind legs as they spoke, and stretching out their fore-paws to him.

'But how am I to help you?' asked the little brother, almost weeping. 'I can kill people, and destroy trees and mountains, but I have no power over men.' And the two elder brothers came up and put their paws on his shoulders, and they all three wept together.

The heart of the bear chief's sister was moved when she saw their misery, and she came gently up behind, and whispered:

'Little boy, gather some moss from the spring over there, and let your brothers smell it.'

With a bound all three were at the spring, and as the youngest plucked a handful of wet moss, the two others sniffed at it with all their might. Then the bearskin fell away from them, and they stood upright once more.

'How can we thank you? how can we thank you?' they stammered, hardly able to speak; and fell at her feet in gratitude. But the bear's sister only smiled, and bade them go home and look after the little girl, who had no one else to protect her.

And this the boys did, and took such good care of their sister that, as she was very small, she soon forgot that she had ever had a father and mother.

[From the *Bureau of Ethnology, U.S.*]

THE SACRED MILK OF KOUMONGOÉ

FAR away, in a very hot country, there once lived a man and woman who had two children, a son named Koané and a daughter called Thakané.

Early in the morning and late in the evenings the parents worked hard in the fields, resting, when the sun was high, under the shade of some tree. While they were absent the little girl kept house alone, for her brother always got up before the dawn, when the air was fresh and cool, and drove out the cattle to the sweetest patches of grass he could find.

One day, when Koané had slept later than usual, his father and mother went to their work before him, and there was only Thakané to be seen busy making the bread for supper.

'Thakané,' he said, 'I am thirsty. Give me a drink from the tree Koumongoé, which has the best milk in the world.'

'Oh, Koané,' cried his sister, 'you know that we are forbidden to touch that tree. What would father say when he came home? For he would be sure to know.'

'Nonsense,' replied Koané, 'there is so much milk in Koumongoé that he will never miss a little. If you won't give it to me, I sha'n't take the cattle out. They will just have to stay all day in the hut, and you know that they will starve.' And he turned from her in a rage, and sat down in the corner.

After a while Thakané said to him : 'It is getting hot, had you not better drive out the cattle now ? '

But Koané only answered sulkily : ' I told you I am not going to drive them out at all. If I have to do without milk, they shall do without grass.'

Thakané did not know what to do. She was afraid to disobey her parents, who would most likely beat her, yet the beasts would be sure to suffer if they were kept in, and she would perhaps be beaten for that too. So at last she took an axe and a tiny earthen bowl, she cut a very small hole in the side of Koumongoé, and out gushed enough milk to fill the bowl.

' Here is the milk you wanted,' said she, going up to Koané, who was still sulking in his corner.

' What is the use of that ? ' grumbled Koané ; ' why, there is not enough to drown a fly. Go and get me three times as much ! '

Trembling with fright, Thakané returned to the tree, and struck it a sharp blow with the axe. In an instant there poured forth such a stream of milk that it ran like a river into the hut.

' Koané ! Koané ! ' cried she, ' come and help me to plug up the hole. There will be no milk left for our father and mother.' But Koané could not stop it any more than Thakané, and soon the milk was flowing through the hut downhill towards their parents in the fields below.

The man saw the white stream a long way off, and guessed what had happened.

' Wife, wife,' he called loudly to the woman, who was working at a little distance : ' Do you see Koumongoé running fast down the hill ? That is some mischief of the children's, I am sure. I must go home and find out what is the matter.' And they both threw down their hoes and hurried to the side of Koumongoé.

Kneeling on the grass, the man and his wife made a cup of their hands and drank the milk from it. And no sooner had they done this, than Koumongoé flowed back again up the hill, and entered the hut.

' Thakané,' said the parents, severely, when they reached

home panting from the heat of the sun, ' what have you been doing? Why did Koumongoé come to us in the fields instead of staying in the garden? '

' It was Koané's fault,' answered Thakané. ' He would not take the cattle to feed until he drank some of the milk from Koumongoé. So, as I did not know what else to do, I gave it to him.'

The father listened to Thakané's words, but made no answer. Instead, he went outside and brought in two sheepskins, which he stained red and sent for a black-smith to forge some iron rings. The rings were then passed over Thakané's arms and legs and neck, and the skins fastened on her before and behind. When all was ready, the man sent for his servants and said :

' I am going to get rid of Thakané.'

' Get rid of your only daughter? ' they answered, in surprise. ' But why? '

' Because she has eaten what she ought not to have eaten. She has touched the sacred tree which belongs to her mother and me alone.' And, turning his back, he called to Thakané to follow him, and they went down the road which led to the dwelling of an ogre.

They were passing along some fields where the corn was ripening, when a rabbit suddenly sprang out at their feet, and standing on its hind legs, it sang :

> Why do you give to the ogre
> Your child, so fair, so fair ?

' You had better ask her,' replied the man, ' she is old enough to give you an answer.'

Then, in her turn, Thakané sang :

> I gave Koumongoé to Koané,
> Koumongoé to the keeper of beasts ;
> For without Koumongoé they could not go to the meadows :
> Without Koumongoé they would starve in the hut ;
> That was why I gave him the Koumongoé of my father.

And when the rabbit heard that, he cried : ' Wretched

man! it is you whom the ogre should eat, and not your beautiful daughter.'

But the father paid no heed to what the rabbit said, and only walked on the faster, bidding Thakané to keep close behind him. By-and-by they met with a troop of

great deer, called elands, and they stopped when they saw
Thakané and sang :

> Why do you give to the ogre
> Your child, so fair, so fair ?

' You had better ask her,' replied the man, ' she is old
enough to give you an answer.'

Then, in her turn, Thakané sang :

> I gave Koumongoé to Koané,
> Koumongoé to the keeper of beasts ;
> For without Koumongoé they could not go to the meadows :
> Without Koumongoé they would starve in the hut ;
> That was why I gave him the Koumongoé of my father.

And the elands all cried : ' Wretched man ! it is
you whom the ogre should eat, and not your beautiful
daughter.'

By this time it was nearly dark, and the father said
they could travel no further that night, and must go to
sleep where they were. Thakané was thankful indeed
when she heard this, for she was very tired, and found
the two skins fastened round her almost too heavy to
carry. So, in spite of her dread of the ogre, she slept till
dawn, when her father woke her, and told her roughly
that he was ready to continue their journey.

Crossing the plain, the girl and her father passed a
herd of gazelles feeding. They lifted their heads, wondering who was out so early, and when they caught sight of
Thakané, they sang :

> Why do you give to the ogre
> Your child, so fair, so fair ?

'You had better ask her,' replied the man, ' she is old
enough to answer for herself.'

Then, in her turn, Thakané sang :

> I gave Koumongoé to Koané,
> Koumongoé to the keeper of beasts ;
> For without Koumongoé they could not go to the meadows :
> Without Koumongoé they would starve in the hut ;
> That was why I gave him the Koumongoé of my father.

And the gazelles all cried: ' Wretched man ! it is you whom the ogre should eat, and not your beautiful daughter.'

At last they arrived at the village where the ogre lived, and they went straight to his hut. He was nowhere to be seen, but in his place was his son Masilo, who was not an ogre at all, but a very polite young man. He ordered his servants to bring a pile of skins for Thakané to sit on, but told her father he must sit on the ground. Then, catching sight of the girl's face, which she had kept bent down, he was struck by its beauty, and put the same question that the rabbit, and the elands, and the gazelles had done.

Thakané answered him as before, and he instantly commanded that she should be taken to the hut of his mother, and placed under her care, while the man should be led to his father. Directly the ogre saw him he bade the servant throw him into the great pot which always stood ready on the fire, and in five minutes he was done to a turn. After that the servant returned to Masilo and related all that had happened.

Now Masilo had fallen in love with Thakané the moment he saw her. At first he did not know what to make of this strange feeling, for all his life he had hated women, and had refused several brides whom his parents had chosen for him. However, they were so anxious that he should marry, that they willingly accepted Thakané as their daughter-in-law, though she did not bring any marriage portion with her.

After some time a baby was born to her, and Thakané thought it was the most beautiful baby that ever was seen. But when her mother-in-law saw it was a girl, she wrung her hands and wept, saying :

' O miserable mother ! Miserable child ! Alas for you ! why were you not a boy ! '

Thakané, in great surprise, asked the meaning of her distress ; and the old woman told her that it was the custom in that country that all the girls who were born should be given to the ogre to eat.

Then Thakané clasped the baby tightly in her arms, and cried :

'But it is not the custom in *my* country ! There, when children die, they are buried in the earth. No one shall take my baby from me.'

That night, when everyone in the hut was asleep, Thakané rose, and carrying her baby on her back, went down to a place where the river spread itself out into a large lake, with tall willows all round the bank. Here, hidden from everyone, she sat down on a stone and began to think what she should do to save her child.

Suddenly she heard a rustling among the willows, and an old woman appeared before her.

' What are you crying for, my dear ? ' said she.

And Thakané answered : ' I was crying for my baby— I cannot hide her for ever, and if the ogre sees her, he will eat her ; and I would rather she was drowned than that.'

' What you say is true,' replied the old woman. ' Give me your child, and let me take care of it. And if you will fix a day to meet me here I will bring the baby.'

Then Thakané dried her eyes, and gladly accepted the old woman's offer. When she got home she told her husband she had thrown it in the river, and as he had watched her go in that direction he never thought of doubting what she said.

On the appointed day, Thakané slipped out when everybody was busy, and ran down the path that led to the lake. As soon as she got there, she crouched down among the willows, and sang softly :

> Bring to me Dilah, Dilah the rejected one,
> Dilah, whom her father Masilo cast out!

And in a moment the old woman appeared holding the baby in her arms. Dilah had become so big and strong, that Thakané's heart was filled with joy and gratitude, and she stayed as long as she dared, playing with her baby. At last she felt she must return to the village, lest she should be missed, and the child was handed back to the old woman, who vanished with her into the lake.

Children grow up very quickly when they live under water, and in less time than anyone could suppose, Dilah had changed from a baby to a woman. Her mother came to visit her whenever she was able, and one day, when they were sitting talking together, they were spied out by a man who had come to cut willows to weave into baskets. He was so surprised to see how like the face of the girl was to Masilo, that he left his work and returned to the village.

'Masilo,' he said, as he entered the hut, 'I have just beheld your wife near the river with a girl who must be your daughter, she is so like you. We have been deceived, for we all thought she was dead.'

When he heard this, Masilo tried to look shocked because his wife had broken the law; but in his heart he was very glad.

'But what shall we do now?' asked he.

'Make sure for yourself that I am speaking the truth by hiding among the bushes the first time Thakané says she is going to bathe in the river, and waiting till the girl appears.'

For some days Thakané stayed quietly at home, and her husband began to think that the man had been mistaken; but at last she said to her husband: 'I am going to bathe in the river.'

'Well, you can go,' answered he. But he ran down quickly by another path, and got there first, and hid himself in the bushes. An instant later, Thakané arrived, and standing on the bank, she sang:

> Bring to me Dilah, Dilah the rejected one,
> Dilah, whom her father Masilo cast out!

Then the old woman came out of the water, holding
the girl, now tall and slender, by the hand. And as
Masilo looked, he saw that she was indeed his daughter,
and he wept for joy that she was not lying dead in the

BRING TO ME DILAH DILAH THE REJECTED ONE

bottom of the lake. The old woman, however, seemed
uneasy, and said to Thakané: 'I feel as if someone was
watching us. I will not leave the girl to-day, but will
take her back with me'; and sinking beneath the surface,
she drew the girl after her. After they had gone, Thakané

returned to the village, which Masilo had managed to reach before her.

All the rest of the day he sat in a corner weeping, and his mother who came in asked : ' Why are you weeping so bitterly, my son ? '

' My head aches,' he answered ; ' it aches very badly.' And his mother passed on, and left him alone.

In the evening he said to his wife : ' I have seen my daughter, in the place where you told me you had drowned her. Instead, she lives at the bottom of the lake, and has now grown into a young woman.'

' I don't know what you are talking about,' replied Thakané. ' I buried my child under the sand on the beach.'

Then Masilo implored her to give the child back to him ; but she would not listen, and only answered : ' If I were to give her back you would only obey the laws of your country and take her to your father, the ogre, and she would be eaten.'

But Masilo promised that he would never let his father see her, and that now she was a woman no one would try to hurt her ; so Thakané's heart melted, and she went down to the lake to consult the old woman.

' What am I to do ? ' she asked, when, after clapping her hands, the old woman appeared before her. ' Yesterday Masilo beheld Dilah, and ever since he has entreated me to give him back his daughter.'

' If I let her go he must pay me a thousand head of cattle in exchange,' replied the old woman. And Thakané carried her answer back to Masilo.

' Why, I would gladly give her two thousand ! ' cried he, ' for she has saved my daughter.' And he bade messengers hasten to all the neighbouring villages, and tell his people to send him at once all the cattle he possessed. When they were all assembled he chose a thousand of the finest bulls and cows, and drove them down to the river, followed by a great crowd wondering what would happen.

Then Thakané stepped forward in front of the cattle and sang :

> Bring to me Dilah, Dilah the rejected one,
> Dilah, whom her father Masilo cast out !

And Dilah came from the waters holding out her hands to Masilo and Thakané, and in her place the cattle sank into the lake, and were driven by the old woman to the great city filled with people, which lies at the bottom.

[*Contes Populaires des Bassoutos.*]

THE WICKED WOLVERINE

ONE day a wolverine was out walking on the hill-side, when, on turning a corner, he suddenly saw a large rock.

'Was that you I heard walking about just now?' he asked, for wolverines are cautious animals, and always like to know the reasons of things.

'No, certainly not,' answered the rock; 'I don't know how to walk.'

'But I *saw* you walking,' continued the wolverine.

'I am afraid that you were not taught to speak the truth,' retorted the rock.

'You need not speak like that, for I have *seen* you walking,' replied the wolverine, 'though I am quite sure that you could never catch *me*!' and he ran a little distance and then stopped to see if the rock was pursuing him; but, to his vexation, the rock was still in the same place. Then the wolverine went up close, and struck the rock a blow with his paw, saying: 'Well, will you catch me *now*?'

'I can't walk, but I can *roll*,' answered the rock.

And the wolverine laughed and said: 'Oh, that will do just as well'; and began to run down the side of the mountain.

At first he went quite slowly, 'just to give the rock a chance,' he thought to himself; but soon he quickened his pace, for he found that the rock was almost at his heels. But the faster the wolverine ran, the faster the rock rolled, and by-and-by the little creature began to get very tired, and was sorry he had not left the rock to itself. Think-

ing that if he could manage to put on a spurt he would
reach the forest of great trees at the bottom of the
mountain, where the rock could not come, he gathered up
all his strength, and instead of running he leaped over
sticks and stones, but, whatever he did, the rock was
always close behind him.   At length he grew so weary
that he could not even see where he was going, and

ALL THE ANIMALS TRY TO GET THE ROCK OFF WOLVERINE'S LEGS

catching his foot in a branch he tripped and fell.   The
rock stopped at once, but there came a shriek from the
wolverine:

'Get off, get off! can't you see that you are on my
legs?'

'Why did you not leave me alone?' asked the rock.
'I did not want to move—I hate moving.   But you

would have it, and I certainly sha'n't move now till I am forced to.'

'I will call my brothers,' answered the wolverine. 'There are many of them in the forest, and you will soon see that they are stronger than you.' And he called, and called, and called, till wolves and foxes and all sorts of other creatures all came running to see what was the matter.

'How *did* you get under that rock?' asked they, making a ring round him; but they had to repeat their question several times before the wolverine would answer, for he, like many other persons, found it hard to confess that he had brought his troubles on himself.

'Well, I was dull, and wanted someone to play with me,' he said at last, in a sulky voice, 'and I challenged the rock to catch me. Of course I thought I could run the fastest; but I tripped, and it rolled on me. It was just an accident.'

'It serves you right for being so silly,' said they; but they pushed and hauled at the rock for a long time without making it move an inch.

'You are no good at all,' cried the wolverine crossly, for it was suffering great pain, 'and if you cannot get me free, I shall see what my friends the lightning and the thunder can do.' And he called loudly to the lightning to come and help him as quickly as possible.

In a few minutes a dark cloud came rolling up the sky, giving out such terrific claps of thunder that the wolves and the foxes and all the other creatures ran helter-skelter in all directions. But, frightened though they were, they did not forget to beg the lightning to take off the wolverine's coat and to free his legs, but to be careful not to hurt him. So the lightning disappeared into the cloud for a moment to gather up fresh strength, and then came rushing down, right upon the rock, which it sent flying in all directions, and took off the wolverine's coat so neatly that, though it was torn into tiny shreds, the wolverine himself was quite unharmed.

'That was rather clumsy of you,' said he, standing up naked in his flesh. ' Surely you could have split the rock without tearing my coat to bits!' And he stooped down to pick up the pieces. It took him a long time, for there were a great many of them, but at last he had them all in his hand.

'I'll go to my sister the frog,' he thought to himself, 'and she will sew them together for me'; and he set off at once for the swamp in which his sister lived.

'Will you sew my coat together? I had an unlucky accident, and it is quite impossible to wear,' he said, when he found her.

'With pleasure,' she answered, for she had always been taught to be polite; and getting her needle and thread she began to fit the pieces. But though she was very good-natured, she was not very clever, and she got some of the bits wrong. When the wolverine, who was very particular about his clothes, came to put it on, he grew very angry.

'What a useless creature you are!' cried he. 'Do you expect me to go about in such a coat as that? Why it bulges all down the back, as if I had a hump, and it is so tight across the chest that I expect it to burst every time I breathe. I knew you were stupid, but I did not think you were as stupid as that.' And giving the poor frog a blow on her head, which knocked her straight into the water, he walked off in a rage to his younger sister the mouse.

'I tore my coat this morning,' he began, when he had found her sitting at the door of her house eating an apple. 'It was all in little bits, and I took it to our sister the frog to ask her to sew it for me. But just look at the way she has done it! You will have to take it to pieces and fit them together properly, and I hope I shall not have to complain again.' For as the wolverine was older than the mouse, he was accustomed to speak to her in this manner. However, the mouse was used to it and only answered : ' I think you had better stay here till it is done, and if there is any alteration needed I can make it.' So the wolverine sat down on a heap of dry ferns, and, picking up the apple, he finished it without even asking the mouse's leave.

At last the coat was ready, and the wolverine put it on.

' Yes, it fits very well,' said he, 'and you have sewn it very neatly. When I pass this way again I will bring you a handful of corn, as a reward '; and he ran off as smart as ever, leaving the mouse quite grateful behind him.

He wandered about for many days, till he reached a place where food was very scarce, and for a whole week he went without any. He was growing desperate, when he suddenly came upon a bear that was lying asleep. 'Ah! here is food at last!' thought he ; but how was he to kill the bear, who was so much bigger than himself? It was no use to try force, he must invent some cunning plan which would get her into his power. At last, after thinking hard, he decided upon something, and going up to the bear, he exclaimed : ' Is that you, my sister ? '

The bear turned round and saw the wolverine, and murmuring to herself, so low that nobody could hear, ' I never heard before that I had a brother,' got up and ran quickly to a tree, up which she climbed. Now the wolverine was very angry when he saw his dinner vanishing in front of him, especially as *he* could not climb trees like the bear, so he followed, and stood at the foot of the tree, shrieking as loud as he could, ' Come down, sister ; our father has sent me to look for you ! You were lost when you were a little girl and went out picking berries, and it was only the other day that we heard from a beaver where you were.' At these words, the bear came a little way down the tree, and the wolverine, seeing this, went on :

' Are you not fond of berries ? *I* am ! And I know a

place where they grow so thick the ground is quite
hidden. Why, look for yourself! That hillside is quite
red with them!'

'I can't see so far,' answered the bear, now climbing
down altogether. 'You must have wonderfully good
eyes! I wish *I* had; but my sight is very short.'

'So was mine till my father smashed a pailful of
cranberries, and rubbed my eyes with them,' replied the
wolverine. 'But if you like to go and gather some of the
berries I will do just as he did, and you will soon be able
to see as far as me.'

It took the bear a long while to gather the berries, for
she was slow about everything, and, besides, it made her
back ache to stoop. But at last she returned with a
sackful, and put them down beside the wolverine. 'That
is splendid, sister!' cried the wolverine. 'Now lie flat
on the ground with your head on this stone, while I
smash them.'

The bear, who was very tired, was only too glad to do
as she was bid, and stretched herself comfortably on the
grass.

'I am ready now,' said the wolverine after a bit; 'just
at first you will find that the berries make your eyes
smart, but you must be careful not to move, or the juice
will run out, and then it will have to be done all over
again.'

So the bear promised to lie very still; but the moment
the cranberries touched her eyes she sprang up with a
roar.

'Oh, you mustn't mind a little pain,' said the wolverine,
'it will soon be over, and then you will see all sorts of
things you have never dreamt of.' The bear sank down
with a groan, and as her eyes were full of cranberry juice,
which completely blinded her, the wolverine took up a
sharp knife and stabbed her to the heart.

Then he took off the skin, and, stealing some fire from
a tent, which his sharp eyes had perceived hidden behind

a rock, he set about roasting the bear bit by bit. He thought the meat was the best he ever had tasted, and when dinner was done he made up his mind to try that same trick again, if ever he was hungry.

And very likely he did !

[Adapted from *Bureau of Ethnology.*]

THE HUSBAND OF THE RAT'S DAUGHTER

ONCE upon a time there lived in Japan a rat and his wife who came of an old and noble race, and had one daughter, the loveliest girl in all the rat world. Her parents were very proud of her, and spared no pains to teach her all she ought to know. There was not another young lady in the whole town who was as clever as she was in gnawing through the hardest wood, or who could drop from such a height on to a bed, or run away so fast if anyone was heard coming. Great attention, too, was paid to her personal appearance, and her skin shone like satin, while her teeth were as white as pearls, and beautifully pointed.

Of course, with all these advantages, her parents expected her to make a brilliant marriage, and, as she grew up, they began to look round for a suitable husband.

But here a difficulty arose. The father was a rat from the tip of his nose to the end of his tail, outside as well as in, and desired that his daughter should wed among her own people. She had no lack of lovers, but her father's secret hopes rested on a fine young rat, with moustaches which almost swept the ground, whose family was still nobler and more ancient than his own. Unluckily, the mother had other views for her precious child. She was one of those people who always despise their own family and surroundings, and take pleasure in thinking that they themselves are made of finer material than the rest of the world. '*Her* daughter should never marry a mere rat,' she declared, holding her head high. 'With her beauty and talents she had a right to look for someone a little better than *that*.'

So she talked, as mothers will, to anyone that would listen to her. What the girl thought about the matter nobody knew or cared—it was not the fashion in the rat world.

Many were the quarrels which the old rat and his wife had upon the subject, and sometimes they bore on their faces certain marks which looked as if they had not kept to words only.

'Reach up to the stars is *my* motto,' cried the lady one day, when she was in a greater passion than usual. 'My daughter's beauty places her higher than anything upon earth,' she cried; 'and I am certainly not going to accept a son-in-law who is beneath her.'

'Better offer her in marriage to the sun,' answered her husband impatiently. 'As far as I know there is nothing greater than he.'

'Well, I *was* thinking of it,' replied the wife, 'and as you are of the same mind, we will pay him a visit to-morrow.'

So the next morning, the two rats, having spent hours in making themselves smart, set out to see the sun, leading their daughter between them.

The journey took some time, but at length they came to the golden palace where the sun lived.

'Noble king,' began the mother, 'behold our daughter! She is so beautiful that she is above everything in the whole world. Naturally, we wish for a son-in-law who, on his side, is greater than all. Therefore we have come to you.'

'I feel very much flattered,' replied the sun, who was so busy that he had not the least wish to marry anybody. 'You do me great honour by your proposal. Only, in one point you are mistaken, and it would be wrong of me to take advantage of your ignorance. There *is* something greater than I am, and that is the cloud. Look!' And as he spoke a cloud spread itself over the sun's face, blotting out his rays.

'Oh, well, we will speak to the cloud,' said the mother. And turning to the cloud she repeated her proposal.

'Indeed I am unworthy of anything so charming,' answered the cloud; 'but you make a mistake again in what you say. There is one thing that is even more powerful than I, and that is the wind. Ah, here he comes, you can see for yourself.'

And she *did* see, for catching up the cloud as he passed, he threw it on the other side of the sky. Then, tumbling father, mother and daughter down to the earth again, he paused for a moment beside them, his foot on an old wall.

When she had recovered her breath, the mother began her little speech once more.

'The wall is the proper husband for your daughter,' answered the wind, whose home consisted of a cave, which he only visited when he was not rushing about elsewhere; 'you can see for yourself that he is greater than I, for he has power to stop me in my flight.' And the mother, who did not trouble to conceal her wishes, turned at once to the wall.

Then something happened which was quite unexpected by everyone.

'I won't marry that ugly old wall, which is as old as my grandfather,' sobbed the girl, who had not uttered one word all this time. 'I would have married the sun, or the cloud, or the wind, because it was my duty, although I love the handsome young rat, and him only. But that horrid old wall—I would sooner die!'

And the wall, rather hurt in his feelings, declared that he had no claim to be the husband of so beautiful a girl.

'It is quite true,' he said, 'that I can stop the wind who can part the clouds who can cover the sun; but there is someone who can do more than all these, and that is the rat. It is the rat who passes through me, and can reduce me to powder, simply with his teeth. If, therefore, you want a son-in-law who is greater than the whole world, seek him among the rats.'

' Ah, what did I tell you ?' cried the father. And his wife, though for the moment angry at being beaten, soon thought that a rat son-in-law was what she had always desired.

So all three returned happily home, and the wedding was celebrated three days after.

[*Contes Populaires.*]

THE MERMAID AND THE BOY

Long, long ago, there lived a king who ruled over a country by the sea. When he had been married about a year, some of his subjects, inhabiting a distant group of islands, revolted against his laws, and it became needful for him to leave his wife and go in person to settle their disputes. The queen feared that some ill would come of it, and implored him to stay at home, but he told her that nobody could do his work for him, and the next morning the sails were spread, and the king started on his voyage.

The vessel had not gone very far when she ran upon a rock, and stuck so fast in a cleft that the strength of the whole crew could not get her off again. To make matters worse, the wind was rising too, and it was quite plain that in a few hours the ship would be dashed to pieces and everybody would be drowned, when suddenly the form of a mermaid was seen dancing on the waves which threatened every moment to overwhelm them.

'There is only one way to free yourselves,' she said to the king, bobbing up and down in the water as she spoke, 'and that is to give me your solemn word that you will deliver to me the first child that is born to you.'

The king hesitated at this proposal. He hoped that some day he might have children in his home, and the thought that he must yield up the heir to his crown was very bitter to him ; but just then a huge wave broke with great force on the ship's side, and his men fell on their knees and entreated him to save them.

So he promised, and this time a wave lifted the vessel

clean off the rocks, and she was in the open sea once more.

The affairs of the islands took longer to settle than the king had expected, and some months passed away before he returned to his palace. In his absence a son had been born to him, and so great was his joy that he quite forgot the mermaid and the price he had paid for the safety of his ship. But as the years went on, and the baby grew into a fine big boy, the remembrance of it came back, and one day he told the queen the whole story. From that moment the happiness of both their lives was ruined. Every night they went to bed wondering if they should find his room empty in the morning, and every day they kept him by their sides, expecting him to be snatched away before their very eyes.

At last the king felt that this state of things could not continue, and he said to his wife :

' After all, the most foolish thing in the world one can do is to keep the boy here in exactly the place in which the mermaid will seek him. Let us give him food and send him on his travels, and perhaps, if the mermaid ever *does* come to seek him, she may be content with some other child.' And the queen agreed that his plan seemed the wisest.

So the boy was called, and his father told him the story of the voyage, as he had told his mother before him. The prince listened eagerly, and was delighted to think that he was to go away all by himself to see the world, and was not in the least frightened ; for though he was now sixteen, he had scarcely been allowed to walk alone beyond the palace gardens. He began busily to make his preparations, and took off his smart velvet coat, putting on instead one of green cloth, while he refused a beautiful bag which the queen offered him to hold his food, and slung a leather knapsack over his shoulders instead, just as he had seen other travellers do. Then he bade farewell to his parents and went his way.

THE MERMAID ASKS FOR THE KING'S CHILD

All through the day he walked, watching with interest the strange birds and animals that darted across his path in the forest or peeped at him from behind a bush. But as evening drew on he became tired, and looked about as he walked for some place where he could sleep. At length he reached a soft mossy bank under a tree, and was just about to stretch himself out on it, when a fearful roar made him start and tremble all over. In another moment something passed swiftly through the air and a lion stood before him.

'What are you doing here?' asked the lion, his eyes glaring fiercely at the boy.

'I am flying from the mermaid,' the prince answered, in a quaking voice.

'Give me some food then,' said the lion, 'it is past my supper time, and I am very hungry.'

The boy was so thankful that the lion did not want to eat *him*, that he gladly picked up his knapsack which lay on the ground, and held out some bread and a flask of wine.

'I feel better now,' said the lion when he had done, 'so now I shall go to sleep on this nice soft moss, and if you like you can lie down beside me.' So the boy and the lion slept soundly side by side, till the sun rose.

'I must be off now,' remarked the lion, shaking the boy as he spoke; 'but cut off the tip of my ear, and keep it carefully, and if you are in any danger just wish yourself a lion and you will become one on the spot. One good turn deserves another, you know.'

The prince thanked him for his kindness, and did as he was bid, and the two then bade each other farewell.

'I wonder how it feels to be a lion,' thought the boy, after he had gone a little way; and he took out the tip of the ear from the breast of his jacket and wished with all his might. In an instant his head had swollen to several times its usual size, and his neck seemed very hot and heavy; and, somehow, his hands became paws, and his skin grew hairy and yellow. But what pleased him most was his long tail with a tuft at the end, which he lashed and switched proudly. ' I like being a lion very much,' he said to himself, and trotted gaily along the road.

After a while, however, he got tired of walking in this unaccustomed way—it made his back ache and his front paws felt sore. So he wished himself a boy again, and in the twinkling of an eye his tail disappeared and his head shrank, and the long thick mane became short and curly. Then he looked out for a sleeping place, and found some dry ferns, which he gathered and heaped up.

But before he had time to close his eyes there was a great noise in the trees near by, as if a big heavy body was crashing through them. The boy rose and turned his head, and saw a huge black bear coming towards him.

' What are you doing here ? ' cried the bear.

' I am running away from the mermaid,' answered the boy ; but the bear took no interest in the mermaid, and only said : ' I am hungry ; give me something to eat.'

The knapsack was lying on the ground among the fern, but the prince picked it up, and, unfastening the strap, took out his second flask of wine and another loaf of bread. ' We will have supper together,' he remarked politely ; but the bear, who had never been taught manners, made no reply, and ate as fast as he could. When he had quite finished, he got up and stretched himself.

' You have got a comfortable-looking bed there,' he observed. ' I really think that, bad sleeper as I am, I might have a good night on it. I can manage to squeeze you in,' he added ; ' you don't take up a great deal of room.' The boy was rather indignant at the bear's cool way of talking ; but as he was too tired to gather more fern, they lay down side by side, and never stirred till sunrise next morning.

I must go now,' said the bear, pulling the sleepy prince on to his feet; 'but first you shall cut off the tip of my ear, and when you are in any danger just wish yourself a bear and you will become one. One good turn deserves another, you know.' And the boy did as he was bid, and he and the bear bade each other farewell.

'I wonder how it feels to be a bear,' thought he to himself when he had walked a little way ; and he took out the tip from the breast of his coat and wished hard that he might become a bear. The next moment his body stretched out and thick black fur covered him all over. As before, his hands were changed into paws, but when he tried to switch his tail he found to his disgust that it would not go any distance. 'Why it is hardly worth calling a tail!' said he. For the rest of the day he remained a bear and continued his journey, but as evening came on the bear-skin, which had been so useful when plunging through brambles in the forest, felt rather heavy, and he wished himself a boy again. He was too much exhausted to take the trouble of cutting any fern or seeking for moss, but just threw himself down under a tree, when exactly above his head he heard a great buzzing as a bumble-bee alighted on a honeysuckle branch. 'What are you doing here?' asked the bee in a cross voice ; 'at your age you ought to be safe at home.'

'I am running away from the mermaid,' replied the boy; but the bee, like the lion and the bear, was one of those people who never listen to the answers to their questions, and only said: 'I am hungry. Give me something to eat.'

The boy took his last loaf and flask out of his knap-sack and laid them on the ground, and they had supper together. 'Well, now I am going to sleep,' observed the bee when the last crumb was gone, 'but as you are not very big I can make room for you beside me,' and he curled up his wings, and tucked in his legs, and he and the prince both slept soundly till morning. Then the bee got up and carefully brushed every scrap of dust off his velvet coat and buzzed loudly in the boy's ear to waken him.

'Take a single hair from one of my wings,' said he, 'and if you are in danger just wish yourself a bee and you will become one. One good turn deserves another, so farewell, and thank you for your supper.' And the bee departed after the boy had pulled out the hair and wrapped it carefully in a leaf.

'It must feel quite different to be a bee from what it does to be a lion or bear,' thought the boy to himself when he had walked for an hour or two. 'I dare say I should get on a great deal faster,' so he pulled out his hair and wished himself a bee.

In a moment the strangest thing happened to him. All his limbs seemed to draw together, and his body to become very short and round; his head grew quite tiny, and instead of his white skin he was covered with the richest, softest velvet. Better than all, he had two lovely gauze wings which carried him the whole day without getting tired.

Late in the afternoon the boy fancied he saw a vast heap of stones a long way off, and he flew straight towards it. But when he reached the gates he saw that it was really a great town, so he wished himself back in his own shape and entered the city.

He found the palace doors wide open and went boldly into a sort of hall which was full of people, and where men and maids were gossiping together. He joined their talk and soon learned from them that the king had only one daughter who had such a hatred to men that she would never suffer one to enter her presence. Her father was in despair, and had had pictures painted of the handsomest princes of all the courts in the world, in the hope that she might fall in love with one of them ; but it was no use ; the princess would not even allow the pictures to be brought into her room.

The Princess on the Seashore

'It is late,' remarked one of the women at last; 'I must go to my mistress.' And, turning to one of the lackeys, she bade him find a bed for the youth.

'It is not necessary,' answered the prince, 'this bench is good enough for me. I am used to nothing better.' And when the hall was empty he lay down for a few minutes. But as soon as everything was quiet in the palace he took out the hair and wished himself a bee, and in this shape he flew upstairs, past the guards, and through the keyhole into the princess's chamber. Then he turned himself into a man again.

At this dreadful sight the princess, who was broad awake, began to scream loudly. 'A man! a man!' cried she; but when the guards rushed in there was only a bumble-bee buzzing about the room. They looked under the bed, and behind the curtains, and into the cupboards, then came to the conclusion that the princess had had a bad dream, and bowed themselves out. The door had scarcely closed on them than the bee disappeared, and a handsome youth stood in his place.

'I *knew* a man was hidden somewhere,' cried the princess, and screamed more loudly than before. Her shrieks brought back the guards, but though they looked in all kinds of impossible places no man was to be seen, and so they told the princess.

'He was here a moment ago—I saw him with my own eyes,' and the guards dared not contradict her, though they shook their heads and whispered to each other that the princess had gone mad on this subject, and saw a man in every table and chair. And they made up their minds that—let her scream as loudly as she might— they would take no notice.

Now the princess saw clearly what they were thinking, and that in future her guards would give her no help, and would perhaps, besides, tell some stories about her to the king, who would shut her up in a lonely tower and prevent her walking in the gardens among her birds and

flowers.   So when, for the third time, she beheld the
prince standing before her, she did not scream but sat up
in bed gazing at him in silent terror.

'Do not be afraid,' he said, 'I shall not hurt you'; and
he began to praise her gardens, of which he had heard
the servants speak, and the birds and flowers which she
loved, till the princess's anger softened, and she answered
him with gentle words.   Indeed, they soon became so
friendly that she vowed she would marry no one else,
and confided to him that in three days her father would
be off to the wars, leaving his sword in her room.   If any
man could find it and bring it to him he would receive her
hand as a reward.   At this point a cock crew, and the
youth jumped up hastily saying : 'Of course I shall ride
with the king to the war, and if I do not return, take your
violin every evening to the seashore and play on it, so
that the very sea-kobolds who live at the bottom of the
ocean may hear it and come to you.'

Just as the princess had foretold, in three days the
king set out for the war with a large following, and
among them was the young prince, who had presented
himself at court as a young noble in search of adventures.
They had left the city many miles behind them, when
the king suddenly discovered that he had forgotten his
sword, and though all his attendants instantly offered
theirs, he declared that he could fight with none but his
own.

'The first man who brings it to me from my daughter's
room,' cried he, 'shall not only have her to wife, but
after my death shall reign in my stead.'

At this the Red Knight, the young prince, and several
more turned their horses to ride as fast as the wind back
to the palace.   But suddenly a better plan entered the
prince's head, and, letting the others pass him, he took his
precious parcel from his breast and wished himself a lion.
Then on he bounded, uttering such dreadful roars that the
horses were frightened and grew unmanageable, and he

easily outstripped them, and soon reached the gates of the palace. Here he hastily changed himself into a bee, and flew straight into the princess's room, where he became a man again. She showed him where the sword hung concealed behind a curtain, and he took it down, saying as he did so : ' Be sure not to forget what you have promised to do.'

The princess made no reply, but smiled sweetly, and slipping a golden ring from her finger she broke it in two and held half out silently to the prince, while the other half she put in her own pocket. He kissed it, and ran down the stairs bearing the sword with him. Some way off he met the Red Knight and the rest, and the Red Knight at first tried to take the sword from him by force. But as the youth proved too strong for him, he gave it up, and resolved to wait for a better opportunity.

This soon came, for the day was hot and the prince was thirsty. Perceiving a little stream that ran into the sea, he turned aside, and, unbuckling the sword, flung himself on the ground for a long drink. Unluckily, the mermaid happened at that moment to be floating on the water not very far off, and knew he was the boy who had been given her before he was born. So she floated gently in to where he was lying, she seized him by the arm, and the waves closed over them both. Hardly had they disappeared, when the Red Knight stole cautiously up, and could hardly believe his eyes when he saw the king's sword on the bank. He wondered what had become of the youth, who an hour before had guarded his treasure so fiercely ; but, after all, that was no affair of his ! So, fastening the sword to his belt, he carried it to the king.

The war was soon over, and the king returned to his people, who welcomed him with shouts of joy. But when the princess from her window saw that her betrothed was not among the attendants riding behind her father, her heart sank, for she knew that some evil must have befallen him, and she feared the Red Knight. She had long ago learned how clever and how wicked he was, and something whispered to her that it was *he* who would gain the credit of having carried back the sword, and would claim her as his bride, though he had never even entered her chamber. And she could do nothing; for although the king loved her, he never let her stand in the way of his plans.

The poor princess was only too right, and everything came to pass exactly as she had foreseen it. The king told her that the Red Knight had won her fairly, and that the wedding would take place next day, and there would be a great feast after it.

In those days feasts were much longer and more splendid than they are now; and it was growing dark when the princess, tired out with all she had gone through, stole up to her own room for a little quiet. But the moon was shining so brightly over the sea that it seemed to draw her towards it, and taking her violin under her arm, she crept down to the shore.

'Listen! listen! said the mermaid to the prince, who was lying stretched on a bed of seaweeds at the bottom of the sea. 'Listen! that is your old love playing, for mermaids know everything that happens upon earth.'

'I hear nothing,' answered the youth, who did not look happy. 'Take me up higher, where the sounds can reach me.'

So the mermaid took him on her shoulders and bore him up midway to the surface. 'Can you hear now?' she asked.

'No,' answered the prince, 'I hear nothing but the water rushing; I must go higher still.'

Then the mermaid carried him to the very top. 'You must surely be able to hear *now*?' said she.

'Nothing but the water,' repeated the youth. So she took him right to the land.

'At any rate you can hear *now*?' she said again.

'The water is still rushing in my ears,' answered he; 'but wait a little, that will soon pass off.' And as he

· LISTEN · LISTEN · SAID · THE · MERMAID · TO · THE · PRINCE ·

[This illustration is reproduced in color between pages 74 and 75.]

spoke he put his hand into his breast, and seizing the hair
wished himself a bee, and flew straight into the pocket of
the princess. The mermaid looked in vain for him, and
floated all night upon the sea; but he never came back,
and never more did he gladden her eyes. But the
princess felt that something strange was about her,
though she knew not what, and returned quickly to the
palace, where the young man at once resumed his own
shape. Oh, what joy filled her heart at the sight of him!
But there was no time to be lost, and she led him right into
the hall, where the king and his nobles were still sitting
at the feast. 'Here is a man who boasts that he can do
wonderful tricks,' said she, 'better even than the Red
Knight's! That cannot be true, of course; but it might
be well to give this impostor a lesson. He pretends, for
instance, that he can turn himself into a lion; but that I
do not believe. I know that you have studied the art of
magic,' she went on, turning to the Red Knight, 'so
suppose you just show him how it is done, and bring
shame upon him.'

Now the Red Knight had never opened a book of magic
in his life; but he was accustomed to think that he could
do everything better than other people without any
teaching at all. So he turned and twisted himself about,
and bellowed and made faces; but he did not become a
lion for all that.

'Well, perhaps it *is* very difficult to change into a
lion. Make yourself a bear,' said the princess. But the
Red Knight found it no easier to become a bear than a
lion.

'Try a bee,' suggested she. 'I have always read that
anyone who can do magic at all can do that.' And the old
knight buzzed and hummed, but he remained a man and
not a bee.

'Now it is your turn,' said the princess to the youth.
'Let us see if you can change yourself into a lion.' And in
a moment such a fierce creature stood before them, that

all the guests rushed out of the hall, treading each other underfoot in their fright. The lion sprang at the Red Knight, and would have torn him in pieces had not the princess held him back, and bidden him to change himself into a man again. And in a second a man took the place of the lion.

'Now become a bear,' said she; and a bear advanced panting and stretching out his arms to the Red Knight, who shrank behind the princess.

By this time some of the guests had regained their courage, and returned as far as the door, thinking that if it was safe for the princess perhaps it was safe for them. The king, who was braver than they, and felt it needful to set them a good example besides, had never left his seat, and when at a new command of the princess the bear once more turned into a man, he was silent from astonishment, and a suspicion of the truth began to dawn on him. ' Was it *he* who fetched the sword ? ' asked the king.

' Yes, it was,' answered the princess ; and she told him the whole story, and how she had broken her gold ring and given him half of it. And the prince took out his half of the ring, and the princess took out hers, and they fitted exactly. Next day the Red Knight was hanged, as he richly deserved, and there was a new marriage feast for the prince and princess.

[*Lappländische Mährchen.*]

SHE PRINCESS THE RED KNIGHT & THE LION

PIVI AND KABO

WHEN birds were men, and men were birds, Pivi and Kabo lived in an island far away, called New Caledonia. Pivi was a cheery little bird that chirps at sunset; Kabo was an ugly black fowl that croaks in the darkness. One day Pivi and Kabo thought that they would make slings, and practise slinging, as the people of the island still do. So they went to a banyan tree, and stripped the bark to make strings for their slings, and next they repaired to the river bank to find stones. Kabo stood on the bank of the river, and Pivi went into the water. The game was for Kabo to sling at Pivi, and for Pivi to dodge the stones, if he could. For some time he dodged them cleverly, but at last a stone from Kabo's sling hit poor Pivi on the leg and broke it. Down went Pivi into the stream, and floated along it, till he floated into a big hollow bamboo, which a woman used for washing her sweet potatoes.

'What is that in my bamboo?' said the woman. And she blew in at one end, and blew little Pivi out at the other, like a pea from a pea-shooter.

'Oh!' cried the woman, 'what a state you are in! What have you been doing?'

'It was Kabo who broke my leg at the slinging game,' said Pivi.

'Well, I am sorry for you,' said the woman; 'will you come with me, and do what I tell you?'

'I will!' said Pivi, for the woman was very kind and pretty. She took Pivi into a shed where she kept her fruit, laid him on a bed of mats, and made him as comfortable as she could, and attended to his broken leg without cutting off the flesh round the bone, as these people usually do.

' You will be still, won't you, Pivi ? ' she said. ' If you hear a little noise you will pretend to be dead. It is the Black Ant who will come and creep from your feet up to your head. Say nothing, and keep quiet, won't you, Pivi ? '

' Certainly, kind lady,' said Pivi, ' I will lie as still as can be.'

' Next will come the big Red Ant—you know him ? '

' Yes, I know him, with his feet like a grasshopper's.'

' He will walk over your body up to your head. Then you must shake all your body. Do you understand, Pivi ? '

' Yes, dear lady, I shall do just as you say.'

' Very good,' said the woman, going out and shutting the door.

Pivi lay still under his coverings, then a tiny noise was heard, and the Black Ant began to march over Pivi, who lay quite still. Then came the big Red Ant skipping along his body, and then Pivi shook himself all over. He jumped up quite well again, he ran to the river, he looked into the water and saw that he was changed from a bird into a fine young man!

' Oh, lady,' he cried, ' look at me now ! I am changed into a man, and so handsome ! '

' Will you obey me again ? ' said the woman.

' Always ; whatever you command I will do it,' said Pivi, politely.

' Then climb up that cocoa-nut tree, with your legs only, not using your hands,' said the woman.

Now the natives can run up cocoa-nut trees like squirrels, some using only one hand ; the girls can do that. But few can climb without using their hands at all.

' At the top of the tree you will find two cocoa-nuts. You must not throw them down, but carry them in your hands ; and you must descend as you went up, using your legs only.'

'I shall try, at least,' said Pivi. And up he went, but it was very difficult, and down he came.

'Here are your cocoa-nuts,' he said, presenting them to the woman.

'Now, Pivi, put them in the shed where you lay, and when the sun sets to cool himself in the sea and rise again not so hot in the dawn you must go and take the nuts.'

All day Pivi played about in the river, as the natives do, throwing fruit and silvery showers of water at each other. When the sun set he went into the hut. But as he drew near he heard sweet voices talking and laughing within.

'What is that? People chattering in the hut! Perhaps they have taken my cocoa-nuts,' said Pivi to himself.

In he went, and there he found two pretty, laughing, teasing girls. He hunted for his cocoanuts, but none were there.

Down he ran to the river. 'Oh, lady, my nuts have been stolen ! ' he cried.

'Come with me, Pivi, and there will be nuts for you,' said the woman.

They went back to the hut, where the girls were laughing and playing.

'Nuts for you ? ' said the woman, 'there are two wives for you, Pivi, take them to your house.'

'Oh, good lady,' cried Pivi, 'how kind you are ! '

So they were married and very happy, when in came cross old Kabo.

'Is this Pivi ? ' said he. 'Yes, it is—no, it isn't. It is not the same Pivi—but there is a kind of likeness. Tell me, *are* you Pivi ? '

'Oh, yes ! ' said Pivi. 'But I am much better looking, and there are my two wives, are they not beautiful ? '

'You are mocking me, Pivi! Your wives? How? Where did you get them? *You*, with wives!'

Then Pivi told Kabo about the kind woman, and all the wonderful things that had happened to him.

'Well, well!' said Kabo, 'but I want to be handsome too, and to have pretty young wives.'

'But how can we manage that?' asked Pivi.

'Oh, we shall do all the same things over again—play at slinging, and, this time, you shall break my leg, Pivi!'

'With all the pleasure in life,' said Pivi, who was always ready to oblige.

So they went slinging, and Pivi broke Kabo's leg, and Kabo fell into the river, and floated into the bamboo, and the woman blew him out, just as before. Then she picked up Kabo, and put him in the shed, and told him what to do when the Black Ant came, and what to do when the Red Ant came. But he didn't!

When the Black Ant came, he shook himself, and behold, he had a twisted leg, and a hump back, and was as black as the ant.

Then he ran to the woman.

'Look, what a figure I am!' he said; but she only told him to climb the tree, as she had told Pivi.

But Kabo climbed with both hands and feet, and he threw down the nuts, instead of carrying them down, and he put them in the hut. And when he went back for them there he found two horrid old black hags, wrangling, and scolding, and scratching! So back he went to Pivi with his two beautiful wives, and Pivi was very sorry, but what could he do? Nothing, but sit and cry.

So, one day, Kabo came and asked Pivi to sail in his canoe to a place where he knew of a great big shell-fish, enough to feed on for a week. Pivi went, and deep in the clear water they saw a monstrous shell-fish, like an oyster, as big as a rock, with the shell wide open.

'We shall catch it, and dry it, and kipper it,' said Pivi, 'and give a dinner to all our friends!'

PIVI DIVES FOR THE SHELLFISH

' I shall dive for it, and break it off the rock,' said Kabo,
' and then you must help me to drag it up into the canoe.'

There the shell-fish lay and gaped, but Kabo, though
he dived in, kept well out of the way of the beast.

Up he came, puffing and blowing : ' Oh, Pivi,' he cried,
' I cannot move it. Jump in and try yourself ! '

Pivi dived, with his spear, and the shell-fish opened
its shell wider yet, and sucked, and Pivi disappeared into
its mouth, and the shell shut up with a snap !

Kabo laughed like a fiend, and then went home.

' Where is Pivi ? ' asked the two pretty girls. Kabo
pretended to cry, and told how Pivi had been swallowed.

' But dry your tears, my darlings,' said Kabo, ' I will
be your husband, and my wives shall be your slaves.
Everything is for the best, in the best of all possible
worlds.'

' No, no ! ' cried the girls, ' we love Pivi. We do not
love anyone else. We shall stay at home, and weep for
Pivi ! '

' Wretched idiots ! ' cried Kabo ; ' Pivi was a scoundrel
who broke my leg, and knocked me into the river.'

Then a little cough was heard at the door, and Kabo
trembled, for he knew it was the cough of Pivi !

' Ah, dear Pivi ! ' cried Kabo, rushing to the door.
' What joy ! I was trying to console your dear wives.'

Pivi said not one word. He waved his hand, and five
and twenty of his friends came trooping down the hill.
They cut up Kabo into little pieces. Pivi turned round,
and there was the good woman of the river.

' Pivi,' she said, ' how did you get out of the living
tomb into which Kabo sent you ? '

' I had my spear with me,' said Pivi. ' It was quite
dry inside the shell, and I worked away at the fish with
my spear, till he saw reason to open his shell, and out I
came.' Then the good woman laughed ; and Pivi and his
two wives lived happy ever afterwards.

[*Moncelon. Bulletin de la Société d'Anthropologie.* Series iii. vol. ix., pp. 613-365.]

THE ELF MAIDEN

ONCE upon a time two young men living in a small village fell in love with the same girl. During the winter, it was all night except for an hour or so about noon, when the darkness seemed a little less dark, and then they used to see which of them could tempt her out for a sleigh ride with the Northern Lights flashing above them, or which could persuade her to come to a dance in some neighbouring barn. But when the spring began, and the light grew longer, the hearts of the villagers leapt at the sight of the sun, and a day was fixed for the boats to be brought out, and the great nets to be spread in the bays of some islands that lay a few miles to the north. Everybody went on this expedition, and the two young men and the girl went with them.

They all sailed merrily across the sea chattering like a flock of magpies, or singing their favourite songs. And when they reached the shore, what an unpacking there was! For this was a noted fishing ground, and here they would live, in little wooden huts, till autumn and bad weather came round again.

The maiden and the two young men happened to share the same hut with some friends, and fished daily from the same boat. And as time went on, one of the youths remarked that the girl took less notice of him than she did of his companion. At first he tried to think that he was dreaming, and for a long while he kept his eyes shut very tight to what he did not want to see, but in spite of his efforts, the truth managed to wriggle

through, and then the young man gave up trying to
deceive himself, and set about finding some way to get
the better of his rival.

The plan that he hit upon could not be carried out for
some months; but the longer the young man thought of
it, the more pleased he was with it, so he made no sign
of his feelings, and waited patiently till the moment came.
This was the very day that they were all going to leave
the islands, and sail back to the mainland for the winter.
In the bustle and hurry of departure, the cunning fisher-
man contrived that their boat should be the last to put
off, and when everything was ready, and the sails about
to be set, he suddenly called out:

' Oh, dear, what shall I do! I have left my best knife
behind in the hut. Run, like a good fellow, and get it for
me, while I raise the anchor and loosen the tiller.'

Not thinking any harm, the youth jumped back on
shore and made his way up the steep bank. At the door
of the hut he stopped and looked back, then started and
gazed in horror. The head of the boat stood out to sea,
and he was left alone on the island.

Yes, there was no doubt of it—he was quite alone;
and he had nothing to help him except the knife which
his comrade had purposely dropped on the ledge of the
window. For some minutes he was too stunned by the
treachery of his friend to think about anything at all,
but after a while he shook himself awake, and determined
that he would manage to keep alive somehow, if it were
only to revenge himself.

So he put the knife in his pocket and went off to a
part of the island which was not so bare as the rest, and
had a small grove of trees. From one of these he cut
himself a bow, which he strung with a piece of cord that
had been left lying about the huts.

When this was ready the young man ran down to the
shore and shot one or two sea-birds, which he plucked
and cooked for supper.

In this way the months slipped by, and Christmas came round again. The evening before, the youth went down to the rocks and into the copse, collecting all the drift wood the sea had washed up or the gale had blown down, and he piled it up in a great stack outside the door, so that he might not have to fetch any all the next day. As soon as his task was done, he paused and looked out towards the mainland, thinking of Christmas Eve last year, and the merry dance they had had. The night was still and cold, and by the help of the Northern Lights he could almost see across to the opposite coast, when, suddenly, he noticed a boat, which seemed steering straight for the island. At first he could hardly stand for joy, the chance of speaking to another man was so delightful; but as the boat drew near there was something, he could not tell what, that was different from the boats which he had been used to all his life, and when it touched the shore he saw that the people that filled it were beings of another world than ours. Then he hastily stepped behind the wood stack, and waited for what might happen next.

The strange folk one by one jumped on to the rocks, each bearing a load of something that they wanted. Among the women he remarked two young girls, more beautiful and better dressed than any of the rest, carrying between them two great baskets full of provisions. The young man peeped out cautiously to see what all this crowd could be doing inside the tiny hut, but in a moment he drew back again, as the girls returned, and looked about as if they wanted to find out what sort of a place the island was.

Their sharp eyes soon discovered the form of a man crouching behind the bundles of sticks, and at first they felt a little frightened, and started as if they would run away. But the youth remained so still, that they took courage and laughed gaily to each other. ' What a strange creature, let us try what he is made of,' said one, and she stooped down and gave him a pinch.

Now the young man had a pin sticking in the sleeve of his jacket, and the moment the girl's hand touched him she pricked it so sharply that the blood came. The girl screamed so loudly that the people all ran out of their huts to see what was the matter. But directly they caught sight of the man they turned and fled in the other direction, and picking up the goods they had brought with them scampered as fast as they could down to the shore. In an instant, boat, people, and goods had vanished completely.

In their hurry they had, however, forgotten two things : a bundle of keys which lay on the table, and the girl whom the pin had pricked, and who now stood pale and helpless beside the wood stack.

' You will have to make me your wife,' she said at last, ' for you have drawn my blood, and I belong to you.'

' Why not? I am quite willing,' answered he. ' But how do you suppose we can manage to live till summer comes round again ? '

' Do not be anxious about that,' said the girl ; ' if you will only marry me all will be well. I am very rich, and all my family are rich also.'

Then the young man gave her his promise to make her his wife, and the girl fulfilled her part of the bargain, and food was plentiful on the island all through the long winter months, though he never knew how it got there. And by-and-by it was spring once more, and time for the fisher-folk to sail from the mainland.

' Where are we to go now ? ' asked the girl, one day, when the sun seemed brighter and the wind softer than usual.

' I do not care where I go,' answered the young man ; ' what do you think ? '

The girl replied that she would like to go somewhere right at the other end of the island, and build a house, far away from the huts of the fishing-folk. And he consented, and that very day they set off in search of a sheltered spot on the banks of a stream, so that it would be easy to get water.

In a tiny bay, on the opposite side of the island, they found the very thing, which seemed to have been made on purpose for them ; and as they were tired with their long walk, they laid themselves down on a bank of moss among some birches and prepared to have a good night's rest, so as to be fresh for work next day. But before she went to sleep the girl turned to her husband, and said : ' If in your dreams you fancy that you hear strange noises, be sure you do not stir, or get up to see what it is.'

' Oh, it is not likely we shall hear any noises in such a quiet place,' answered he, and fell sound asleep.

Suddenly he was awakened by a great clatter about his ears, as if all the workmen in the world were sawing and hammering and building close to him. He was just going to spring up and go to see what it meant, when he luckily remembered his wife's words and lay still. But the time till morning seemed very long, and with the first ray of sun they both rose, and pushed aside the branches of the birch trees. There, in the very place they had chosen, stood a beautiful house—doors and windows, and everything all complete !

' Now you must fix on a spot for your cow-stalls,' said the girl, when they had breakfasted off wild cherries ; ' and take care it is the proper size, neither too large nor too small.' And the husband did as he was bid, though he wondered what use a cow-house could be, as they had no cows to put in it. But as he was a little afraid of his wife, who knew so much more than he, he asked no questions.

This night also he was awakened by the same sounds as before, and in the morning they found, near the stream, the most beautiful cow-house that ever was seen, with stalls and milk-pails and stools all complete, indeed, everything that a cow-house could possibly want, except the cows. Then the girl bade him measure out the ground for a storehouse, and this, she said, might be as large as he

pleased; and when the storehouse was ready she proposed
that they should set off to pay her parents a visit.

THE ELF MAIDEN'S HOUSE

The old people welcomed them heartily, and summoned
their neighbours, for many miles round, to a great feast
in their honour. In fact, for several weeks there was no

work done on the farm at all; and at length the young man and his wife grew tired of so much play, and declared that they must return to their own home. But, before they started on the journey, the wife whispered to her husband : 'Take care to jump over the threshold as quick as you can, or it will be the worse for you.'

The young man listened to her words, and sprang over the threshold like an arrow from a bow; and it was well he did, for, no sooner was he on the other side, than his father-in-law threw a great hammer at him, which would have broken both his legs, if it had only touched them.

When they had gone some distance on the road home, the girl turned to her husband and said : 'Till you step inside the house, be sure you do not look back, whatever you may hear or see.'

And the husband promised, and for a while all was still; and he thought no more about the matter till he noticed at last that the nearer he drew to the house the louder grew the noise of the trampling of feet behind him. As he laid his hand upon the door he thought he was safe, and turned to look. There, sure enough, was a vast herd of cattle, which had been sent after him by his father-in-law when he found that his daughter had been cleverer than he. Half of the herd were already through the fence and cropping the grass on the banks of the stream, but half still remained outside and faded into nothing, even as he watched them.

However, enough cattle were left to make the young man rich, and he and his wife lived happily together, except that every now and then the girl vanished from his sight, and never told him where she had been. For a long time he kept silence about it; but one day, when he had been complaining of her absence, she said to him : 'Dear husband, I am bound to go, even against my will, and there is only one way to stop me. Drive a nail into the threshold, and then I can never pass in or out.'

And so he did.

[*Lappländische Mährchen.*]

HOW SOME WILD ANIMALS BECAME TAME ONES

Once upon a time there lived a miller who was so rich that, when he was going to be married, he asked to the feast not only his own friends but also the wild animals who dwelt in the hills and woods round about. The chief of the bears, the wolves, the foxes, the horses, the cows, the goats, the sheep, and the reindeer, all received invitations; and as they were not accustomed to weddings they were greatly pleased and flattered, and sent back messages in the politest language that they would certainly be there.

The first to start on the morning of the wedding-day was the bear, who always liked to be punctual; and, besides, he had a long way to go, and his hair, being so thick and rough, needed a good brushing before it was fit to be seen at a party. However, he took care to awaken very early, and set off down the road with a light heart. Before he had walked very far he met a boy who came whistling along, hitting at the tops of the flowers with a stick.

'Where are you going?' said he, looking at the bear in surprise, for he was an old acquaintance, and not generally so smart.

'Oh, just to the miller's marriage,' answered the bear carelessly. 'Of course, I would much rather stay at home, but the miller was so anxious I should be there that I really could not refuse.'

'Don't go, don't go!' cried the boy. 'If you do you

will never come back ! You have got the most beautiful skin in the world—just the kind that everyone is wanting, and they will be sure to kill you and strip you of it.'

'I had not thought of that,' said the bear, whose face turned white, only nobody could see it. 'If you are certain that they would be so wicked—but perhaps you are jealous because nobody has invited *you* ? '

'Oh, nonsense ! ' replied the boy angrily, ' do as you see. It is your skin, and not mine ; *I* don't care what becomes of it ! ' And he walked quickly on with his head in the air.

The bear waited until he was out of sight, and then followed him slowly, for he felt in his heart that the boy's advice was good, though he was too proud to say so.

The boy soon grew tired of walking along the road, and turned off into the woods, where there were bushes he could jump and streams he could wade ; but he had not gone far before he met the wolf.

'Where are you going ? ' asked he, for it was not the first time he had seen him.

'Oh, just to the miller's marriage,' answered the wolf, as the bear had done before him. ' It is rather tiresome, of course—weddings are always so stupid ; but still one must be good-natured ! '

'Don't go ! ' said the boy again. 'Your skin is so thick and warm, and winter is not far off now. They will kill you, and strip it from you.'

The wolf's jaw dropped in astonishment and terror. ' Do you *really* think that would happen ? ' he gasped.

'Yes, to be sure, I do,' answered the boy. 'But it is your affair, not mine. So good-morning,' and on he went. The wolf stood still for a few minutes, for he was trembling all over, and then crept quietly back to his cave.

Next the boy met the fox, whose lovely coat of silvery grey was shining in the sun.

'You look very fine ! ' said the boy, stopping to admire him, ' are you going to the miller's wedding too ? '

'Yes,' answered the fox; 'it is a long journey to take for such a thing as that, but you know what the miller's friends are like—so dull and heavy! It is only kind to go and amuse them a little.'

'You poor fellow,' said the boy pityingly. 'Take my advice and stay at home. If you once enter the miller's gate his dogs will tear you in pieces.'

'Ah, well, such things *have* occurred, I know,' replied the fox gravely. And without saying any more he trotted off the way he had come.

His tail had scarcely disappeared, when a great noise of crashing branches was heard, and up bounded the horse, his black skin glistening like satin.

'Good-morning,' he called to the boy as he galloped past, 'I can't wait to talk to you now. I have promised the miller to be present at his wedding-feast, and they won't sit down till I come.'

'Stop! stop!' cried the boy after him, and there was something in his voice that made the horse pull up. 'What is the matter?' asked he.

'You don't know what you are doing,' said the boy. 'If once you go there you will never gallop through these woods any more. You are stronger than many men, but they will catch you and put ropes round you, and you will have to work and to serve them all the days of your life.'

The horse threw back his head at these words, and laughed scornfully.

'Yes, I am stronger than many men,' answered he, 'and all the ropes in the world would not hold me. Let them bind me as fast as they will, I can always break loose, and return to the forest and freedom.'

And with this proud speech he gave a whisk of his long tail, and galloped away faster than before.

But when he reached the miller's house everything happened as the boy had said. While he was looking at the guests and thinking how much handsomer and stronger he was than any of them, a rope was suddenly flung over his head, and he was thrown down and a bit thrust between his teeth. Then, in spite of his struggles, he was dragged to a stable, and shut up for several days without any food, till his spirit was broken and his coat had lost its gloss. After that he was harnessed to a plough, and had plenty of time to remember all he had lost through not listening to the counsel of the boy.

When the horse had turned a deaf ear to his words the boy wandered idly along, sometimes gathering wild strawberries from a bank, and sometimes plucking wild cherries from a tree, till he reached a clearing in the middle of the forest. Crossing this open space was a beautiful milk-white cow with a wreath of flowers round her neck.

'Good-morning,' she said pleasantly, as she came up to the place where the boy was standing.

'Good-morning,' he returned. 'Where are you going in such a hurry?'

'To the miller's wedding; I am rather late already, for the wreath took such a long time to make, so I can't stop.'

'Don't go,' said the boy earnestly; 'when once they have tasted your milk they will never let you leave them, and you will have to serve them all the days of your life.'

'Oh, nonsense; what do *you* know about it?' answered the cow, who always thought she was wiser than other people. 'Why, I can run twice as fast as any of them! I should like to see anybody try to keep me against my will.' And, without even a polite bow, she went on her way, feeling very much offended.

But everything turned out just as the boy had said. The company had all heard of the fame of the cow's milk, and persuaded her to give them some, and then her doom was sealed. A crowd gathered round her, and held her horns so that she could not use them, and, like the horse, she was shut in the stable, and only let out in the mornings, when a long rope was tied round her head, and she was fastened to a stake in a grassy meadow.

And so it happened to the goat and to the sheep.

Last of all came the reindeer, looking as he always did, as if some serious business was on hand.

' Where are you going? ' asked the boy, who by this time was tired of wild cherries, and was thinking of his dinner.

' I am invited to the wedding,' answered the reindeer, ' and the miller has begged me on no account to fail him.'

' O fool! ' cried the boy, ' have you no sense at all? Don't you know that when you get there they will hold you fast, for neither beast nor bird is as strong or as swift as you? '

' That is exactly why I am quite safe,' replied the reindeer. ' I am so strong that no one can bind me, and so swift that not even an arrow can catch me. So, good-bye for the present, you will soon see me back.'

But none of the animals that went to the miller's wedding ever came back. And because they were self-willed and conceited, and would not listen to good advice, they and their children have been the servants of men to this very day.

[*Lappländische Mährchen.*]

FORTUNE AND THE WOOD-CUTTER

SEVERAL hundreds of years ago there lived in a forest a wood-cutter and his wife and children. He was very poor, having only his axe to depend upon, and two mules to carry the wood he cut to the neighbouring town; but he worked hard, and was always out of bed by five o'clock, summer and winter.

This went on for twenty years, and though his sons were now grown up, and went with their father to the forest, everything seemed to go against them, and they remained as poor as ever. In the end the wood-cutter lost heart, and said to himself:

'What is the good of working like this if I never am a penny the richer at the end? I shall go to the forest no more! And perhaps, if I take to my bed, and do not run after Fortune, one day she may come to me.'

So the next morning he did not get up, and when six o'clock struck, his wife, who had been cleaning the house, went to see what was the matter.

'Are you ill?' she asked wonderingly, surprised at not finding him dressed. 'The cock has crowed ever so often. It is high time for you to get up.'

'Why should I get up?' asked the man, without moving.

'Why? to go to the forest, of course.'

'Yes; and when I have toiled all day I hardly earn enough to give us one meal.'

'But what can we do, my poor husband?' said she. 'It is just a trick of Fortune's, who would never smile upon us.'

'Well, I have had my fill of Fortune's tricks,' cried
he. 'If she wants me she can find me here. But I have
done with the wood for ever.'

'My dear husband, grief has driven you mad! Do
you think Fortune will come to anybody who does not
go after her? Dress yourself, and saddle the mules,
and begin your work. Do you know that there is not a
morsel of bread in the house?'

'I don't care if there isn't, and I am not going to the
forest. It is no use your talking; nothing will make me
change my mind.'

The distracted wife begged and implored in vain; her
husband persisted in staying in bed, and at last, in despair,
she left him and went back to her work.

An hour or two later a man from the nearest village
knocked at the door, and when she opened it, he said to
her: 'Good-morning, mother. I have got a job to do,
and I want to know if your husband will lend me your
mules, as I see he is not using them, and can lend me a
hand himself?'

'He is upstairs; you had better ask him,' answered
the woman. And the man went up, and repeated his
request.

'I am sorry, neighbour, but I have sworn not to leave
my bed, and nothing will make me break my vow.'

'Well, then, will you lend me your two mules? I will
pay you something for them.'

'Certainly, neighbour. Take them and welcome.'

So the man left the house, and leading the mules
from the stable, placed two sacks on their back, and drove
them to a field where he had found a hidden treasure.
He filled the sacks with the money, though he knew
perfectly well that it belonged to the sultan, and was
driving them quietly home again, when he saw two
soldiers coming along the road. Now the man was aware
that if he was caught he would be condemned to death,
so he fled back into the forest. The mules, left to

themselves, took the path that led to their master's stable.

The wood-cutter's wife was looking out of the window when the mules drew up before the door, so heavily laden that they almost sank under their burdens. She lost no time in calling her husband, who was still lying in bed.

'Quick, quick! get up as fast as you can. Our two mules have returned with sacks on their backs, so heavily laden with something or other that the poor beasts can hardly stand up.'

'Wife, I have told you a dozen times already that I am not going to get up. Why can't you leave me in peace?'

As she found she could get no help from her husband the woman took a large knife and cut the cords which bound the sacks on to the animals' backs. They fell at once to the ground, and out poured a rain of gold pieces, till the little court-yard shone like the sun.

'A treasure!' gasped the woman, as soon as she could speak from surprise. 'A treasure!' And she ran off to tell her husband.

'Get up! get up!' she cried. 'You were quite right not to go to the forest, and to await Fortune in your bed; she has come at last! Our mules have returned home laden with all the gold in the world, and it is now lying in the court. No one in the whole country can be as rich as we are!'

In an instant the wood-cutter was on his feet, and running to the court, where he paused, dazzled by the glitter of the coins which lay around him.

'You see, my dear wife, that I was right,' he said at last. 'Fortune is so capricious, you can never count on her. Run after her, and she is sure to fly from you; stay still, and she is sure to come.'

[*Traditions Populaires de l'Asie Mineure.*]

THE ENCHANTED HEAD

ONCE upon a time an old woman lived in a small cottage near the sea with her two daughters. They were very poor, and the girls seldom left the house, as they worked all day long making veils for the ladies to wear over their faces, and every morning, when the veils were finished, the mother took them over the bridge and sold them in the city. Then she bought the food that they needed for the day, and returned home to do her share of veil-making.

One morning the old woman rose even earlier than usual, and set off for the city with her wares. She was just crossing the bridge when, suddenly, she knocked up against a human head, which she had never seen there before. The woman started back in horror; but what was her surprise when the head spoke, exactly as if it had a body joined on to it.

'Take me with you, good mother!' it said imploringly; 'take me with you back to your house.'

At the sound of these words the poor woman nearly went mad with terror. Have that horrible thing always at home? Never! never! And she turned and ran back as fast as she could, not knowing that the head was jumping, dancing, and rolling after her. But when she reached her own door it bounded in before her, and stopped in front of the fire, begging and praying to be allowed to stay.

All that day there was no food in the house, for the veils had not been sold, and they had no money to buy anything with. So they all sat silent at their work, inwardly cursing the head which was the cause of their misfortunes.

When evening came, and there was no sign of supper, the head spoke, for the first time that day:

'Good mother, does no one ever eat here? During all the hours I have spent in your house not a creature has touched anything.'

'No,' answered the old woman, 'we are not eating anything.'

'And why not, good mother?'

'Because we have no money to buy any food.'

'Is it your custom never to eat?'

'No, for every morning I go into the city to sell my veils, and with the few shillings I get for them I buy all we want. To-day I did not cross the bridge, so of course I had nothing for food.'

'Then *I* am the cause of your having gone hungry all day?' asked the head.

'Yes, you are,' answered the old woman.

'Well, then, I will give you money and plenty of it, if you will only do as I tell you. In an hour, as the clock strikes twelve, you must be on the bridge at the place where you met me. When you get there call out "Ahmed," three times, as loud as you can. Then a negro will appear, and you must say to him: "The head, your master, desires you to open the trunk, and to give me the green purse which you will find in it."'

'Very well, my lord,' said the old woman, 'I will set off at once for the bridge.' And wrapping her veil round her she went out.

Midnight was striking as she reached the spot where she had met the head so many hours before.

'Ahmed! Ahmed! Ahmed!' cried she, and immediately a huge negro, as tall as a giant, stood on the bridge before her.

'What do you want?' asked he.

' The head, your master, desires you to open the trunk, and to give me the green purse which you will find in it.'

' I will be back in a moment, good mother,' said he. And three minutes later he placed a purse full of sequins in the old woman's hand.

No one can imagine the joy of the whole family at the sight of all this wealth. The tiny, tumble-down cottage was rebuilt, the girls had new dresses, and their mother ceased selling veils. It was such a new thing to them to have money to spend, that they were not as careful as they might have been, and by-and-by there was not a single coin left in the purse. When this happened their hearts sank within them, and their faces fell.

' Have you spent your fortune ? ' asked the head from its corner, when it saw how sad they looked. ' Well, then, go at midnight, good mother, to the bridge, and call out " Mahomet ! " three times, as loud as you can. A negro will appear in answer, and you must tell him to open the trunk, and to give you the red purse which he will find there.'

The old woman did not need twice telling, but set off at once for the bridge.

' Mahomet ! Mahomet ! Mahomet ! ' cried she, with all her might ; and in an instant a negro, still larger than the last, stood before her.

' What do you want ? ' asked he.

' The head, your master, bids you open the trunk, and to give me the red purse which you will find in it.'

' Very well, good mother, I will do so,' answered the negro, and, the moment after he had vanished, he re-appeared with the purse in his hand.

This time the money seemed so endless that the old woman built herself a new house, and filled it with the most beautiful things that were to be found in the shops. Her daughters were always wrapped in veils that looked as if they were woven out of sunbeams, and their dresses shone with precious stones. The neighbours wondered where all this sudden wealth had sprung from, but nobody knew about the head.

'Good mother,' said the head, one day, 'this morning you are to go to the city and ask the sultan to give me his daughter for my bride.'

'Do what?' asked the old woman in amazement. 'How can I tell the sultan that a head without a body wishes to become his son-in-law? They will think that I am mad, and I shall be hooted from the palace and stoned by the children.'

'Do as I bid you,' replied the head; 'it is my will.'

The old woman was afraid to say anything more, and, putting on her richest clothes, started for the palace. The sultan granted her an audience at once, and, in a trembling voice, she made her request.

'Are you mad, old woman?' said the sultan, staring at her.

'The wooer is powerful, O Sultan, and nothing is impossible to him.'

'Is that true?'

'It is, O Sultan; I swear it,' answered she.

'Then let him show his power by doing three things, and I will give him my daughter.'

'Command, O gracious prince,' said she.

'Do you see that hill in front of the palace?' asked the sultan.

'I see it,' answered she.

'Well, in forty days the man who has sent you must make that hill vanish, and plant a beautiful garden in its place. That is the first thing. Now go, and tell him what I say.'

So the old woman returned and told the head the sultan's first condition.

'It is well,' he replied; and said no more about it.

For thirty-nine days the head remained in its favourite corner. The old woman thought that the task set before him was beyond his powers, and that no more would be heard about the sultan's daughter. But on the thirty-ninth evening after her visit to the palace, the head suddenly spoke.

'Good mother,' he said, 'you must go to-night to the bridge, and when you are there cry "Ali! Ali! Ali!" as loud as you can. A negro will appear before you, and you will tell him that he is to level the hill, and to make, in its place, the most beautiful garden that ever was seen.'

'I will go at once,' answered she.

It did not take her long to reach the bridge which led to the city, and she took up her position on the spot where she had first seen the head, and called loudly 'Ali! Ali! Ali.' In an instant a negro appeared before her, of such a huge size that the old woman was half frightened; but his voice was mild and gentle as he said: 'What is it that you want?'

'Your master bids you level the hill that stands in front of the sultan's palace and in its place to make the most beautiful garden in the world.'

'Tell my master he shall be obeyed,' replied Ali; 'it shall be done this moment.' And the old woman went home and gave Ali's message to the head.

Meanwhile the sultan was in his palace waiting till the fortieth day should dawn, and wondering that not one spadeful of earth should have been dug out of the hill.

'If that old woman has been playing me a trick,' thought he, 'I will hang her! And I will put up a gallows to-morrow on the hill itself.'

But when to-morrow came there was no hill, and when the sultan opened his eyes he could not imagine why the room was so much lighter than usual, and what was the reason of the sweet smell of flowers that filled the air.

'Can there be a fire?' he said to himself; 'the sun never came in at this window before. I must get up and see.' So he rose and looked out, and underneath him

flowers from every part of the world were blooming, and
creepers of every colour hung in chains from tree to tree.

Then he remembered. ' Certainly that old woman's
son is a clever magician ! ' cried he ; ' I never met anyone
as clever as that. What shall I give him to do next?
Let me think. Ah ! I know.' And he sent for the old
woman, who by the orders of the head, was waiting
below.

' Your son has carried out my wishes very nicely,' he
said. ' The garden is larger and better than that of any
other king. But when I walk across it I shall need some
place to rest on the other side. In forty days he must
build me a palace, in which every room shall be filled
with different furniture from a different country, and each
more magnificent than any room that ever was seen.'
And having said this he turned round and went away.

' Oh ! he will never be able to do that,' thought she ;
' it is much more difficult than the hill.' And she walked
home slowly, with her head bent.

' Well, what am I to do next ? ' asked the head cheerfully. And the old woman told her story.

' Dear me ! is that all ? why it is child's play,' answered
the head ; and troubled no more about the palace for
thirty-nine days. Then he told the old woman to go to
the bridge and call for Hassan.

' What do you want, old woman ? ' asked Hassan, when
he appeared, for he was not as polite as the others had
been.

' Your master commands you to build the most magnificent palace that ever was seen,' replied she ; ' and you
are to place it on the borders of the new garden.'

' He shall be obeyed,' answered Hassan. And when the
sultan woke he saw, in the distance, a palace built of soft
blue marble, resting on slender pillars of pure gold.

' That old woman's son is certainly all-powerful,' cried
he ; ' what shall I bid him do now ? ' And after thinking

THE PRINCESS SEES THE MAGIC HEAD

some time he sent for the old woman, who was expecting the summons.

'The garden is wonderful, and the palace the finest in the world,' said he, ' so fine, that my servants would cut but a sorry figure in it. Let your son fill it with forty slaves whose beauty shall be unequalled, all exactly like each other, and of the same height.'

This time the king thought he had invented something totally impossible, and was quite pleased with himself for his cleverness.

Thirty-nine days passed, and at midnight on the night of the last the old woman was standing on the bridge.

'Bekir! Bekir! Bekir!' cried she. And a negro appeared, and inquired what she wanted.

'The head, your master, bids you find forty slaves of unequalled beauty, and of the same height, and place them in the sultan's palace on the other side of the garden.'

And when, on the morning of the fortieth day, the sultan went to the blue palace, and was received by the forty slaves, he nearly lost his wits from surprise.

' I will assuredly give my daughter to the old woman's son,' thought he. 'If I were to search all the world through I could never find a more powerful son-in-law.'

And when the old woman entered his presence he informed her that he was ready to fulfil his promise, and she was to bid her son appear at the palace without delay.

This command did not at all please the old woman, though, of course, she made no objections to the sultan.

'All has gone well so far,' she grumbled, when she told her story to the head, ' but what do you suppose the sultan will say, when he sees his daughter's husband?'

'Never mind what he says! Put me on a silver dish and carry me to the palace.'

So it was done, though the old woman's heart beat as she laid down the dish with the head upon it.

At the sight before him the king flew into a violent rage.

'I will never marry my daughter to such a monster,' he cried. But the princess placed her hand gently on his arm.

'You have given your word, my father, and you cannot break it,' said she.

'But, my child, it is impossible for you to marry such a being,' exclaimed the sultan.

'Yes, I will marry him. He has a beautiful head, and I love him already.'

So the marriage was celebrated, and great feasts were held in the palace, though the people wept tears to think of the sad fate of their beloved princess. But when the merry-making was done, and the young couple were alone, the head suddenly disappeared, or, rather, a body was added to it, and one of the handsomest young men that ever was seen stood before the princess.

'A wicked fairy enchanted me at my birth,' he said, 'and for the rest of the world I must always be a head only. But for you, and you only, I am a man like other men.'

'And that is all I care about,' said the princess.

[*Traditions populaires de toutes les nations (Asie Mineure)*].

THE SISTER OF THE SUN

A LONG time ago there lived a young prince whose favourite playfellow was the son of the gardener who lived in the grounds of the palace. The king would have preferred his choosing a friend from the pages who were brought up at court; but the prince would have nothing to say to them, and as he was a spoilt child, and allowed his way in all things, and the gardener's boy was quiet and well-behaved, he was suffered to be in the palace, morning, noon, and night.

The game the children loved the best was a match at archery, for the king had given them two bows exactly alike, and they would spend whole days in trying to see which could shoot the highest. This is always very dangerous, and it was a great wonder they did not put their eyes out; but somehow or other they managed to escape.

One morning, when the prince had done his lessons, he ran out to call his friend, and they both hurried off to the lawn which was their usual playground. They took their bows out of the little hut where their toys were kept, and began to see which could shoot the highest. At last they happened to let fly their arrows both together, and when they fell to earth again the tail feather of a golden hen was found sticking in one. Now the question began to arise whose was the lucky arrow, for they were both alike, and look as closely as you would you could see no difference between them. The prince declared that the arrow was his, and the gardener's boy was quite sure

it was *his*—and on this occasion he was perfectly right;
but, as they could not decide the matter, they went
straight to the king.

When the king had heard the story, he decided that
the feather belonged to his son; but the other boy would
not listen to this and claimed the feather for himself. At
length the king's patience gave way, and he said angrily:

'Very well; if you are so sure that the feather is
yours, yours it shall be; only you will have to seek till
you find a golden hen with a feather missing from her
tail. And if you fail to find her your head will be the
forfeit.'

The boy had need of all his courage to listen silently
to the king's words. He had no idea where the golden
hen might be, or even, if he discovered that, how he was
to get to her. But there was nothing for it but to do the
king's bidding, and he felt that the sooner he left the
palace the better. So he went home and put some food
into a bag, and then set forth, hoping that some accident
might show him which path to take.

After walking for several hours he met a fox, who
seemed inclined to be friendly, and the boy was so glad to
have anyone to talk to that he sat down and entered into
conversation.

'Where are you going?' asked the fox.

'I have got to find a golden hen who has lost a feather
out of her tail,' answered the boy; 'but I don't know
where she lives or how I shall catch her!'

'Oh, I can show you the way!' said the fox, who was
really very good-natured. 'Far towards the east, in that
direction, lives a beautiful maiden who is called "The
Sister of the Sun." She has three golden hens in her
house. Perhaps the feather belongs to one of them.'

The boy was delighted at this news, and they walked
on all day together, the fox in front, and the boy behind.
When evening came they lay down to sleep, and put the
knapsack under their heads for a pillow.

Suddenly, about midnight, the fox gave a low whine, and drew nearer to his bedfellow. ' Cousin,' he whispered very low, 'there is someone coming who will take the knapsack away from me. Look over there ! ' And the boy, peeping through the bushes, saw a man.

' Oh, I don't think he will rob us ! ' said the boy ; and when the man drew near, he told them his story, which so much interested the stranger that he asked leave to travel with them, as he might be of some use. So when the sun rose they set out again, the fox in front as before, the man and boy following.

After some hours they reached the castle of the Sister of the Sun, who kept the golden hens among her treasures. They halted before the gate and took counsel as to which of them should go in and see the lady herself.

' I think it would be best for me to enter and steal the hens,' said the fox ; but this did not please the boy at all.

' No, it is my business, so it is right that I should go,' answered he.

' You will find it a very difficult matter to get hold of the hens,' replied the fox.

' Oh, nothing is likely to happen to me,' returned the boy.

' Well, go then,' said the fox, ' but be careful not to make any mistake. Steal only the hen which has the feather missing from her tail, and leave the others alone.'

The man listened, but did not interfere, and the boy entered the court of the palace.

He soon spied the three hens strutting proudly about, though they were really anxiously wondering if there were not some grains lying on the ground that they might be glad to eat. And as the last one passed by him, he saw she had one feather missing from her tail.

At this sight the youth darted forward and seized the hen by the neck so that she could not struggle. Then, tucking her comfortably under his arm, he made straight for the gate. Unluckily, just as he was about to go through it he looked back and caught a glimpse of wonderful splendours from an open door of the palace. 'After all, there is no hurry,' he said to himself; 'I may as well see something now I *am* here,' and turned back, forgetting all about the hen, which escaped from under his arm, and ran to join her sisters.

He was so much fascinated by the sight of all the beautiful things which peeped through the door that he scarcely noticed that he had lost the prize he had won; and he did not remember there was such a thing as a hen in the world when he beheld the Sister of the Sun sleeping on a bed before him.

For some time he stood staring; then he came to himself with a start, and feeling that he had no business there, softly stole away, and was fortunate enough to recapture the hen, which he took with him to the gate. On the threshold he stopped again. 'Why should I not look at the Sister of the Sun?' he thought to himself; 'she is asleep, and will never know.' And he turned back for the second time and entered the chamber, while the hen wriggled herself free as before. When he had gazed his fill he went out into the courtyard and picked up his hen who was seeking for corn.

As he drew near the gate he paused. 'Why did I not give her a kiss?' he said to himself; 'I shall never kiss any woman so beautiful.' And he wrung his hands with regret, so that the hen fell to the ground and ran away.

'But I can do it still!' he cried with delight, and he rushed back to the chamber and kissed the sleeping maiden on the forehead. But, alas! when he came out again he found that the hen had grown so shy that she would not let him come near her. And, worse than that, her sisters began to cluck so loud that the Sister of the Sun was awakened by the noise. She jumped up in haste from her bed, and going to the door she said to the boy:

'You shall never, never, have my hen till you bring

THE GOLDEN HEN WILL NOT BE CAUGHT NAPPING

me back my sister who was carried off by a giant to his castle, which is a long way off.'

Slowly and sadly the youth left the palace and told his story to his friends, who were waiting outside the gate, how he had actually held the hen three times in his arms and had lost her.

'I knew that we should not get off so easily,' said the fox, shaking his head ; ' but there is no more time to waste. Let us set off at once in search of the sister. Luckily, I know the way.'

They walked on for many days, till at length the fox, who, as usual, was going first, stopped suddenly.

' The giant's castle is not far now,' he said, ' but when we reach it you two must remain outside while I go and fetch the princess. Directly I bring her out you must both catch hold of her tight, and get away as fast as you can ; while I return to the castle and talk to the giants— for there are many of them—so that they may not notice the escape of the princess.'

A few minutes later they arrived at the castle, and the fox, who had often been there before, slipped in without difficulty. There were several giants, both young and old, in the hall, and they were all dancing round the princess. As soon as they saw the fox they cried out : ' Come and dance too, old fox ; it is a long time since we have seen you.'

So the fox stood up, and did his steps with the best of them ; but after a while he stopped and said :

'I know a charming new dance that I should like to show you ; but it can only be done by two people. If the princess will honour me for a few minutes, you will soon see how it is done.'

' Ah, that is delightful ; we want something new,' answered they, and placed the princess between the out-stretched arms of the fox. In one instant he had knocked over the great stand of lights that lighted the hall, and in the darkness had borne the princess to the gate. His comrades seized hold of her, as they had been bidden, and the fox was back again in the hall before anyone had missed him. He found the giants busy trying to kindle a fire and get some light; but after a bit someone cried out:

'Where is the princess?'

'Here, in my arms,' replied the fox. 'Don't be afraid; she is quite safe.' And he waited until he thought that his comrades had gained a good start, and put at least five or six mountains between themselves and the giants. Then he sprang through the door, calling, as he went: 'The maiden is here; take her if you can!'

At these words the giants understood that their prize had escaped, and they ran after the fox as fast as their great legs could carry them, thinking that they should soon come up with the fox, who they supposed had the princess on his back. The fox, on his side, was far too clever to choose the same path that his friends had taken, but wound in and out of the forest, till at last even *he* was tired out, and fell fast asleep under a tree. Indeed, he was so exhausted with his day's work that he never heard the approach of the giants, and their hands were already stretched out to seize his tail when his eyes opened, and with a tremendous bound he was once more beyond their reach. All the rest of the night the fox ran and ran; but when bright red spread over the east, he stopped and waited till the giants were close upon him. Then he turned, and said quietly: 'Look, there is the Sister of the Sun!'

The giants raised their eyes all at once, and were instantly turned into pillars of stone. The fox then made each pillar a low bow, and set off to join his friends.

He knew a great many short cuts across the hills, so it was not long before he came up with them, and all four travelled night and day till they reached the castle of the Sister of the Sun. What joy and feasting there was throughout the palace at the sight of the princess whom they had mourned as dead ! and they could not make enough of the boy who had gone through such dangers in order to rescue her. The golden hen was given to him at once, and, more than that, the Sister of the Sun told him that, in a little time, when he was a few years older, she would herself pay a visit to his home and become his wife. The boy could hardly believe his ears when he heard what was in store for him, for this was the most beautiful princess in all the world ; and however thick the darkness might be, it fled away at once from the light of a star on her forehead.

So the boy set forth on his journey home, with his friends for company ; his heart full of gladness when he thought of the promise of the princess. But, one by one, his comrades dropped off at the places where they had first met him, and he was quite alone when he reached his native town and the gates of the palace. With the golden hen under his arm he presented himself before the king, and told his adventures, and how he was going to have for a wife a princess so wonderful and unlike all other princesses, that the star on her forehead could turn night into day. The king listened silently, and when the boy had done, he said quietly : ' If I find that your story is not true I will have you thrown into a cask of pitch.'

' It is true—every word of it,' answered the boy ; and went on to tell that the day and even the hour were fixed when his bride was to come and seek him.

But as the time drew near, and nothing was heard of the princess, the youth became anxious and uneasy, especially when it came to his ears that the great cask was being filled with pitch, and that sticks were laid underneath to make a fire to boil it with. All day long the boy stood at the window, looking over the sea by which the princess must travel ; but there were no signs of her, not even the tiniest white sail. And, as he stood, soldiers came and laid hands on him, and led him up to the cask, where a big fire was blazing, and the horrid black pitch boiling and bubbling over the sides. He looked and shuddered, but there was no escape ; so he shut his eyes to avoid seeing.

The word was given for him to mount the steps which led to the top of the cask, when, suddenly, some men were seen running with all their might, crying as they went that a large ship with its sails spread was making straight for the city. No one knew what the ship was, or whence it came ; but the king declared that he would not have the boy burned before its arrival, there would always be time enough for that.

At length the vessel was safe in port, and a whisper went through the watching crowd that on board was the Sister of the Sun, who had come to marry the young peasant, as she had promised. In a few moments more she had landed, and desired to be shown the way to the cottage which her bridegroom had so often described to her ; and whither he had been led back by the king's order at the first sign of the ship.

'Don't you know me?' asked the Sister of the Sun, bending over him where he lay, almost driven out of his senses with terror.

'No, no ; I don't know you,' answered the youth, without raising his eyes.

'Kiss me,' said the Sister of the Sun ; and the youth obeyed her, but still without looking up.

'Don't you know me *now*?' asked she.

'No, I don't know you—I don't know you,' he replied, with the manner of a man whom fear had driven mad.

At this the Sister of the Sun grew rather frightened, and beginning at the beginning, she told him the story of his meeting with her, and how she had come a long way in order to marry him. And just as she had finished in walked the king, to see if what the boy had said was really true. But hardly had he opened the door of the cottage when he was almost blinded by the light that filled it ; and he remembered what he had been told about the star on

the forehead of the princess. He staggered back as if
he had been struck, then a curious feeling took hold of
him, which he had never felt before, and falling on his
knees before the Sister of the Sun he implored her to
give up all thought of the peasant boy, and to share his

The King falls in love with the Sister of the Sun

throne. But she only laughed, and said she had a finer
throne of her own, if she wanted to sit on it, and that she
was free to please herself, and would have no husband
but the boy whom she would never have seen except for
the king himself.

'I shall marry him to-morrow,' ended she ; and ordered the preparations to be set on foot at once.

When the next day came, however, the bridegroom's father informed the princess that, by the law of the land, the marriage must take place in the presence of the king ; but he hoped his majesty would not long delay his arrival. An hour or two passed, and everyone was waiting and watching, when at last the sound of trumpets was heard and a grand procession was seen marching up the street. A chair covered with velvet had been made ready for the king, and he took his seat upon it, and, looking round upon the assembled company, he said :

'I have no wish to forbid this marriage ; but, before I can allow it to be celebrated, the bridegroom must prove himself worthy of such a bride by fulfilling three tasks. And the first is that in a single day he must cut down every tree in an entire forest.'

The youth stood aghast at the king's words. He had never cut down a tree in his life, and had not the least idea how to begin. And as for a whole forest——! But the princess saw what was passing in his mind, and whispered to him :

'Don't be afraid. In my ship you will find an axe, which you must carry off to the forest. When you have cut down one tree with it just say : " So let the forest fall," and in an instant all the trees will be on the ground. But pick up three chips of the tree you have felled, and put them in your pocket.'

And the young man did exactly as he was bid, and soon returned with the three chips safe in his coat.

The following morning the princess declared that she had been thinking about the matter, and that, as she was not a subject of the king, she saw no reason why she should be bound by his laws ; and she meant to be married that very day. But the bridegroom's father told her that it was all very well for her to talk like that, but it was quite different for his son, who would pay with his head for any disobedience to the king's commands. However, in consideration of what the youth had done the day before, he hoped his majesty's heart might be softened, especially as he had sent a message that they might expect him at once. With this the bridal pair had to be content, and be as patient as they could till the king's arrival.

He did not keep them long, but they saw by his face that nothing good awaited them.

'The marriage cannot take place,' he said shortly, 'till the youth has joined to their roots all the trees he cut down yesterday.'

This sounded much more difficult than what he had done before, and he turned in despair to the Sister of the Sun.

'It is all right,' she whispered encouragingly. 'Take this water and sprinkle it on one of the fallen trees, and say to it : "So let all the trees of the forest stand upright," and in a moment they will be erect again.'

And the young man did what he was told, and left the forest looking exactly as it had done before.

Now, surely, thought the princess, there was no longer any need to put off the wedding ; and she gave orders that all should be ready for the following day. But again the old man interfered, and declared that without the king's permission no marriage could take place. For the third time his majesty was sent for, and for the third time he proclaimed that he could not give his consent until the bridegroom should have slain a serpent which dwelt in a broad river that flowed at the back of the castle. Everyone knew stories of this terrible serpent, though no one had actually seen it ; but from time to time a child strayed from home and never came back, and then mothers would forbid the other children to go near the river, which had juicy fruits and lovely flowers growing along its banks.

So no wonder the youth trembled and turned pale when he heard what lay before him.

'You will succeed in this also,' whispered the Sister of

the Sun, pressing his hand, 'for in my ship is a magic sword
which will cut through everything. Go down to the river
and unfasten a boat which lies moored there, and throw
the chips into the water. When the serpent rears up its
body you will cut off its three heads with one blow of your
sword. Then take the tip of each tongue and go with it
to-morrow morning into the king's kitchen. If the king
himself should enter, just say to him : " Here are three
gifts I offer you in return for the services you demanded
of me ! " and throw the tips of the serpent's tongues at
him, and hasten to the ship as fast as your legs will carry
you. But be sure you take great care never to look
behind you.'

The young man did exactly what the princess had
told him. The three chips which he flung into the river
became a boat, and, as he steered across the stream, the
serpent put up its head and hissed loudly. The youth
had his sword ready, and in another second the three
heads were bobbing on the water. Guiding his boat till
he was beside them, he stooped down and snipped off
the ends of the tongues, and then rowed back to the
other bank. Next morning he carried them into the
royal kitchen, and when the king entered, as was his
custom, to see what he was going to have for dinner, the
bridegroom flung them in his face, saying : ' Here is a
gift for you in return for the services you asked of me.'
And, opening the kitchen door, he fled to the ship.
Unluckily he missed the way, and in his excitement ran
backwards and forwards, without knowing whither he
was going. At last, in despair, he looked round, and saw
to his amazement that both the city and palace had
vanished completely. Then he turned his eyes in the
other direction and, far, far away, he caught sight of the
ship with her sails spread, and a fair wind behind her.

This dreadful spectacle seemed to take away his
senses, and all day long he wandered about, without
knowing where he was going, till, in the evening, he

noticed some smoke from a little hut of turf near by. He went straight up to it and cried : 'O mother, let me come in for pity's sake ! ' The old woman who lived in the hut beckoned to him to enter, and hardly was he inside when he cried again : 'O mother, can you tell me anything of the Sister of the Sun ? '

But the old woman only shook her head. 'No, I know nothing of her,' said she.

The young man turned to leave the hut, but the old woman stopped him, and, giving him a letter, begged him to carry it to her next eldest sister, saying : 'If you should get tired on the way, take out the letter and rustle the paper.'

This advice surprised the young man a good deal, as he did not see how it could help him ; but he did not answer, and went down the road without knowing where he was going. At length he grew so tired he could walk no more ; then he remembered what the old woman had said. After he had rustled the leaves only once all fatigue disappeared, and he strode gaily over the grass till he came to another little turf hut.

'Let me in, I pray you, dear mother,' cried he. And the door opened in front of him. 'Your sister has sent you this letter,' he said, and added quickly : 'O mother ! can you tell me anything of the Sister of the Sun ? '

'No, I know nothing of her,' answered she. But as he turned hopelessly away, she stopped him.

'If you happen to pass my eldest sister's house, will you give her this letter ? ' said she. 'And if you should get tired on the road, just take it out of your pocket and rustle the paper.'

So the young man put the letter in his pocket, and walked all day over the hills till he reached a little turf hut, exactly like the other two.

'Let me in, I pray you, dear mother,' cried he. And as he entered he added : 'Here is a letter from your sister, and—can you tell me anything of the Sister of the Sun ? '

'Yes, I can,' answered the old woman. 'She lives in the castle on the Banka. Her father lost a battle only a few days ago because you had stolen his sword from him, and the Sister of the Sun herself is almost dead of grief. But, when you see her, stick a pin into the palm of her hand, and suck the drops of blood that flow. Then she will grow calmer, and will know you again. Only, beware; for before you reach the castle on the Banka fearful things will happen.'

He thanked the old woman with tears of gladness for the good news she had given him, and continued his journey. But he had not gone very far when, at a turn of the road, he met with two brothers, who were quarrelling over a piece of cloth.

'My good men, what are you fighting about?' said he. 'That cloth does not look worth much!'

'Oh, it is ragged enough,' answered they, 'but it was left us by our father, and if any man wraps it round him no one can see him; and we each want it for our own.'

'Let me put it round me for a moment,' said the youth, 'and then I will tell you whose it ought to be!'

The brothers were pleased with this idea, and gave him the stuff; but the moment he had thrown it over his shoulder he disappeared as completely as if he had never been there at all.

Meanwhile the young man walked briskly along, till he came up with two other men, who were disputing over a table-cloth.

'What is the matter?' asked he, stopping in front of them.

'If this cloth is spread on a table,' answered they, 'the table is instantly covered with the most delicious food; and we each want to have it.'

'Let me try the table-cloth,' said the youth, 'and I will tell you whose it ought to be.'

The two men were quite pleased with this idea, and handed him the cloth. He then hastily threw the first piece of stuff round his shoulders and vanished from sight, leaving the two men grieving over their own folly.

The young man had not walked far before he saw two more men standing by the road-side, both grasping the same stout staff, and sometimes one seemed on the point of getting it, and sometimes the other.

'What are you quarrelling about? You could cut a dozen sticks from the wood each just as good as that!' said the young man. And as he spoke the fighters both stopped and looked at him.

'Ah! you may think so,' said one, 'but a blow from one end of this stick will kill a man, while a touch from the other end will bring him back to life. You won't easily find another stick like that!'

'No; that is true,' answered the young man. 'Let me just look at it, and I will tell you whose it ought to be.'

The men were pleased with the idea, and handed him the staff.

'It is very curious, certainly,' said he; 'but which end is it that restores people to life? After all, anyone can be killed by a blow from a stick if it is only hard enough!' But when he was shown the end he threw the stuff over his shoulders and vanished.

At last he saw another set of men, who were struggling for the possession of a pair of shoes.

'Why can't you leave that pair of old shoes alone?' said he. 'Why, you could not walk a yard in them!'

'Yes, they are old enough,' answered they; 'but whoever puts them on and wishes himself at a particular place, gets there without going.'

'That sounds very clever,' said the youth. 'Let me try them, and then I shall be able to tell you whose they ought to be.'

The idea pleased the men, and they handed him the shoes; but the moment they were on his feet he cried:

'I wish to be in the castle on the Banka!' And before

he knew it, he was there, and found the Sister of the Sun dying of grief. He knelt down by her side, and pulling out a pin he stuck it into the palm of her hand, so that a drop of blood gushed out. This he sucked, as he had been told to do by the old woman, and immediately the princess came to herself, and flung her arms round his neck. Then she told him all her story, and what had happened since the ship had sailed away without him. 'But the worst misfortune of all,' she added, 'was a battle which my father lost because you had vanished with his magic sword ; and out of his whole army hardly one man was left.'

' Show me the battle-field,' said he. And she took him to a wild heath, where the dead were lying as they fell, waiting for burial. One by one he touched them with the end of his staff, till at length they all stood before him. Throughout the kingdom there was nothing but joy; and *this* time the wedding was *really* celebrated. And the bridal pair lived happily in the castle on the Banka till they died.

[*Lappländische Mährchen.*]

THE PRINCE AND THE THREE FATES

ONCE upon a time a little boy was born to a king who ruled over a great country through which ran a wide river. The king was nearly beside himself with joy, for he had always longed for a son to inherit his crown, and he sent messages to beg all the most powerful fairies to come and see this wonderful baby. In an hour or two, so many were gathered round the cradle, that the child seemed in danger of being smothered; but the king, who was watching the fairies eagerly, was disturbed to see them looking grave. 'Is there anything the matter?' he asked anxiously.

The fairies looked at him, and all shook their heads at once.

'He is a beautiful boy, and it is a great pity; but what *is* to happen *will* happen,' said they. 'It is written in the books of fate that he must die, either by a crocodile, or a serpent, or by a dog. If we could save him we would; but that is beyond our power.'

And so saying they vanished.

For a time the king stood where he was, horror-stricken at what he had heard; but, being of a hopeful nature, he began at once to invent plans to save the prince from the dreadful doom that awaited him. He instantly sent for his master builder, and bade him construct a strong castle on the top of a mountain, which should be fitted with the most precious things from the king's own palace, and every kind of toy a child could wish to play with. And, besides, he gave the strictest orders that a guard should walk round the castle night and day.

For four or five years the baby lived in the castle alone with his nurses, taking his airings on the broad terraces, which were surrounded by walls, with a moat beneath them, and only a drawbridge to connect them with the outer world.

One day, when the prince was old enough to run quite fast by himself, he looked from the terrace across the moat, and saw a little soft fluffy ball of a dog jumping and playing on the other side. Now, of course, all dogs had been kept from him for fear that the fairies' prophecy should come true, and he had never even beheld one before. So he turned to the page who was walking behind him, and said:

'What is that funny little thing which is running so fast over there?'

'That is a dog, prince,' answered the page.

'Well, bring me one like it, and we will see which can run the faster.' And he watched the dog till it had disappeared round the corner.

The page was much puzzled to know what to do. He had strict orders to refuse the prince nothing; yet he remembered the prophecy, and felt that this was a serious matter. At last he thought he had better tell the king the whole story, and let him decide the question.

'Oh, get him a dog if he wants one,' said the king, 'he will only cry his heart out if he does not have it.' So a puppy was found, exactly like the other; they might have been twins, and perhaps they were.

Years went by, and the boy and the dog played together till the boy grew tall and strong. The time came at last when he sent a message to his father, saying:

'Why do you keep me shut up here, doing nothing? I know all about the prophecy that was made at my birth, but I would far rather be killed at once than live an idle, useless life here. So give me arms, and let me go, I pray you; me and my dog too.'

And again the king listened to his wishes, and he and his dog were carried in a ship to the other side of the river, which was so broad here it might almost have been the sea. A black horse was waiting for him, tied to a tree, and he mounted and rode away wherever his fancy took him, the dog always at his heels. Never was any prince so happy as he, and he rode and rode till at length he came to a king's palace.

The king who lived in it did not care about looking after his country, and seeing that his people lived cheerful and contented lives. He spent his whole time in making riddles, and inventing plans which he had much better have let alone. At the period when the young prince reached the kingdom he had just completed a wonderful house for his only child, a daughter. It had seventy windows, each seventy feet from the ground, and he had sent the royal herald round the borders of the neighbouring kingdoms to proclaim that whoever could climb up the walls to the window of the princess should win her for his wife.

The fame of the princess's beauty had spread far and wide, and there was no lack of princes who wished to try their fortune. Very funny the palace must have looked each morning, with the dabs of different colour on the white marble as the princes were climbing up the walls. But though some managed to get further than others, nobody was anywhere near the top.

They had already been spending several days in this manner when the young prince arrived, and as he was pleasant to look upon, and civil to talk to, they welcomed him to the house which had been given to them, and saw that his bath was properly perfumed after his long journey. ' Where do you come from ? ' they said at last. ' And whose son are you ? '

But the young prince had reasons for keeping his own secret, and he answered :

' My father was master of the horse to the king of my

country, and after my mother died he married another wife. At first all went well, but as soon as she had babies of her own she hated me, and I fled, lest she should do me harm.'

The hearts of the other young men were touched as soon as they heard this story, and they did everything they could think of to make him forget his past sorrows.

'What are you doing here?' said the youth, one day.

'We spend our whole time climbing up the walls of the palace, trying to reach the windows of the princess,' answered the young men; 'but, as yet, no one has reached within ten feet of them.'

'Oh, let me try too,' cried the prince; 'but to-morrow I will wait and see what you do before I begin.'

So the next day he stood where he could watch the young men go up, and he noted the places on the wall that seemed most difficult, and made up his mind that when his turn came he would go up some other way.

Day after day he was to be seen watching the wooers, till, one morning, he felt that he knew the plan of the walls by heart, and took his place by the side of the others. Thanks to what he had learned from the failure of the rest, he managed to grasp one little rough projection after another, till at last, to the envy of his friends, he stood on the sill of the princess's window. Looking up from below, they saw a white hand stretched forth to draw him in.

Then one of the young men ran straight to the king's palace, and said: 'The wall has been climbed, and the prize is won!'

'By whom?' cried the king, starting up from his throne; 'which of the princes may I claim as my son-in-law?'

'The youth who succeeded in climbing to the princess's window is not a prince at all,' answered the young man. 'He is the son of the master of the horse to the great king who dwells across the river, and he fled from his own country to escape from the hatred of his stepmother.

At this news the king was very angry, for it had never entered his head that anyone *but* a prince would seek to woo his daughter.

'Let him go back to the land whence he came,' he shouted in wrath ; 'does he expect me to give my daughter to an exile?' And he began to smash the drinking vessels in his fury ; indeed, he quite frightened the young man, who ran hastily home to his friends, and told the youth what the king had said.

Now the princess, who was leaning from her window, heard his words and bade the messenger go back to the king her father and tell him that she had sworn a vow never to eat or drink again if the youth was taken from her. The king was more angry than ever when he received this message, and ordered his guards to go at once to the palace and put the successful wooer to death ; but the princess threw herself between him and his murderers.

'Lay a finger on him, and I shall be dead before sunset,' said she ; and as they saw that she meant it, they left the palace, and carried the tale to her father.

By this time the king's anger was dying away, and he began to consider what his people would think of him if he broke the promise he had publicly given. So he ordered the princess to be brought before him, and the young man also, and when they entered the throne room he was so pleased with the noble air of the victor that his wrath quite melted away, and he ran to him and embraced him.

'Tell me who you are?' he asked, when he had recovered himself a little, 'for I will never believe that you have not royal blood in your veins.'

But the prince still had his reasons for being silent, and only told the same story. However, the king had taken such a fancy to the youth that he said no more, and the marriage took place the following day, and great herds of cattle and a large estate were given to the young couple.

After a little while the prince said to his wife : 'My life is in the hands of three creatures—a crocodile, a serpent, and a dog.'

'Ah, how rash you are!' cried the princess, throwing her arms round his neck. 'If you know that, how can you have that horrid beast about you? I will give orders to have him killed at once.'

But the prince would not listen to her.

'Kill my dear little dog, who has been my playfellow since he was a puppy?' exclaimed he. 'Oh, never would I allow that.' And all that the princess could get from him was that he would always wear a sword, and have somebody with him when he left the palace.

When the prince and princess had been married a few months, the prince heard that his stepmother was dead, and his father was old and ill, and longing to have his eldest son by his side again. The young man could not remain deaf to such a message, and he took a tender farewell of his wife, and set out on his journey home. It was a long way, and he was forced to rest often on the road, and so it happened that, one night, when he was sleeping in a city on the banks of the great river, a huge crocodile came silently up and made its way along a passage to the prince's room. Fortunately one of his guards woke up as it was trying to steal past them, and shut the crocodile up in a large hall, where a giant watched over it, never leaving the spot except during the night, when the crocodile slept. And this went on for more than a month.

Now, when the prince found that he was not likely to leave his father's kingdom again, he sent for his wife, and bade the messenger tell her that he would await her coming in the town on the banks of the great river.

THE PRINCESS AND THE SNAKE

[*This illustration is reproduced in color between pages 74 and 75.*]

This was the reason why he delayed his journey so long,
and narrowly escaped being eaten by the crocodile.
During the weeks that followed the prince amused himself as best he could, though he counted the minutes to
the arrival of the princess, and when she did come, he at
once prepared to start for the court. That very night,
however, while he was asleep, the princess noticed something strange in one of the corners of the room. It was
a dark patch, and seemed, as she looked, to grow longer
and longer, and to be moving slowly towards the cushions
on which the prince was lying. She shrank in terror, but,
slight as was the noise, the thing heard it, and raised its
head to listen. Then she saw it was the long flat head
of a serpent, and the recollection of the prophecy rushed
into her mind. Without waking her husband, she glided
out of bed, and taking up a heavy bowl of milk which
stood on a table, laid it on the floor in the path of the
serpent—for she knew that no serpent in the world can
resist milk. She held her breath as the snake drew near,
and watched it throw up its head again as if it was
smelling something nice, while its forky tongue darted
out greedily. At length its eyes fell upon the milk, and
in an instant it was lapping it so fast that it was a
wonder the creature did not choke, for it never took its
head from the bowl as long as a drop was left in it.
After that it dropped on the ground and slept heavily.
This was what the princess had been waiting for, and,
catching up her husband's sword, she severed the snake's
head from its body.

The morning after this adventure the prince and
princess set out for the king's palace, but found, when
they reached it, that he was already dead. They gave
him a magnificent burial, and then the prince had to
examine the new laws which had been made in his
absence, and do a great deal of business besides, till he
grew quite ill from fatigue, and was obliged to go away to
one of his palaces on the banks of the river, in order to

rest. Here he soon got better, and began to hunt, and to shoot wild duck with his bow; and wherever he went, his dog, now grown very old, went with him.

One morning the prince and his dog were out as usual, and in chasing their game they drew near the bank of the river. The prince was running at full speed after his dog when he almost fell over something that looked like a log of wood, which was lying in his path. To his surprise a voice spoke to him, and he saw that the thing which he had taken for a branch was really a crocodile.

'You cannot escape from me,' it was saying, when he had gathered his senses again. 'I am your fate, and wherever you go, and whatever you do, you will always find me before you. There is only one means of shaking off my power. If you can dig a pit in the dry sand which will remain full of water, my spell will be broken. If not death will come to you speedily. I give you this one chance. Now go.'

The young man walked sadly away, and when he reached the palace he shut himself into his room, and for the rest of the day refused to see anyone, not even his wife. At sunset, however, as no sound could be heard through the door, the princess grew quite frightened, and made such a noise that the prince was forced to draw back the bolt and let her come in. 'How pale you look,' she cried, 'has anything hurt you? Tell me, I pray you, what is the matter, for perhaps I can help!'

So the prince told her the whole story, and of the impossible task given him by the crocodile.

'How can a sand hole remain full of water?' asked he. 'Of course it will all run through. The crocodile called it a "chance"; but he might as well have dragged me into the river at once. He said truly that I cannot escape him.'

'Oh, if *that* is all,' cried the princess, 'I can set you free myself, for my fairy godmother taught me to know the use of plants and in the desert not far from here there grows a little four-leaved herb which will keep the water in the pit for a whole year. I will go in search of it at dawn, and you can begin to dig the hole as soon as you like.'

To comfort her husband, the princess had spoken lightly and gaily ; but she knew very well she had no light task before her. Still, she was full of courage and energy, and determined that, one way or another, her husband should be saved.

It was still starlight when she left the palace on a snow-white donkey, and rode away from the river straight to the west. For some time she could see nothing before her but a flat waste of sand, which became hotter and hotter as the sun rose higher and higher. Then a dreadful thirst seized her and the donkey, but there was no stream to quench it, and if there had been she would hardly have had time to stop, for she still had far to go, and must be back before evening, or else the crocodile might declare that the prince had not fulfilled his conditions. So she spoke cheering words to her donkey, who brayed in reply, and the two pushed steadily on.

Oh ! how glad they both were when they caught sight of a tall rock in the distance. They forgot that they were thirsty, and that the sun was hot ; and the ground seemed to fly under their feet, till the donkey stopped of its own accord in the cool shadow. But though the donkey might rest the princess could not, for the plant, as she knew, grew on the very top of the rock, and a wide chasm ran round the foot of it. Luckily she had brought a rope with her, and making a noose at one end, she flung it across with all her might. The first time it slid back slowly into the ditch, and she had to draw it up, and throw it again, but at length the noose caught on something, the princess could not see what, and had to trust her whole weight to this little bridge, which might snap and let her fall deep down among the rocks. And in that case her death was as certain as that of the prince.

But nothing so dreadful happened. The princess got safely to the other side, and then became the worst part of her task. As fast as she put her foot on a ledge of the rock the stone broke away from under her, and left her in the same place as before. Meanwhile the hours were passing, and it was nearly noon.

The heart of the poor princess was filled with despair, but she would not give up the struggle. She looked round till she saw a small stone above her which seemed rather stronger than the rest, and by only poising her foot lightly on those that lay between, she managed by a great effort to reach it. In this way, with torn and bleeding hands, she gained the top; but here such a violent wind was blowing that she was almost blinded with dust, and was obliged to throw herself on the ground, and feel about after the precious herb.

For a few terrible moments she thought that the rock was bare, and that her journey had been to no purpose. Feel where she would, there was nothing but grit and stones, when, suddenly, her fingers touched something soft in a crevice. It was a plant, that was clear; but was it the right one? See she could not, for the wind was blowing more fiercely than ever, so she lay where she was and counted the leaves. One, two, three—yes! yes! there were four! And plucking a leaf she held it safe in her hand while she turned, almost stunned by the wind, to go down the rock.

When once she was safely over the side all became still in a moment, and she slid down the rock so fast that it was only a wonder that she did not land in the chasm. However, by good luck, she stopped quite close to her rope bridge and was soon across it. The donkey brayed joyfully at the sight of her, and set off home at his best speed, never seeming to know that the earth under his feet was nearly as hot as the sun above him.

On the bank of the great river he halted, and the princess rushed up to where the prince was standing by the pit he had digged in the dry sand, with a huge water pot beside it. A little way off the crocodile lay blinking in the sun, with his sharp teeth and whity-yellow jaws wide open.

THE POOL IN THE SAND

At a signal from the princess the prince poured the water in the hole, and the moment it reached the brim the princess flung in the four-leaved plant. Would the charm work, or would the water trickle away slowly through the sand, and the prince fall a victim to that horrible monster? For half an hour they stood with their eyes rooted to the spot, but the hole remained as full as at the beginning, with the little green leaf floating on the top. Then the prince turned with a shout of triumph, and the crocodile sulkily plunged into the river.

The prince had escaped for ever the second of his three fates!

He stood there looking after the crocodile, and rejoicing that he was free, when he was startled by a wild duck which flew past them, seeking shelter among the rushes that bordered the edge of the stream. In another instant his dog dashed by in hot pursuit, and knocked heavily against his master's legs. The prince staggered, lost his balance and fell backwards into the river, where the mud and the rushes caught him and held him fast. He shrieked for help to his wife, who came running; and luckily brought her rope with her. The poor old dog was drowned, but the prince was pulled to shore. ' My wife,' he said, ' has been stronger than my fate.'

[Adapted from *Les Contes Populaires de l'Egypte Ancienne.*]

THE FOX AND THE LAPP

Once upon a time a fox lay peeping out of his hole, watching the road that ran by at a little distance, and hoping to see something that might amuse him, for he was feeling very dull and rather cross. For a long while he watched in vain; everything seemed asleep, and not even a bird stirred overhead. The fox grew crosser than ever, and he was just turning away in disgust from his place when he heard the sound of feet coming over the snow. He crouched eagerly down at the edge of the road and said to himself: ' I wonder what would happen if I were to pretend to be dead! This is a man driving a reindeer sledge, I know the tinkling of the harness. And at any rate I shall have an adventure, and that is always something!'

So he stretched himself out by the side of the road, carefully choosing a spot where the driver could not help seeing him, yet where the reindeer would not tread on him; and all fell out just as he had expected. The sledge-driver pulled up sharply, as his eyes lighted on the beautiful animal lying stiffly beside him, and jumping out he threw the fox into the bottom of the sledge, where the goods he was carrying were bound tightly together by ropes. The fox did not move a muscle though his bones were sore from the fall, and the driver got back to his seat again and drove on merrily.

But before they had gone very far, the fox, who was near the edge, contrived to slip over, and when the Laplander saw him stretched out on the snow he pulled up his reindeer and put the fox into one of the other sledges that was fastened behind, for it was market-day at the nearest town, and the man had much to sell.

They drove on a little further, when some noise in the forest made the man turn his head, just in time to see the fox fall with a heavy thump on to the frozen snow. 'That beast is bewitched!' he said to himself, and then he threw the fox into the last sledge of all, which had a cargo of fishes. This was exactly what the cunning creature wanted, and he wriggled gently to the front and bit the cord which tied the sledge to the one before it so that it remained standing in the middle of the road.

Now there were so many sledges that the Lapp did not notice for a long while that one was missing; indeed, he would have entered the town without knowing if snow had not suddenly begun to fall. Then he got down to secure more firmly the cloths that kept his goods dry, and going to the end of the long row, discovered that the sledge containing the fish and the fox was missing. He quickly unharnessed one of his reindeer and rode back along the way he had come, to find the sledge standing safe in the middle of the road; but as the fox had bitten off the cord close to the noose there was no means of moving it away.

The fox meanwhile was enjoying himself mightily. As soon as he had loosened the sledge, he had taken his favourite fish from among the piles neatly arranged for sale, and had trotted off to the forest with it in his mouth. By-and-by he met a bear, who stopped and said : ' Where did you find that fish, Mr. Fox ? '

' Oh, not far off,' answered he ; ' I just stuck my tail in the stream close by the place where the elves dwell, and the fish hung on to it of itself.'

' Dear me,' snarled the bear, who was hungry and not in a good temper, ' if the fish hung on to your tail, I suppose he will hang on to mine.'

' Yes, certainly, grandfather,' replied the fox, ' if you have patience to suffer what I suffered.'

'Of course I can,' replied the bear, 'what nonsense you talk! Show me the way.'

So the fox led him to the bank of a stream, which, being in a warm place, had only lightly frozen in places, and was at this moment glittering in the spring sunshine.

'The elves bathe here,' he said, 'and if you put in your tail the fish will catch hold of it. But it is no use being in a hurry, or you will spoil everything.'

THE ELVES AND THE BEAR

Then he trotted off, but only went out of sight of the bear, who stood still on the bank with his tail deep in the water. Soon the sun set and it grew very cold and the ice formed rapidly, and the bear's tail was fixed as tight as if a vice had held it; and when the fox saw that everything had happened just as he had planned it, he called out loudly:

'Be quick, good people, and come with your bows and spears. A bear has been fishing in your brook!'

And in a moment the whole place was full of little creatures each one with a tiny bow and a spear hardly big enough for a baby ; but both arrows and spears could sting, as the bear knew very well, and in his fright he gave such a tug to his tail that it broke short off, and he rolled away into the forest as fast as his legs could carry him.   At this sight the fox held his sides for laughing, and then scampered away in another direction.   By-and-by he came to a fir tree, and crept into a hole under the root.   After that he did something very strange.

Taking one of his hind feet between his two front paws, he said softly :

' What would you do, my foot, if someone was to betray me ? '

' I would run so quickly that he should not catch you.'

' What would you do, mine ear, if someone was to betray me ? '

' I would listen so hard that I should hear all his plans.'

' What would you do, my nose, if someone was to betray me ? '

' I would smell so sharply that I should know from afar that he was coming.'

' What would you do, my tail, if someone was to betray me ? '

' I would steer you so straight a course that you would soon be beyond his reach.   Let us be off ; I feel as if danger was near.'

But the fox was comfortable where he was, and did not hurry himself to take his tail's advice.   And before very long he found he was too late, for the bear had come round by another path, and guessing where his enemy was began to scratch at the roots of the tree.   The fox made himself as small as he could, but a scrap of his tail peeped out, and the bear seized it and held it tight. Then the fox dug his claws into the ground, but he was not strong enough to pull against the bear, and slowly he was dragged forth and his body flung over the bear's neck. In this manner they set out down the road, the fox's tail being always in the bear's mouth.

After they had gone some way, they passed a tree-stump, on which a bright coloured woodpecker was tapping.

'Ah! those were better times when I used to paint all the birds such gay colours,' sighed the fox.

'What are you saying, old fellow?' asked the bear.

'I? Oh, I was saying nothing,' answered the fox drearily. 'Just carry me to your cave and eat me up as quick as you can.'

The bear was silent, and thought of his supper; and the two continued their journey till they reached another tree with a woodpecker tapping on it.

'Ah! those were better times when I used to paint all the birds such gay colours,' said the fox again to himself.

'Couldn't you paint me too?' asked the bear suddenly.

But the fox shook his head; for he was always acting, even if no one was there to see him do it.

'You bear pain so badly,' he replied, in a thoughtful voice, 'and you are impatient besides, and could never put up with all that is necessary. Why, you would first have to dig a pit, and then twist ropes of willow, and drive in posts and fill the hole with pitch, and, last of all, set it on fire. Oh, no; you would never be able to do all that.'

'It does not matter a straw how hard the work is,' answered the bear eagerly, 'I will do it every bit.' And as he spoke he began tearing up the earth so fast that soon a deep pit was ready, deep enough to hold him.

'That is all right,' said the fox at last, 'I see I was mistaken in you. Now sit here, and I will bind you.' So the bear sat down on the edge of the pit, and the fox sprang on his back, which he crossed with the willow ropes, and then set fire to the pitch. It burnt up in an

instant, and caught the bands of willow and the bear's
rough hair; but he did not stir, for he thought that the
fox was rubbing the bright colours into his skin, and that
he would soon be as beautiful as a whole meadow of
flowers. But when the fire grew hotter still he moved
uneasily from one foot to the other, saying, imploringly :
' It is getting rather warm, old man.'   But all the answer
he got was: 'I thought you would never be able to suffer
pain like those little birds.'

The bear did not like being told that he was not as
brave as a bird, so he set his teeth and resolved to endure
anything sooner than speak again ; but by this time the
last willow band had burned through, and with a push
the fox sent his victim tumbling into the grass, and ran
off to hide himself in the forest.   After a while he stole
cautiously and found, as he expected, nothing left but a
few charred bones.   These he picked up and put in a bag,
which he slung over his back.

By-and-by he met a Lapp driving his team of reindeer along the road, and as he drew near, the fox rattled
the bones gaily.

' That sounds like silver or gold,' thought the man to
himself.   And he said politely to the fox :

'Good-day, friend !   What have you got in your bag
that makes such a strange sound ? '

' All the wealth my father left me,' answered the fox.
' Do you feel inclined to bargain ? '

' Well, I don't mind,' replied the Lapp, who was a
prudent man, and did not wish the fox to think him too
eager ; ' but show me first what money you have got.'

'Ah, but I can't do that,' answered the fox, 'my bag
is sealed up.   But if you will give me those three reindeer, you shall take it as it is, with all its contents.

The Lapp did not quite like it, but the fox spoke with
such an air that his doubts melted away.   He nodded,
and stretched out his hand ; the fox put the bag into it,
and unharnessed the reindeer he had chosen.

' Oh, I forgot ! ' he exclaimed, turning round, as he was about to drive them in the opposite direction, ' you must be sure not to open the bag until you have gone at least five miles, right on the other side of those hills out there. If you do, you will find that all the gold and silver has changed into a parcel of charred bones.' Then he whipped up his reindeer, and was soon out of sight.

For some time the Lapp was satisfied with hearing the bones rattle, and thinking to himself what a good bargain he had made, and of all the things he would buy with the money. But, after a bit, this amusement ceased to content him, and besides, what was the use of planning when you did not know for certain how rich you were ? Perhaps there might be a great deal of silver and only a little gold in the bag ; or a great deal of gold, and only a little silver. Who could tell ? He would not, of course, take the money out to count it, for that might bring him bad luck. But there could be no harm in just one peep ! So he slowly broke the seal, and untied the strings, and, behold, a heap of burnt bones lay before him ! In a minute he knew he had been tricked, and flinging the bag to the ground in a rage, he ran after the fox as fast as his snow-shoes would carry him.

Now the fox had guessed exactly what would happen, and was on the look out. Directly he saw the little speck coming towards him, he wished that the man's snow-shoes might break, and that very instant the Lapp's shoes snapped in two. The Lapp did not know that this was the fox's work, but he had to stop and fetch one of his other reindeer, which he mounted, and set off again in pursuit of his enemy. The fox soon heard him coming, and this time he wished that the reindeer might fall and break its leg. And so it did ; and the man felt it was a hopeless chase, and that he was no match for the fox.

So the fox drove on in peace till he reached the cave where all his stores were kept, and then he began to wonder whom he could get to help him kill his reindeer,

for though he could steal reindeer he was too small to
kill them. 'After all, it will be quite easy,' thought he,
and he bade a squirrel, who was watching him on a tree
close by, take a message to all the robber beasts of the
forest, and in less than half an hour a great crashing of
branches was heard, and bears, wolves, snakes, mice, frogs,
and other creatures came pressing up to the cave.

When they heard why they had been summoned, they
declared themselves ready each one to do his part. The
bear took his crossbow from his neck and shot the reindeer in the chin ; and, from that day to this, every reindeer
has a mark in that same spot, which is always known as
the bear's arrow. The wolf shot him in the thigh, and
the sign of his arrow still remains ; and so with the mouse
and the viper and all the rest, even the frog ; and at the
last the reindeer all died. And the fox did nothing, but
looked on.

'I really must go down to the brook and wash myself,' said he (though he was perfectly clean), and he went
under the bank and hid himself behind a stone. From
there he set up the most frightful shrieks, so that the
animals fled away in all directions. Only the mouse and
the ermine remained where they were, for they thought
that they were much too small to be noticed.

The fox continued his shrieks till he felt sure that the
animals must have got to a safe distance ; then he crawled
out of his hiding-place and went to the bodies of the reindeer, which he now had all to himself. He gathered a
bundle of sticks for a fire, and was just preparing to cook
a steak, when his enemy, the Lapp, came up, panting with
haste and excitement.

'What are you doing there?' cried he ; 'why did you
palm off those bones on me? And why, when you had got
the reindeer, did you kill them? '

'Dear brother,' answered the fox with a sob, 'do not
blame me for this misfortune. It is my comrades who
have slain them in spite of my prayers.'

The man made no reply, for the white fur of the ermine, who was crouching with the mouse behind some stones, had just caught his eye. He hastily seized the iron hook which hung over the fire and flung it at the little creature ; but the ermine was too quick for him, and the hook only touched the top of its tail, and that has remained black to this day. As for the mouse, the Lapp threw a half-burnt stick after him, and though it was not hot enough to hurt him, his beautiful white skin was smeared all over with it, and all the washing in the world would not make him clean again. And the man would have been wiser if he had let the ermine and the mouse alone, for when he turned round again he found he was alone.

Directly the fox noticed that his enemy's attention had wandered from himself he watched his chance, and stole softly away till he had reached a clump of thick bushes, when he ran as fast as he could, till he reached a river, where a man was mending his boat.

' Oh, I wish, I do wish, I had a boat to mend too ! ' he cried, sitting up on his hind-legs and looking into the man's face.

' Stop your silly chatter ! ' answered the man crossly, ' or I will give you a bath in the river.'

' Oh, I wish, I do wish, I had a boat to mend,' cried the fox again, as if he had not heard. And the man grew angry and seized him by the tail, and threw him far out in the stream close to the edge of an island ; which was just what the fox wanted. He easily scrambled up, and, sitting on the top, he called : ' Hasten, hasten, O fishes, and carry me to the other side ! ' And the fishes left the stones where they had been sleeping, and the pools where they had been feeding, and hurried to see who could get to the island first.

' I have won,' shouted the pike. ' Jump on my back, dear fox, and you will find yourself in a trice on the opposite shore.'

'No, thank you,' answered the fox, 'your back is much too weak for me. I should break it.'

'Try mine,' said the eel, who had wriggled to the front.

'No, thank you,' replied the fox again, 'I should slip over your head and be drowned.'

'You won't slip on *my* back,' said the perch, coming forward.

'No; but you are really *too* rough,' returned the fox.

'Well, you can have no fault to find with *me*,' put in the trout.

'Good gracious! are *you* here?' exclaimed the fox. 'But I'm afraid to trust myself to you either.'

At this moment a fine salmon swam slowly up.

'Ah, yes, you are the person I want,' said the fox; 'but come near, so that I may get on your back, without wetting my feet.'

So the salmon swam close under the island, and when he was touching it the fox seized him in his claws and drew him out of the water, and put him on a spit, while he kindled a fire to cook him by. When everything was ready, and the water in the pot was getting hot, he popped him in, and waited till he thought the salmon was nearly boiled. But as he stooped down the water gave a sudden fizzle, and splashed into the fox's eyes, blinding him. He started backwards with a cry of pain, and sat still for some minutes, rocking himself to and fro. When he was a little better he rose and walked down a road till he met a grouse, who stopped and asked what was the matter.

'Have you a pair of eyes anywhere about you?' asked the fox politely.

'No, I am afraid I haven't,' answered the grouse, and passed on.

A little while after the fox heard the buzzing of an early bee, whom a gleam of sun had tempted out.

'Do you happen to have an extra pair of eyes any-where?' asked the fox.

'I am sorry to say I have only those I am using,' replied the bee. And the fox went on till he nearly fell over an asp who was gliding across the road.

'I should be *so* glad if you would tell me where I could get a pair of eyes,' said the fox. 'I suppose you don't happen to have any you could lend me?'

'Well, if you only want them for a short time, perhaps I could manage,' answered the asp; 'but I can't do without them for long.'

'Oh, it is only for a very short time that I need them,' said the fox; 'I have a pair of my own just behind that hill, and when I find them I will bring yours back to you. Perhaps you will keep these till then.' So he took the eyes out of his own head and popped them into the head of the asp, and put the asp's eyes in their place. As he was running off he cried over his shoulder: 'As long as the world lasts the asps' eyes will go down in the heads of foxes from generation to generation.'

And so it has been; and if you look at the eyes of an asp you will see that they are all burnt; and though thousands of years have gone by since the fox was going about playing tricks upon everybody he met, the asp still bears the traces of the day when the sly creature cooked the salmon.

[*Lappländische Mährchen.*]

KISA THE CAT

ONCE upon a time there lived a queen who had a beautiful cat, the colour of smoke, with china-blue eyes, which she was very fond of. The cat was constantly with her, and ran after her wherever she went, and even sat up proudly by her side when she drove out in her fine glass coach.

'Oh, pussy,' said the queen one day, 'you are happier than I am! For you have a dear little kitten just like yourself, and I have nobody to play with but you.'

'Don't cry,' answered the cat, 'laying her paw on her mistress's arm. Crying never does any good. I will see what can be done.'

The cat was as good as her word. As soon as she returned from her drive she trotted off to the forest to consult a fairy who dwelt there, and very soon after the queen had a little girl, who seemed made out of snow and sunbeams. The queen was delighted, and soon the baby began to take notice of the kitten as she jumped about the room, and would not go to sleep at all unless the kitten lay curled up beside her.

Two or three months went by, and though the baby was still a baby, the kitten was fast becoming a cat, and one evening when, as usual, the nurse came to look for her, to put her in the baby's cot, she was nowhere to be found. What a hunt there was for that kitten, to be sure! The servants, each anxious to find her, as the queen was certain to reward the lucky man, searched in the most impossible places. Boxes were opened that would hardly have held the kitten's paw ; books were taken from bookshelves, lest the kitten should have got behind them, drawers were pulled out, for perhaps the kitten might have got shut in. But it was all no use. The kitten had plainly run away, and nobody could tell if it would ever choose to come back.

Years passed away, and one day, when the princess was playing ball in the garden, she happened to throw her ball farther than usual, and it fell into a clump of rose-bushes. The princess of course ran after it at once, and she was stooping down to feel if it was hidden in the long grass, when she heard a voice calling her : ' Ingibjörg ! Ingibjörg ! ' it said, ' have you forgotten me ? I am Kisa, your sister ! '

' But I never *had* a sister,' answered Ingibjörg, very much puzzled ; for she knew nothing of what had taken place so long ago.

' Don't you remember how I always slept in your cot beside you, and how you cried till I came ? But girls have no memories at all ! Why, I could find my way straight up to that cot this moment, if I was once inside the palace.'

' Why did you go away then ? ' asked the princess. But before Kisa could answer, Ingibjörg's attendants arrived breathless on the scene, and were so horrified at the sight of a strange cat, that Kisa plunged into the bushes and went back to the forest.

The princess was very much vexed with her ladies-in-waiting for frightening away her old playfellow, and told the queen who came to her room every evening to bid her good-night.

' Yes, it is quite true what Kisa said,' answered the queen ; ' I should have liked to see her again. Perhaps, some day, she will return, and then you must bring her to me.'

Next morning it was very hot, and the princess declared that she must go and play in the forest, where it was always cool, under the big shady trees. As usual, her attendants let her do anything she pleased, and, sitting down on a mossy bank where a little stream tinkled by, soon fell sound asleep. The princess saw with delight that they would pay no heed to her, and wandered on and on, expecting every moment to see some fairies dancing round a ring, or some little brown elves peeping at her from behind a tree. But, alas! she met none of these; instead, a horrible giant came out of his cave and ordered her to follow him. The princess felt much afraid, as he was so big and ugly, and began to be sorry that she had not stayed within reach of help; but as there was no use in disobeying the giant, she walked meekly behind.

They went a long way, and Ingibjörg grew very tired, and at length began to cry.

'I don't like girls who make horrid noises,' said the giant, turning round. 'But if you *want* to cry, I will give you something to cry for.' And drawing an axe from his belt, he cut off both her feet, which he picked up and put in his pocket. Then he went away.

Poor Ingibjörg lay on the grass in terrible pain, and wondering if she should stay there till she died, as no one would know where to look for her. How long it was since she had set out in the morning she could not tell— it seemed years to her, of course; but the sun was still high in the heavens when she heard the sound of wheels, and then, with a great effort, for her throat was parched with fright and pain, she gave a shout.

'I am coming!' was the answer; and in another moment a cart made its way through the trees, driven by Kisa, who used her tail as a whip to urge the horse to go faster. Directly Kisa saw Ingibjörg lying there, she jumped quickly down, and lifting the girl carefully in her two front paws, laid her upon some soft hay, and drove back to her own little hut.

In the corner of the room was a pile of cushions, and these Kisa arranged as a bed. Ingibjörg, who by this time was nearly fainting from all she had gone through, drank greedily some milk, and then sank back on the cushions while Kisa fetched some dried herbs from a cupboard, soaked them in warm water and tied them on the bleeding legs. The pain vanished at once, and Ingibjörg looked up and smiled at Kisa.

'You will go to sleep now,' said the cat, ' and you will not mind if I leave you for a little while. I will lock the door, and no one can hurt you.' But before she had finished the princess was asleep. Then Kisa got into the cart, which was standing at the door, and catching up the reins, drove straight to the giant's cave.

Leaving her cart behind some trees, Kisa crept gently up to the open door, and, crouching down, listened to what the giant was telling his wife, who was at supper with him.

'The first day that I can spare I shall just go back and kill her,' he said ; ' it would never do for people in the forest to know that a mere girl can defy me ! ' And he and his· wife were so busy calling Ingibjörg all sorts of names for her bad behaviour, that they never noticed Kisa stealing into a dark corner, and upsetting a whole bag of salt into the great pot before the fire.

'Dear me, how thirsty I am ! ' cried the giant by-and-by.

'So am I,' answered his wife. 'I do wish I had not taken that last spoonful of broth ; I am sure something was wrong with it.'

'If I don't get some water I shall die,' went on the giant. And rushing out of the cave, followed by his wife, he ran down the path which led to the river.

Then Kisa entered the hut, and lost no time in searching every hole till she came upon some grass, under which Ingibjörg's feet were hidden, and putting them in her cart, drove back again to her own hut.

Ingibjörg was thankful to see her, for she had lain, too frightened to sleep, trembling at every noise.

'Oh, is it you?' she cried joyfully, as Kisa turned the key. And the cat came in, holding up the two neat little feet in their silver slippers.

'In two minutes they shall be as tight as ever they

KISA THE CAT CARRIES OFF
INGIBJORG'S FEET
FROM THE GIANT'S CAVE

were!' said Kisa. And taking some strings of the magic grass which the giant had carelessly heaped on them, she bound the feet on to the legs above.

' Of course you won't be able to walk for some time ; you must not expect *that*,' she continued. ' But if you are very good, perhaps, in about a week, I may carry you home again.'

And so she did ; and when the cat drove the cart up to the palace gate, lashing the horse furiously with her tail, and the king and queen saw their lost daughter sitting beside her, they declared that no reward could be too great for the person who had brought her out of the giant's hands.

' We will talk about that by-and-by,' said the cat, as she made her best bow, and turned her horse's head.

The princess was very unhappy when Kisa left her without even bidding her farewell. She would neither eat nor drink, nor take any notice of all the beautiful dresses her parents bought for her.

' She will die, unless we can make her laugh,' one whispered to the other. ' Is there anything in the world that we have left untried ? '

' Nothing, except marriage,' answered the king. And he invited all the handsomest young men he could think of to the palace, and bade the princess choose a husband from among them.

It took her some time to decide which she admired the most, but at last she fixed upon a young prince, whose eyes were like the pools in the forest, and his hair of bright gold. The king and the queen were greatly pleased, as the young man was the son of a neighbouring king, and they gave orders that a splendid feast should be got ready.

When the marriage was over, Kisa suddenly stood before them, and Ingibjörg rushed forward and clasped her in her arms.

' I have come to claim my reward,' said the cat. ' Let me sleep for this night at the foot of your bed.'

' Is that *all* ? ' asked Ingibjörg, much disappointed.

' It is enough,' answered the cat. And when the

morning dawned, it was no cat that lay upon the bed, but a beautiful princess.

' My mother and I were both enchanted by a spiteful fairy,' said she, ' and we could not free ourselves till we had done some kindly deed that had never been wrought before. My mother died without ever finding a chance of doing anything new, but I took advantage of the evil act of the giant to make you as whole as ever.'

Then they were all more delighted than before, and the princess lived in the court until she, too, married, and went away to govern one of her own.

[Adapted from *Neuislandischen Volksmärchen*]

THE LION AND THE CAT

FAR away on the other side of the world there lived, long ago, a lion and his younger brother, the wild cat, who were so fond of each other that they shared the same hut. The lion was much the bigger and stronger of the two—indeed, he was much bigger and stronger than any of the beasts that dwelt in the forest; and, besides, he could jump farther and run faster than all the rest. If strength and swiftness could gain him a dinner he was sure never to be without one, but when it came to cunning, both the grizzly bear and the serpent could get the better of him, and he was forced to call in the help of the wild cat.

Now the young wild cat had a lovely golden ball, so beautiful that you could hardly look at it except through a piece of smoked glass, and he kept it hidden in the thick fur muff that went round his neck. A very large old animal, since dead, had given it to him when he was hardly more than a baby, and had told him never to part with it, for as long as he kept it no harm could ever come near him.

In general the wild cat did not need to use his ball, for the lion was fond of hunting, and could kill all the food that they needed; but now and then his life would have been in danger had it not been for the golden ball.

One day the two brothers started to hunt at daybreak, but as the cat could not run nearly as fast as the lion, he had quite a long start. At least he *thought* it was a long one, but in a very few bounds and springs the lion reached his side.

'There is a bear sitting on that tree,' he whispered softly. 'He is only waiting for us to pass, to drop down on my back.'

'Ah, you are so big that he does not see I am behind you,' answered the wild cat. And, touching the ball, he just said : 'Bear, die !' And the bear tumbled dead out of the tree, and rolled over just in front of them.

For some time they trotted on without any adventures, till just as they were about to cross a strip of long grass on the edge of the forest, the lion's quick ears detected a faint rustling noise.

'That is a snake,' he cried, stopping short, for he was much more afraid of snakes than of bears.

'Oh, it is all right,' answered the cat. 'Snake, die !' And the snake died, and the two brothers skinned it. They then folded the skin up into a very small parcel, and the cat tucked it into his mane, for snakes' skins can do all sorts of wonderful things, if you are lucky enough to have one of them.

All this time they had had no dinner, for the snake's flesh was not nice, and the lion did not like eating bear— perhaps because he never felt sure that the bear was *really* dead, and would not jump up alive when his enemy went near him. Most people are afraid of *some* thing, and bears and serpents were the only creatures that caused the lion's heart to tremble. So the two brothers set off again and soon reached the side of a hill where some fine deer were grazing.

'Kill one of those deer for your own dinner,' said the boy-brother, 'but catch me another alive. I want him.'

The lion at once sprang towards them with a loud roar, but the deer bounded away, and they were all three soon lost to sight. The cat waited for a long while, but finding that the lion did not return, went back to the house where they lived.

It was quite dark when the lion came home, where his brother was sitting curled up in one corner.

'Did you catch the deer for me?' asked the boy-brother, springing up.

'Well, no,' replied the man-brother. 'The fact is, that I did not get up to them till we had run half way across the world and left the wind far behind us. Think what a trouble it would have been to drag it here! So—I just ate them both.'

The cat said nothing, but he did not feel that he loved his big brother. He had thought a great deal about that deer, and had meant to get on his back to ride him as a horse, and go to see all the wonderful places the lion talked to him about when he was in a good temper. The more he thought of it the more sulky he grew, and in the morning, when the lion said that it was time for them to start to hunt, the cat told him that he might kill the bear and snake by himself, as *he* had a headache, and would rather stay at home. The little fellow knew quite well that the lion would not dare to go out without him and his ball for fear of meeting a bear or a snake.

The quarrel went on, and for many days neither of the brothers spoke to each other, and what made them still more cross was, that they could get very little to eat, and we know that people are often cross when they are hungry. At last it occurred to the lion that if he could only steal the magic ball he could kill bears and snakes for himself, and then the cat might be as sulky as he liked for anything that it would matter. But how was the stealing to be done? The cat had the ball hung round his neck day and night, and he was such a light sleeper that it was useless to think of taking it while he slept. No! the only thing was to get him to lend it of his own accord, and after some days the lion (who was not at all clever) hit upon a plan that he thought would do.

'Dear me, how dull it is here!' said the lion one afternoon, when the rain was pouring down in such torrents that, however sharp your eyes or your nose might be, you could not spy a single bird or beast among the bushes. ' Dear me, how dull, how dreadfully dull I am. Couldn't we have a game of catch with that golden ball of yours ? '

' I don't care about playing catch, it does not amuse me,' answered the cat, who was as cross as ever; for no cat, even to this day, ever forgets an injury done to him.

' Well, then, lend me the ball for a little, and I will play by myself,' replied the lion, stretching out a paw as he spoke.

' You can't play in the rain, and if you did, you would only lose it in the bushes,' said the cat.

' Oh, no, I won't; I will play in here. Don't be so ill-natured.' And with a very bad grace the cat untied the string and threw the golden ball into the lion's lap, and composed himself to sleep again.

For a long while the lion tossed it up and down gaily, feeling that, however sound asleep the boy-brother might *look*, he was sure to have one eye open; but gradually he began to edge closer to the opening, and at last gave such a toss that the ball went up high into the air, and he could not see what became of it.

' Oh, how stupid of me ! ' he cried, as the cat sprang up angrily, ' let us go at once and search for it. It can't really have fallen very far.' But though they searched that day and the next, and the next after that, they never found it, because it never came down.

After the loss of his ball the cat refused to live with the lion any longer, but wandered away to the north, always hoping he might meet with his ball again. But months passed, and years passed, and though he travelled over hundreds of miles, he never saw any traces of it.

At length, when he was getting quite old, he came to a place unlike any that he had ever seen before, where a big river rolled right to the foot of some high mountains. The ground all about the river bank was damp and marshy, and as no cat likes to wet its feet, this one climbed a tree that rose high above the water, and thought sadly of his lost ball, which would have helped him out of this horrible place. Suddenly he saw a beautiful ball, for all the world like his own, dangling from a branch of the tree he was on. He longed to get at it; but was the branch strong enough to bear his weight? It was no use, after all he had done, getting drowned in the water. However, it could do no harm, if he was to go a little way; he could always manage to get back somehow.

So he stretched himself at full length upon the branch, and wriggled his body cautiously along. To his delight it seemed thick and stout. Another movement, and, by stretching out his paw, he would be able to draw the string towards him, when the branch gave a loud crack, and the cat made haste to wriggle himself back the way he had come.

But when cats make up their minds to do anything they generally *do* it; and this cat began to look about to see if there was really no way of getting at his ball. Yes! there was, and it was much surer than the other, though rather more difficult. Above the bough where the ball hung was another bough much thicker, which he knew could not break with his weight; and by holding on tight to this with all his four paws he could just manage to touch the ball with his tail. He would thus be able to whisk the ball to and fro till, by-and-by, the string would become quite loose, and it would fall to the ground. It might take some time, but the lion's little brother was patient, like most cats.

Well, it all happened just as the cat intended it should, and when the ball dropped on the ground the cat ran down the tree like lightning, and, picking it up, tucked it away in the snake's skin round his neck. Then he began jumping along the shore of the Big Water from one place to another, trying to find a boat, or even a log of wood, that would take him across. But there was nothing ; only, on the other side, he saw two girls cooking, and though he shouted to them at the top of his voice, they were too far off to hear what he said. And, what was worse, the ball suddenly fell out of its snake's skin bag right into the river.

Now, it is not at all an uncommon thing for balls to tumble into rivers, but in that case they generally either fall to the bottom and stay there, or else bob about on the top of the water close to where they first touched it. But this ball, instead of doing either of these things, went straight across to the other side, and there one of the girls saw it when she stooped to dip some water into her pail.

'Oh! what a lovely ball!' cried she, and tried to catch it in her pail ; but the ball always kept bobbing just out of her reach.

'Come and help me!' she called to her sister, and after a long while they had the ball safe inside the pail. They were delighted with their new toy, and one or the other held it in her hand till bedtime came, and then it was a long time before they could make up their minds where it would be safest for the night. At last they locked it in a cupboard in one corner of their room, and as there was no hole anywhere the ball could not possibly get out. After that they went to sleep.

In the morning the first thing they both did was to run to the cupboard and unlock it, but when the door opened they started back, for, instead of the ball, there stood a handsome young man.

'Ladies,' he said, 'how can I thank you for what you have done for me? Long, long ago, I was en-chanted by a wicked fairy, and condemned to keep the shape of a ball till I should meet with two maidens, who would take me to their own home. But where was I to meet them ? For hundreds of years I have lived in the depths of the forest, where nothing but wild beasts ever

came, and it was only when the lion threw me into the
sky that I was able to fall to earth near this river.   Where
there is a river, sooner or later people will come ; so,
hanging myself on a tree, I watched and waited.   For a
moment I lost heart when I fell once more into the
hands of my old master the wild cat, but my hopes rose
again as I saw he was making for the river bank opposite
where you were standing.   That was my chance, and I
took it.   And now, ladies, I have only to say that, if ever I
can do anything to help you, go to the top of that high
mountain and knock three times at the iron door at the
north side, and I will come to you.'

So, with a low bow, he vanished from before them,
leaving the maidens weeping at having lost in one
moment both the ball and the prince.

[Adapted from *North American Indian Legends.*]

WHICH WAS THE FOOLISHEST?

In a little village that stood on a wide plain, where you could see the sun from the moment he rose to the moment he set, there lived two couples side by side. The men, who worked under the same master, were quite good friends, but the wives were always quarrelling, and the subject they quarrelled most about was—which of the two had the stupidest husband.

Unlike most women—who think that anything that belongs to them must be better than what belongs to anyone else—each thought her own husband the more foolish of the two.

'You should just see what he does!' one said to her neighbour. 'He puts on the baby's frock upside down, and, one day, I found him trying to feed her with boiling soup, and her mouth was scalded for days after. Then he picks up stones in the road and sows them instead of potatoes, and one day he wanted to go into the garden from the top window, because he declared it was a shorter way than through the door.'

'That is bad enough, of course,' answered the other; 'but it is really *nothing* to what I have to endure every day from *my* husband. If, when I am busy, I ask him to go and feed the poultry, he is certain to give them some poisonous stuff instead of their proper food, and when I visit the yard next I find them all dead. Once he even took my best bonnet, when I had gone away to my sick mother, and when I came back I found he had given it to the hen to lay her eggs in. And you know yourself that, only last week, when I sent him to buy a cask of butter, he returned driving a hundred and fifty ducks which someone had induced him to take, and not one of them would lay.'

' Yes, I am afraid he *is* trying,' replied the first; ' but let us put them to the proof, and see which of them is the most foolish.'

So, about the time that she expected her husband home from work, she got out her spinning-wheel, and sat busily turning it, taking care not even to look up from her work when the man came in. For some minutes he stood with his mouth open watching her, and as she still remained silent, he said at last :

' Have you gone mad, wife, that you sit spinning without anything on the wheel ? '

' *You* may think that there is nothing on it,' answered she, ' but I can assure you that there is a large skein of wool, so fine that nobody can see it, which will be woven into a coat for you.'

' Dear me ! ' he replied, ' what a clever wife I have got ! If you had not told me I should never have known that there was any wool on the wheel at all. But now I really do seem to see something.'

The woman smiled and was silent, and after spinning busily for an hour more, she got up from her stool, and began to weave as fast as she could. At last she got up, and said to her husband : ' I am too tired to finish it to-night, so I shall go to bed, and to-morrow I shall only have the cutting and stitching to do.'

So the next morning she got up early, and after she had cleaned her house, and fed her chickens, and put everything in its place again, she bent over the kitchen table, and the sound of her big scissors might be heard snip ! snap ! as far as the garden. Her husband could not see anything to snip at; but then he was so stupid that was not surprising ! '

After the cutting came the sewing. The woman

patted and pinned and fixed and joined, and then, turning
to the man, she said:

'Now it is ready for you to try on.' And she
made him take off his coat, and stand up in front of
her, and once more she patted and pinned and fixed and
joined, and was very careful in smoothing out every
wrinkle.

'It does not feel very warm,' observed the man at
last, when he had borne all this patiently for a long time.

'That is because it is so fine,' answered she; 'you do
not want it to be as thick as the rough clothes you wear
every day.'

He *did*, but was ashamed to say so, and only answered:
'Well, I am sure it must be beautiful since you say so,
and I shall be smarter than anyone in the whole village.
"What a splendid coat!" they will exclaim when they
see me. But it is not everybody who has a wife as
clever as mine.'

Meanwhile the other wife was not idle. As soon as
her husband entered she looked at him with such a look
of terror that the poor man was quite frightened.

'Why do you stare at me so? Is there anything the
matter?' asked he.

'Oh! go to bed at once,' she cried; 'you must be very
ill indeed to look like that!'

The man was rather surprised at first, as he felt
particularly well that evening; but the moment his wife
spoke he became quite certain that he had something
dreadful the matter with him, and grew quite pale.

'I dare say it would be the best place for me,' he
answered, trembling; and he suffered his wife to take him
upstairs, and to help him off with his clothes.

'If you sleep well during the night there *may* be a
chance for you,' said she, shaking her head, as she tucked
him up warmly; 'but if not——' And of course the
poor man never closed an eye till the sun rose.

'How do you feel this morning?' asked the woman,
coming in on tip-toe when her house-work was finished.

' Oh, bad ; very bad indeed,' answered he ; ' I have not slept for a moment. Can you think of nothing to make me better ? '

' I will try everything that is possible,' said the wife, who did not in the least wish her husband to die, but was determined to show that he was more foolish than the other man. ' I will get some dried herbs and make you a drink, but I am very much afraid that it is too late. Why did you not tell me before ? '

' I thought perhaps the pain would go off in a day or two ; and, besides, I did not want to make you unhappy,' answered the man, who was by this time quite sure he had been suffering tortures, and had borne them like a hero. ' Of course, if I had had any idea how ill I really was, I should have spoken at once.'

' Well, well, I will see what can be done,' said the wife, ' but talking is not good for you. Lie still, and keep yourself warm.'

All that day the man lay in bed, and whenever his wife entered the room and asked him, with a shake of the head, how he felt, he always replied that he was getting worse. At last, in the evening, she burst into tears, and when he inquired what was the matter, she sobbed out :

' Oh, my poor, poor husband, are you really dead ? I must go to-morrow and order your coffin.'

Now, when the man heard this, a cold shiver ran through his body, and all at once he knew that he was as well as he had ever been in his life.

' Oh, no, no ! ' he cried, ' I feel quite recovered ! Indeed, I think I shall go out to work.'

You will do no such thing,' replied his wife. ' Just keep quite quiet, for before the sun rises you will be a dead man.'

The man was very frightened at her words, and lay absolutely still while the undertaker came and measured him for his coffin ; and his wife gave orders to the grave-digger about his grave. That evening the coffin was sent home, and in the morning at nine o'clock the woman put him on a long flannel garment, and called to the under-taker's men to fasten down the lid and carry him to the grave, where all their friends were waiting them.   Just as the body was being placed in the ground the other woman's husband came running up, dressed, as far as any-one could see, in no clothes at all.   Everybody burst into shouts of laughter at the sight of him, and the men laid down the coffin and laughed too, till their sides nearly split.   The dead man was so astonished at this behaviour, that he peeped out of a little window in the side of the coffin, and cried out:

'I should laugh as loudly as any of you, if I were not a dead man.'

When they heard the voice coming from the coffin the other people suddenly stopped laughing, and stood as if they had been turned into stone.   Then they rushed with one accord to the coffin, and lifted the lid so that the man could step out amongst them.

'Were you really not dead after all?' asked they. 'And if not, why did you let yourself be buried?'

At this the wives both confessed that they had each wished to prove that her husband was stupider than the other.   But the villagers declared that they could not decide which was the most foolish—the man who allowed himself to be persuaded that he was wearing fine clothes when he was dressed in nothing, or the man who let him-self be buried when he was alive and well.

So the women quarrelled just as much as they did before, and no one ever knew whose husband was the most foolish.

[Adapted from the *Neuisländische Volksmärchen.*]

ASMUND AND SIGNY

Long, long ago, in the days when fairies, witches, giants, and ogres still visited the earth, there lived a king who reigned over a great and beautiful country. He was married to a wife whom he dearly loved, and had two most promising children—a son called Asmund, and a daughter who was named Signy.

The king and queen were very anxious to bring their children up well, and the young prince and princess were taught everything likely to make them clever and accomplished. They lived at home in their father's palace, and he spared no pains to make their lives happy.

Prince Asmund dearly loved all outdoor sports and an open-air life, and from his earliest childhood he had longed to live entirely in the forest close by. After many arguments and entreaties he succeeded in persuading the king to give him two great oak trees for his very own.

'Now,' said he to his sister, 'I will have the trees hollowed out, and then I will make rooms in them and furnish them so that I shall be able to live out in the forest.'

'Oh, Asmund!' exclaimed Signy, 'what a delightful idea! Do let me come too, and live in one of your trees. I will bring all my pretty things and ornaments, and the trees are so near home we shall be quite safe in them.'

Asmund, who was extremely fond of his sister, readily consented, and they had a very happy time together, carrying over all their pet treasures, and Signy's jewels and other ornaments, and arranging them in the pretty little rooms inside the trees.

Unfortunately sadder days were to come. A war with another country broke out, and the king had to lead his army against their enemy. During his absence the queen fell ill, and after lingering for some time she died, to the great grief of her children. They made up their minds to live altogether for a time in their trees, and for this purpose they had provisions enough stored up inside to last them a year.

Now, I must tell you, in another country a long way off, there reigned a king who had an only son named Ring. Prince Ring had heard so much about the beauty and goodness of Princess Signy that he determined to marry her if possible. So he begged his father to let him have a ship for the voyage, set sail with a favourable wind, and after a time landed in the country where Signy lived.

The prince lost no time in setting out for the royal palace, and on his way there he met such a wonderfully lovely woman that he felt he had never seen such beauty before in all his life. He stopped her and at once asked who she was.

'I am Signy, the king's daughter,' was the reply.

Then the prince inquired why she was wandering about all by herself, and she told him that since her mother's death she was so sad that whilst her father was away she preferred being alone.

Ring was quite deceived by her, and never guessed that she was not Princess Signy at all, but a strong, gigantic, wicked witch bent on deceiving him under a beautiful shape. He confided to her that he had travelled all the way from his own country for her sake, having fallen in love with the accounts he had heard of her beauty, and he then and there asked her to be his wife.

The witch listened to all he said and, much pleased,

ended by accepting his offer; but she begged him to return to his ship for a little while as she wished to go some way further into the forest, promising to join him later on.

Prince Ring did as she wished and went back to his ship to wait, whilst she walked on into the forest till she reached the two oak trees.

Here she resumed her own gigantic shape, tore up the trees by their roots, threw one of them over her back and clasped the other to her breast, carried them down to the shore and waded out with them to the ship.

She took care not to be noticed as she reached the ship, and directly she got on board she once more changed to her former lovely appearance and told the prince that her luggage was now all on board, and that they need wait for nothing more.

The prince gave orders to set sail at once, and after a fine voyage landed in his own country, where his parents and his only sister received him with the greatest joy and affection.

The false Signy was also very kindly welcomed. A beautiful house was got ready for her, and Prince Ring had the two oaks planted in the garden just in front of her windows so that she might have the pleasure of seeing them constantly. He often went to visit the witch, whom he believed to be Princess Signy, and one day he asked: ' Don't you think we might be married before long?'

' Yes,' said she, quite pleased, ' I am quite ready to marry you whenever you like.'

' Then,' replied Ring, ' let us decide on this day fortnight. And see, I have brought you some stuff to make your wedding-dress of.' So saying he gave her a large piece of the most beautiful brocade, all woven over with gold threads, and embroidered with pearls and other jewels.

The prince had hardly left her before the witch resumed her proper shape and tore about the room, raging and storming and flinging the beautiful silk on the floor.

'What was *she* to do with such things?' she roared. '*She* did not know how to sew or make clothes, and she was sure to die of starvation into the bargain if her brother Ironhead did not come soon and bring her some raw meat and bones, for she really could eat nothing else.'

As she was raving and roaring in this frantic manner part of the floor suddenly opened and a huge giant rose up carrying a great chest in his arms. The witch was enchanted at this sight, and eagerly helped her brother to set down and open the chest, which was full of the ghastly food she had been longing for. The horrid pair set to and greedily devoured it all, and when the chest was quite empty the giant put it on his shoulder and dis-appeared as he had come, without leaving any trace of his visit.

But his sister did not keep quiet for long, and tore and pulled at the rich brocade as if she wanted to destroy it, stamping about and shouting angrily.

Now, all this time Prince Asmund and his sister sat in their trees just outside the window and saw all that was going on.

'Dear Signy,' said Asmund, 'do try to get hold of that piece of brocade and make the clothes yourself, for really we shall have no rest day or night with such a noise.'

'I will try,' said Signy; 'it won't be an easy matter, but it's worth while taking some trouble to have a little peace.'

So she watched for an opportunity and managed to carry off the brocade the first time the witch left her room. Then she set to work, cutting out and sewing as best she could, and by the end of six days she had turned it into an elegant robe with a long train and a mantle. When it was finished she climbed to the top

SIGNY AT THE WINDOW

of her tree and contrived to throw the clothes on to a
table through the open window.

How delighted the witch was when she found the
clothes all finished! The next time Prince Ring came to
see her she gave them to him, and he paid her many
compliments on her skilful work, after which he took
leave of her in the most friendly manner. But he had
scarcely left the house when the witch began to rage as
furiously as ever, and never stopped till her brother Ironhead appeared.

When Asmund saw all these wild doings from his
tree he felt he could no longer keep silence. He went to
Prince Ring and said : ' Do come with me and see the
strange things that are happening in the new princess's
room.'

The prince was not a little surprised, but he consented
to hide himself with Asmund behind the panelling of the
room, from where they could see all that went on through
a little slit. The witch was raving and roaring as usual,
and said to her brother :

' Once I am married to the king's son I shall be better
off than now. I shall take care to have all that pack of
courtiers put to death, and then I shall send for all my
relations to come and live here instead. I fancy the
giants will enjoy themselves very much with me and my
husband.'

When Prince Ring heard this he fell into such a rage
that he ordered the house to be set on fire, and it was
burnt to the ground, with the witch and her brother
in it.

Asmund then told the prince about the two oak trees
and took him to see them. The prince was quite astonished at them and at all their contents, but still more
so at the extreme beauty of Signy. He fell in love with
her at once, and entreated her to marry him, which, after
a time, she consented to do. Asmund, on his side, asked
for the hand of Prince Ring's sister, which was gladly

granted him, and the double wedding was celebrated with great rejoicings.

After this Prince Asmund and his bride returned to his country to live with the king his father. The two couples often met, and lived happily for many, many years. And that is the end of the story.

[From *Isländische Mährchen.*]

RÜBEZAHL

OVER all the vast under-world the mountain Gnome Rübezahl was lord; and busy enough the care of his dominions kept him. There were the endless treasure chambers to be gone through, and the hosts of gnomes to be kept to their tasks. Some built strong barriers to hold back the fiery rivers in the earth's heart, and some had scalding vapours to change dull stones to precious metal, or were hard at work filling every cranny of the rocks with diamonds and rubies; for Rübezahl loved all pretty things. Sometimes the fancy would take him to leave those gloomy regions, and come out upon the green earth for a while, and bask in the sunshine and hear the birds sing. And as gnomes live many hundreds of years he saw strange things. For, the first time he came up, the great hills were covered with thick forests, in which wild animals roamed, and Rübezahl watched the fierce fights between bear and bison, or chased the grey wolves, or amused himself by rolling great rocks down into the desolate valleys, to hear the thunder of their fall echoing among the hills. But the next time he ventured above ground, what was his surprise to find everything changed! The dark woods were hewn down, and in their place appeared blossoming orchards surrounding cosy-looking thatched cottages; from every chimney the blue smoke curled peacefully into the air, sheep and oxen fed in the flowery meadows, while from the shade of the hedges came the music of the shepherd's pipe. The strangeness and pleasantness of the sight so delighted the gnome that he never thought of resenting the intrusion of these unexpected guests, who, without saying ' by your leave ' or ' with your leave,' had made themselves so very much at home upon his hills ; nor did he wish to interfere with their doings, but left them in quiet possession of their homes, as a good householder leaves in peace the swallows who have built their nests under his eaves. He was indeed greatly minded to make friends with this being called 'man,' so, taking the form of an old field labourer, he entered the service of a farmer. Under his care all the crops flourished exceedingly, but the master proved to be wasteful and ungrateful, and Rübezahl soon left him, and went to be shepherd to his next neighbour. He tended the flock so diligently, and knew so well where to lead the sheep to the sweetest pastures, and where among the hills to look for any who strayed away, that they too prospered under his care, and not one was lost or torn by wolves ; but this new master was a hard man, and begrudged him his well-earned wages. So he ran away and went to serve the judge. Here he upheld the law with might and main, and was a terror to thieves and evildoers ; but the judge was a bad man, who took bribes, and despised the law. Rübezahl would not be the tool of an unjust man, and so he told his master, who thereupon ordered him to be thrown into prison. Of course that did not trouble the gnome at all, he simply got out through the keyhole, and went away down to his underground palace, very much disappointed by his first experience of mankind. But, as time went on, he forgot the disagreeable things that had happened to him, and thought he would take another look at the upper world.

So he stole into the valley, keeping himself carefully hidden in copse or hedgerow, and very soon met with an adventure ; for, peeping through a screen of leaves, he saw before him a green lawn where stood a charming maiden, fresh as the spring, and beautiful to look upon.

The Gnome falls in love with the Princess

Around her upon the grass lay her young companions, as if they had thrown themselves down to rest after some merry game. Beyond them flowed a little brook, into which a waterfall leapt from a high rock, filling the air with its pleasant sound, and making a coolness even in the sultry noontide. The sight of the maiden so pleased the gnome that, for the first time, he wished himself a mortal; and, longing for a better view of the gay company, he changed himself into a raven and perched upon an oak-tree which overhung the brook. But he soon found that this was not at all a good plan. He could only see with a raven's eyes, and feel as a raven feels; and a nest of field-mice at the foot of the tree interested him far more than the sport of the maidens. When he understood this he flew down again in a great hurry into the thicket, and took the form of a handsome young man—that was the best way—and he fell in love with the girl then and there. The fair maiden was the daughter of the king of the country, and she often wandered in the forest with her play fellows gathering the wild flowers and fruits, till the midday heat drove the merry band to the shady lawn by the brook to rest, or to bathe in the cool waters. On this particular morning the fancy took them to wander off again into the wood. This was Master Rübezahl's opportunity. Stepping out of his hiding-place he stood in the midst of the little lawn, weaving his magic spells, till slowly all about him changed, and when the maidens returned at noon to their favourite resting-place they stood lost in amazement, and almost fancied that they must be dreaming. The red rocks had become white marble and alabaster; the stream that murmured and struggled before in its rocky bed, flowed in silence now in its smooth channel, from which a clear fountain leapt, to fall again in showers of diamond drops, now on this side now on that, as the wandering breeze scattered it.

Daisies and forget-me-nots fringed its brink, while tall hedges of roses and jasmine ringed it round, making the sweetest and daintiest bower imaginable. To the right and left of the waterfall opened out a wonderful grotto, its walls and arches glittering with many-coloured rock-crystals, while in every niche were spread out strange fruits and sweetmeats, the very sight of which made the princess long to taste them. She hesitated a while, however, scarcely able to believe her eyes, and not knowing if she should enter the enchanted spot or fly from it. But at length curiosity prevailed, and she and her companions explored to their heart's content, and tasted and examined everything, running hither and thither in high glee, and calling merrily to each other.

At last, when they were quite weary, the princess cried out suddenly that nothing would content her but to bathe in the marble pool, which certainly did look very inviting ; and they all went gaily to this new amusement. The princess was ready first, but scarcely had she slipped over the rim of the pool when down—down—down she sank, and vanished in its depths before her frightened playmates could seize her by so much as a lock of her floating golden hair !

Loudly did they weep and wail, running about the brink of the pool, which looked so shallow and so clear, but which had swallowed up their princess before their eyes. They even sprang into the water and tried to dive after her, but in vain ; they only floated like corks in the enchanted pool, and could not keep under water for a second.

They saw at last that there was nothing for it but to carry to the king the sad tidings of his beloved daughter's disappearance. And what great weeping and lamentation there was in the palace when the dreadful news was told ! The king tore his robes, dashed his golden crown from his head, and hid his face in his purple mantle for grief and anguish at the loss of the princess. After the first outburst of wailing, however, he took heart and hurried off to see for himself the scene of this strange adventure, thinking, as people will in sorrow, that there might be some mistake after all. But when he reached the spot, behold, all was changed again! The glittering grotto described to him by the maidens had completely vanished, and so had the marble bath, the bower of jasmine; instead, all was a tangle of flowers, as it had been of old. The king was so much perplexed that he threatened the princess's playfellows with all sorts of punishments if they would not confess something about her disappearance; but as they only repeated the same story he presently put down the whole affair to the work of some sprite or goblin, and tried to console himself for his loss by ordering a grand hunt; for kings cannot bear to be troubled about anything long.

Meanwhile the princess was not at all unhappy in the palace of her elfish lover.

When the water-nymphs, who were hiding in readiness, had caught her and dragged her out of the sight of her terrified maidens, she herself had not had time to be frightened. They swam with her quickly by strange underground ways to a palace so splendid that her father's seemed but a poor cottage in comparison with it, and when she recovered from her astonishment she found herself seated upon a couch, wrapped in a wonderful robe of satin fastened with a silken girdle, while beside her knelt a young man who whispered the sweetest speeches imaginable in her ear. The gnome, for he it was, told her all about himself and his great underground kingdom, and presently led her through the many rooms and halls of the palace, and showed her the rare and wonderful things displayed in them till she was fairly dazzled at the sight of so much splendour. On three sides of the castle lay a lovely garden with masses of gay, sweet flowers, and velvet lawns all cool and shady, which pleased the eye of the princess. The fruit trees were hung with golden and rosy apples, and nightingales sang in every bush, as the gnome and the princess wandered in the leafy alleys, sometimes gazing at the moon, sometimes pausing to gather the rarest flowers for her adornment. And all the time he was thinking to himself that never, during the hundreds of years he had lived, had he seen so charming a maiden. But the princess felt no such happiness; in spite of all the magic delights around her she was sad, though she tried to seem content for fear of displeasing the gnome. However, he soon perceived her melancholy, and in a thousand ways strove to dispel the cloud, but in vain. At last he said to himself: 'Men are sociable creatures, like bees or ants. Doubtless this lovely mortal is pining for company. Who is there I can find for her to talk to?'

Thereupon he hastened into the nearest field and dug up a dozen or so of different roots—carrots, turnips, and radishes—and laying them carefully in an elegant basket brought them to the princess, who sat pensive in the shade of the rose-bower.

'Loveliest daughter of earth,' said the gnome, 'banish all sorrow; no more shall you be lonely in my dwelling. In this basket is all you need to make this spot delightful to you. Take this little many-coloured wand, and with a touch give to each root the form you desire to see.'

With this he left her, and the princess, without an instant's delay, opened the basket, and touching a turnip, cried eagerly: 'Brunhilda, my dear Brunhilda! come to me quickly!' And sure enough there was Brunhilda, joyfully hugging and kissing her beloved princess, and chattering as gaily as in the old days.

This sudden appearance was so delightful that the princess could hardly believe her own eyes, and was quite beside herself with the joy of having her dear playfellow with her once more. Hand in hand they wandered about the enchanted garden, and gathered the golden apples from the trees, and when they were tired of this amusement the princess led her friend through all the

RUBEZAHL AND THE PRINCESS

[*This illustration is reproduced in color between pages 74 and 75.*]

wonderful rooms of the palace, until at last they came to the one in which were kept all the marvellous dresses and ornaments the gnome had given to his hoped-for bride. There they found so much to amuse them that the hours passed like minutes. Veils, girdles, and necklaces were tried on and admired, the imitation Brunhilda knew so well how to behave herself, and showed so much taste that nobody would ever have suspected that she was nothing but a turnip after all. The gnome, who had secretly been keeping an eye upon them, was very pleased with himself for having so well understood the heart of a woman ; and the princess seemed to him even more charming than before. She did not forget to touch the rest of the roots with her magic wand, and soon had all her maidens about her, and even, as she had two tiny radishes to spare, her favourite cat, and her little dog whose name was Beni.

And now all went cheerfully in the castle. The princess gave to each of the maidens her task, and never was mistress better served. For a whole week she enjoyed the delight of her pleasant company undisturbed. They all sang, they danced, they played from morning to night ; only the princess noticed that day by day the fresh young faces of her maidens grew pale and wan, and the mirror in the great marble hall showed her that she alone still kept her rosy bloom, while Brunhilda and the rest faded visibly. They assured her that all was well with them ; but, nevertheless, they continued to waste away, and day by day it became harder to them to take part in the games of the princess, till at last, one fine morning, when the princess started from bed and hastened out to join her gay playfellows, she shuddered and started back at the sight of a group of shrivelled crones, with bent backs and trembling limbs, who supported their tottering steps with staves and crutches, and coughed dismally. A little nearer to the hearth lay the once frolicsome Beni, with all four feet stretched stiffly out, while the sleek cat seemed too weak to raise his head from his velvet cushion.

The horrified princess fled to the door to escape from the sight of this mournful company, and called loudly for the gnome, who appeared at once, humbly anxious to do her bidding.

'Malicious Sprite,' she cried, 'why do you begrudge me my playmates—the greatest delight of my lonely hours? Isn't this solitary life in such a desert bad enough without your turning the castle into a hospital for the aged? Give my maidens back their youth and health this very minute, or I will never love you!'

'Sweetest and fairest of damsels,' cried the gnome, 'do not be angry; everything that is in my power I will do—but do not ask the impossible. So long as the sap was fresh in the roots the magic staff could keep them in the forms you desired, but as the sap dried up they withered away. But never trouble yourself about that, dearest one, a basket of fresh turnips will soon set matters right, and you can speedily call up again every form you wish to see. The great green patch in the garden will provide you with a more lively company.'

So saying the gnome took himself off. And the princess with her magic wand touched the wrinkled old women, and left them the withered roots they really were, to be thrown upon the rubbish heap; and with light feet skipped off across to the meadow to take possession of the freshly filled basket. But to her surprise she could not find it anywhere. Up and down the garden she searched, spying into every corner, but not a sign of it was to be found. By the trellis of grape vines she met the gnome, who was so much embarrassed at the sight of her that she became aware of his confusion while he was still quite a long way off.

'You are trying to tease me,' she cried, as soon as she saw him. 'Where have you hidden the basket? I have been looking for it at least an hour.'

'Dear queen of my heart,' answered he, 'I pray you to forgive my carelessness. I promised more than I could perform. I have sought all over the land for the roots you desire ; but they are gathered in, and lie drying in musty cellars, and the fields are bare and desolate, for below in the valley winter reigns, only here in your presence spring is held fast, and wherever your foot is set the gay flowers bloom. Have patience for a little, and then without fail you shall have your puppets to play with.'

Almost before the gnome had finished, the disappointed princess turned away, and marched off to her own apartments, without deigning to answer him.

The gnome, however, set off above ground as speedily as possible, and disguising himself as a farmer, bought an ass in the nearest market-town, and brought it back loaded with sacks of turnip, carrot, and radish seed. With this he sowed a great field, and sent a vast army of his goblins to watch and tend it, and to bring up the fiery rivers from the heart of the earth near enough to warm and encourage the sprouting seeds. Thus fostered they grew and flourished marvellously, and promised a goodly crop.

The princess wandered about the field day by day, no other plants or fruits in all her wonderful garden pleased her as much as these roots ; but still her eyes were full of discontent. And, best of all, she loved to while away the hours in a shady fir-wood, seated upon the bank of a little stream, into which she would cast the flowers she had gathered and watch them float away.

The gnome tried hard by every means in his power to please the princess and win her love, but little did he guess the real reason of his lack of success. He imagined that she was too young and inexperienced to care for him ; but that was a mistake, for the truth was that another image already filled her heart. The young Prince Ratibor, whose lands joined her father's, had won the heart of

the princess ; and the lovers had been looking forward
to the coming of their wedding-day when the bride's
mysterious disappearance took place.   The sad news
drove Ratibor distracted, and as the days went on, and
nothing could be heard of the princess, he forsook his
castle and the society of men, and spent his days in the
wild forests, roaming about and crying her name aloud
to the trees and rocks.   Meanwhile, the maiden, in her
gorgeous prison, sighed in secret over her grief, not wish-
ing to arouse the gnome's suspicions.   In her own mind
she was wondering if by any means she might escape
from her captivity, and at last she hit upon a plan.

By this time spring once more reigned in the valley,
and the gnome sent the fires back to their places in
the deeps of the earth, for the roots which they had
kept warm through all the cruel winter had now come to
their full size.   Day by day the princess pulled up some
of them, and made experiments with them, conjuring up
now this longed-for person, and now that, just for the
pleasure of seeing them as they appeared ; but she really
had another purpose in view.

One day she changed a tiny turnip into a bee, and
sent him off to bring her some news of her lover.

' Fly, dear little bee, towards the east,' said she, ' to my
beloved Ratibor, and softly hum into his ear that I love
him only, but that I am a captive in the gnome's palace
under the mountains.   Do not forget a single word of
my greeting, and bring me back a message from my
beloved.'

So the bee spread his shining wings and flew away to
do as he was bidden ; but before he was out of sight a
greedy swallow made a snatch at him, and to the great
grief of the princess her messenger was eaten up then
and there.

After that, by the power of the wonderful wand she
summoned a cricket, and taught him this greeting :

' Hop, little cricket, to Ratibor, and chirp in his ear

that I love him only, but that I am held captive by the gnome in his palace under the mountains.'

So the cricket hopped off gaily, determined to do his best to deliver his message ; but, alas ! a long-legged stork who was prancing along the same road caught him in her cruel beak, and before he could say a word he had disappeared down her throat.

These two unlucky ventures did not prevent the princess from trying once more.

This time she changed the turnip into a magpie.

'Flutter from tree to tree, chattering bird,' said she, 'till you come to Ratibor, my love. Tell him that I am a captive, and bid him come with horses and men, the third day from this, to the hill that rises from the Thorny Valley.'

The magpie listened, hopped awhile from branch to branch, and then darted away, the princess watching him anxiously as far as she could see.

Now Prince Ratibor was still spending his life in wandering about the woods, and not even the beauty of the spring could soothe his grief.

One day, as he sat in the shade of an oak tree, dreaming of his lost princess, and sometimes crying her name aloud, he seemed to hear another voice reply to his, and, starting up, he gazed around him, but he could see no one, and he had just made up his mind that he must be mistaken, when the same voice called again, and, looking up sharply, he saw a magpie which hopped to and fro among the twigs. Then Ratibor heard with surprise that the bird was indeed calling him by name.

'Poor chatterpie,' said he ; 'who taught you to say that name, which belongs to an unlucky mortal who wishes the earth would open and swallow up him and his memory for ever ? '

Thereupon he caught up a great stone, and would have hurled it at the magpie, if it had not at that moment uttered the name of the princess.

This was so unexpected that the prince's arm fell helplessly to his side at the sound, and he stood motionless.

But the magpie in the tree, who, like all the rest of his family, was not happy unless he could be for ever chattering, began to repeat the message the princess had taught him ; and as soon as he understood it, Prince Ratibor's heart was filled with joy. All his gloom and misery vanished in a moment, and he anxiously questioned the welcome messenger as to the fate of the princess.

But the magpie knew no more than the lesson he had learnt, so he soon fluttered away ; while the prince hurried back to his castle to gather together a troop of horsemen, full of courage for whatever might befall.

The princess meanwhile was craftily pursuing her plan of escape. She left off treating the gnome with coldness and indifference ; indeed, there was a look in her eyes which encouraged him to hope that she might some day return his love, and the idea pleased him mightily. The next day, as soon as the sun rose, she made her appearance decked as a bride, in the wonderful robes and jewels which the fond gnome had prepared for her. Her golden hair was braided and crowned with myrtle blossoms, and her flowing veil sparkled with gems. In these magnificent garments she went to meet the gnome upon the great terrace.

'Loveliest of maidens,' he stammered, bowing low before her, 'let me gaze into your dear eyes, and read in them that you will no longer refuse my love, but will make me the happiest being the sun shines upon.'

So saying he would have drawn aside her veil; but the princess only held it more closely about her.

'Your constancy has overcome me,' she said; 'I can no longer oppose your wishes. But believe my words, and suffer this veil still to hide my blushes and tears.'

'Why tears, beloved one ? ' cried the gnome anxiously ; 'every tear of yours falls upon my heart like a drop of molten gold. Greatly as I desire your love, I do not ask a sacrifice.'

'Ah!' cried the false princess, 'why do you misunderstand my tears? My heart answers to your tenderness, and yet I am fearful. A wife cannot always charm, and though *you* will never alter, the beauty of mortals is as a flower that fades. How can I be sure that you will always be as loving and charming as you are now?'

'Ask some proof, sweetheart,' said he. 'Put my obedience and my patience to some test by which you can judge of my unalterable love.'

'Be it so,' answered the crafty maiden. 'Then give me just one proof of your goodness. Go! count the turnips in yonder meadow. My wedding feast must not lack guests. They shall provide me with bride-maidens too. But beware lest you deceive me, and do not miss a single one. That shall be the test of your truth towards me.'

Unwilling as the gnome was to lose sight of his beautiful bride for a moment, he obeyed her commands without delay, and hurried off to begin his task. He skipped along among the turnips as nimbly as a grasshopper, and had soon counted them all; but, to be quite certain that he had made no mistake, he thought he would just run over them again. This time, to his great annoyance, the number was different; so he reckoned them for the third time, but now the number was not the same as either of the previous ones! And this was hardly to be wondered at, as his mind was full of the princess's pretty looks and words.

As for the maiden, no sooner was her deluded lover fairly out of sight than she began to prepare for flight. She had a fine fresh turnip hidden close at hand, which she changed into a spirited horse, all saddled and bridled, and, springing upon its back, she galloped away over hill and dale till she reached the Thorny Valley, and flung herself into the arms of her beloved Prince Ratibor.

Meanwhile the toiling gnome went through his task over and over again till his back ached and his head swam, and he could no longer put two and two together; but as he felt tolerably certain of the exact number of turnips in the field, big and little together, he hurried back eager to prove to his beloved one what a delightful and submissive husband he would be. He felt very well satisfied with himself as he crossed the mossy lawn to the place where he had left her; but, alas! she was no longer there.

He searched every thicket and path, he looked behind every tree, and gazed into every pond, but without success; then he hastened into the palace and rushed from room to room, peering into every hole and corner and calling her by name; but only echo answered in the marble halls— there was neither voice nor footstep.

Then he began to perceive that something was amiss, and, throwing off the mortal form that encumbered him, he flew out of the palace, and soared high into the air, and saw the fugitive princess in the far distance just as the swift horse carried her across the boundary of his dominions.

Furiously did the enraged gnome fling two great clouds together, and hurl a thunderbolt after the flying maiden, splintering the rocky barriers which had stood a thousand years. But his fury was vain, the thunder-clouds melted away into a soft mist, and the gnome, after flying about for a while in despair, bewailing to the four winds his unhappy fate, went sorrowfully back to the palace, and stole once more through every room, with many sighs and lamentations. He passed through the gardens which for him had lost their charm, and the sight of the princess's footprints on the golden sand of the pathway renewed his grief. All was lonely, empty, sorrowful; and the forsaken gnome resolved that he would have no more dealings with such false creatures as he had found men to be.

Thereupon he stamped three times upon the earth, and the magic palace, with all its treasures, vanished away into the nothingness out of which he had called it ; and the gnome fled once more to the depths of his underground kingdom.

While all this was happening, Prince Ratibor was hurrying away with his prize to a place of safety. With great pomp and triumph he restored the lovely princess to her father, and was then and there married to her, and took her back with him to his own castle.

But long after she was dead, and her children too, the villagers would tell the tale of her imprisonment underground, as they sat carving wood in the winter nights.

[*Volksmährchen der Deutschen.*]

STORY OF THE KING WHO WOULD BE
STRONGER THAN FATE

ONCE upon a time, far away in the east country, there lived a king who loved hunting so much that, when once there was a deer in sight, he was careless of his own safety. Indeed, he often became quite separated from his nobles and attendants, and in fact was particularly fond of lonely adventures. Another of his favourite amusements was to give out that he was not well, and could not be seen ; and then, with the knowledge only of his faithful Grand Wazeer, to disguise himself as a pedlar, load a donkey with cheap wares, and travel about. In this way he found out what the common people said about him, and how his judges and governors fulfilled their duties.

One day his queen presented him with a baby daughter as beautiful as the dawn, and the king himself was so happy and delighted that, for a whole week, he forgot to hunt, and spent the time in public and private rejoicing.

Not long afterwards, however, he went out after some deer which were to be found in a far corner of his forests. In the course of the beat his dogs disturbed a beautiful snow-white stag, and directly he saw it the king determined that he would have it at any cost. So he put the spurs to his horse, and followed it as hard as he could gallop. Of course all his attendants followed at the best speed that they could manage ; but the king was so splendidly mounted, and the stag was so swift, that, at the end of an hour, the king found that only his favourite hound and

himself were in the chase ; all the rest were far, far behind
and out of sight.

Nothing daunted, however, he went on and on, till he
perceived that he was entering a valley with great rocky
mountains on all sides, and that his horse was getting
very tired and trembled at every stride. Worse than all
evening was already drawing on, and the sun would
soon set. In vain had he sent arrow after arrow at the
beautiful stag. Every shot fell short, or went wide of the
mark ; and at last, just as darkness was setting in, he
lost sight altogether of the beast. By this time his horse
could hardly move from fatigue, his hound staggered
panting along beside him, he was far away amongst
mountains where he had never been before, and had quite
missed his way, and not a human creature or dwelling
was in sight.

All this was very discouraging, but the king would not
have minded if he had not lost that beautiful stag. That
troubled him a good deal, but he never worried over what
he could not help, so he got down from his horse, slipped
his arm through the bridle, and led the animal along the
rough path in hopes of discovering some shepherd's hut,
or, at least, a cave or shelter under some rock, where he
might pass the night.

Presently he heard the sound of rushing water, and
made towards it. He toiled over a steep rocky shoulder
of a hill, and there, just below him, was a stream dashing
down a precipitous glen, and, almost beneath his feet,
twinkling and flickering from the level of the torrent, was
a dim light as of a lamp. Towards this light the king
with his horse and hound made his way, sliding and
stumbling down a steep, stony path. At the bottom the
king found a narrow grassy ledge by the brink of the
stream, across which the light from a rude lantern in
the mouth of a cave shed a broad beam of uncertain
light. At the edge of the stream sat an old hermit with a
long white beard, who neither spoke nor moved as the

king approached, but sat throwing into the stream dry leaves which lay scattered about the ground near him.

'Peace be upon you,' said the king, giving the usual country salutation.

'And upon you peace,' answered the hermit; but still he never looked up, nor stopped what he was doing.

For a minute or two the king stood watching him. He noticed that the hermit threw two leaves in at a time, and watched them attentively. Sometimes both were carried rapidly down by the stream; sometimes only one leaf was carried off, and the other, after whirling slowly round and round on the edge of the current, would come circling back on an eddy to the hermit's feet. At other times both leaves were held in the backward eddy, and failed to reach the main current of the noisy stream.

'What are you doing?' asked the king at last, and the hermit replied that he was reading the fates of men; every one's fate, he said, was settled from the beginning, and, whatever it were, there was no escape from it. The king laughed.

'I care little,' he said, 'what my fate may be; but I should be curious to know the fate of my little daughter.'

'I cannot say,' answered the hermit.

'Do you not know, then?' demanded the king.

'I might know,' returned the hermit, 'but it is not always wisdom to know much.'

But the king was not content with this reply, and began to press the old man to say what he knew, which for a long time he would not do. At last, however, the king urged him so greatly that he said:

'The king's daughter will marry the son of a poor slave-girl called Puruna, who belongs to the king of the land of the north. There is no escaping from Fate.'

The king was wild with anger at hearing these words, but he was also very tired; so he only laughed, and answered that he hoped there would be a way out of *that* fate anyhow. Then he asked if the hermit could shelter

him and his beasts for the night, and the hermit said
' Yes ' ; so, very soon the king had watered and tethered
his horse, and, after a supper of bread and parched peas,
lay down in the cave, with the hound at his feet, and
tried to go to sleep. But instead of sleeping he only lay
awake and thought of the hermit's prophecy; and the
more he thought of it the angrier he felt, until he gnashed
his teeth and declared that it should never, never come
true.

Morning came, and the king got up, pale and sulky,
and, after learning from the hermit which path to take,
was soon mounted and found his way home without
much difficulty. Directly he reached his palace he
wrote a letter to the king of the land of the north,
begging him, as a favour, to sell him his slave girl
Puruna and her son, and saying that, if he consented, he
would send a messenger to receive them at the river
which divided the kingdoms.

For five days he awaited the reply, and hardly slept
or ate, but was as cross as could be all the time. On the
fifth day his messenger returned with a letter to say that
the king of the land of the north would not sell, but he
would give, the king the slave girl and her son. The king
was overjoyed. He sent for his Grand Wazeer and told
him that he was going on one of his lonely expeditions,
and that the Wazeer must invent some excuse to account
for his absence. Next he disguised himself as an ordinary
messenger, mounted a swift camel, and sped away to the
place where the slave girl was to be handed over to him.
When he got there he gave the messengers who brought
her a letter of thanks and a handsome present for their
master and rewards for themselves; and then without
delay he took the poor woman and her tiny boy-baby up
on to his camel and rode off to a wild desert.

After riding for a day and a night, almost without
stopping, he came to a great cave where he made the
woman dismount, and, taking her and the baby into the

cave, he drew his sword and with one blow chopped her head off. But although his anger made him cruel enough for anything so dreadful, the king felt that he could not turn his great sword on the helpless baby, who he was sure must soon die in this solitary place without its mother; so he left it in the cave where it was, and, mounting his camel, rode home as fast as he could.

Now, in a small village in his kingdom there lived an old widow who had no children or relations of any kind. She made her living mostly by selling the milk of a flock of goats; but she was very, very poor, and not very strong, and often used to wonder how she would live if she got too weak or ill to attend to her goats. Every morning she drove the goats out into the desert to graze on the shrubs and bushes which grew there, and every evening they came home of themselves to be milked and to be shut up safely for the night.

One evening the old woman was astonished to find that her very best nanny-goat returned without a drop of milk. She thought that some naughty boy or girl was playing a trick upon her and had caught the goat on its way home and stolen all the milk. But when evening after evening the goat remained almost dry she determined to find out who the thief was. So the next day she followed the goats at a distance and watched them while they grazed. At length, in the afternoon, the old woman noticed this particular nanny-goat stealing off by herself away from the herd and she at once went after her. On and on the goat walked for some way, and then disappeared into a cave in the rocks. The old woman followed the goat into the cave and then, what should she see but the animal giving her milk to a little boy-baby, whilst on the ground near by lay the sad remains of the baby's dead mother! Wondering and frightened, the old woman thought at last that this little baby might be a son to her in her old age, and that he would grow up and in time to come be her comfort and support. So she carried home the baby to her hut, and next day she took a spade to the cave and dug a grave where she buried the poor mother.

Years passed by, and the baby grew up into a fine handsome lad, as daring as he was beautiful, and as industrious as he was brave. One day, when the boy, whom the old woman had named Nur Mahomed, was about seventeen years old, he was coming from his day's work in the fields, when he saw a strange donkey eating the cabbages in the garden which surrounded their little cottage. Seizing a big stick, he began to beat the intruder and to drive him out of his garden. A neighbour passing by called out to him—' Hi! I say! why are you beating the pedlar's donkey like that?'

' The pedlar should keep him from eating my cabbages,' said Nur Mahomed; ' if he comes this evening here again I'll cut off his tail for him!'

Whereupon he went off indoors, whistling cheerfully. It happened that this neighbour was one of those people who make mischief by talking too much; so, meeting the pedlar in the ' serai,' or inn, that evening, he told him what had occurred, and added : ' Yes; and the young spit-fire said that if beating the donkey would not do, he would beat you also, and cut your nose off for a thief!'

A few days later, the pedlar having moved on, two men appeared in the village inquiring who it was who had threatened to ill-treat and to murder an innocent pedlar. They declared that the pedlar, in fear of his life, had complained to the king; and that they had been sent to bring the lawless person who had said these things before the king himself. Of course they soon found out about the donkey eating Nur Mahomed's cabbages, and about the young man's hot words; but although the lad assured them that he had never said anything about murdering anyone, they replied they were ordered to arrest him, and bring him to take his trial before the king. So, in spite of his protests, and the wails of his mother, he was carried off, and in due time brought before the king. Of course Nur Mahomed never guessed that the supposed pedlar happened to have been the king himself, although nobody knew it.

But as he was very angry at what he had been told, he declared that he was going to make an example of this young man, and intended to teach him that even poor travelling pedlars could get justice in *his* country, and be protected from such lawlessness. However, just as he was going to pronounce some very heavy sentence, there was a stir in the court, and up came Nur Mahomed's old mother, weeping and lamenting, and begging to be heard. The king ordered her to speak, and she began to plead for the boy, declaring how good he was, and how he was the support of her old age, and if he were put in prison she would die. The king asked her who she was. She replied that she was his mother.

'His mother?' said the king; 'you are too old, surely, to have so young a son!'

Then the old woman, in her fright and distress, confessed the whole story of how she found the baby, and how she rescued and brought him up, and ended by beseeching the king for mercy.

It is easy to guess how, as the story came out, the king looked blacker and blacker, and more and more grim, until at last he was half fainting with rage and astonishment. This, then, was the baby he had left to die, after cruelly murdering his mother! Surely fate might have spared him this! He wished he had sufficient excuse to put the boy to death, for the old hermit's prophecy came back to him as strongly as ever; and yet the young man had done nothing bad enough to deserve such a punishment. Everyone would call him a tyrant if he were to give such an order—in fact, he dared not try it!

At length he collected himself enough to say :—'If this young man will enlist in my army I will let him off. We have need of such as him, and a little discipline will do him good.' Still the old woman pleaded that she

could not live without her son, and was nearly as terrified
at the idea of his becoming a soldier as she was at the
thought of his being put in prison. But at length the
king—determined to get the youth into his clutches—
pacified her by promising her a pension large enough to
keep her in comfort; and Nur Mahomed, to his own
great delight, was duly enrolled in the king's army.

As a soldier Nur Mahomed seemed to be in luck.
He was rather surprised, but much pleased, to find that
he was always one of those chosen when any difficult
or dangerous enterprise was afoot; and, although he had
the narrowest escapes on some occasions, still, the very
desperateness of the situations in which he found himself
gave him special chances of displaying his courage. And
as he was also modest and generous, he became a favourite
with his officers and his comrades.

Thus it was not very surprising that, before very long,
he became enrolled amongst the picked men of the king's
bodyguard. The fact is, that the king had hoped to have
got him killed in some fight or another; but, seeing that,
on the contrary, he throve on hard knocks, he was now
determined to try more direct and desperate methods.

One day, soon after Nur Mahomed had entered the
bodyguard, he was selected to be one of the soldiers told
off to escort the king through the city. The procession
was marching on quite smoothly, when a man, armed
with a dagger, rushed out of an alley straight towards the
king. Nur Mahomed, who was the nearest of the guards,
threw himself in the way, and received the stab that had
been apparently intended for the king. Luckily the blow
was a hurried one, and the dagger glanced on his breast-
bone, so that, although he received a severe wound, his
youth and strength quickly got the better of it. The
king was, of course, obliged to take some notice of this
brave deed, and as a reward made him one of his own
attendants.

After this the strange adventures the young man

passed through were endless. Officers of the bodyguard were often sent on all sorts of secret and difficult errands, and such errands had a curious way of becoming necessary when Nur Mahomed was on duty. Once, while he was taking a journey, a foot-bridge gave way under him ; once he was attacked by armed robbers ; a rock rolled down upon him in a mountain pass ; a heavy stone coping fell from a roof at his feet in a narrow city alley. Altogether, Nur Mahomed began to think that, somewhere or other, he had made an enemy ; but he was light-hearted, and the thought did not much trouble him. He escaped somehow every time, and felt amused rather than anxious about the next adventure.

It was the custom of that city that the officer for the day of the palace guards should receive all his food direct from the king's kitchen. One day, when Nur Mahomed's turn came to be on duty, he was just sitting down to a delicious stew that had been sent in from the palace, when one of those gaunt, hungry dogs, which, in eastern countries, run about the streets, poked his nose in at the open guard-room door, and looked at Nur Mahomed with mouth watering and nostrils working. The kind-hearted young man picked out a lump of meat, went to the door, and threw it outside to him. The dog pounced upon it, and gulped it down greedily, and was just turning to go, when it staggered, fell, rolled over, and died. Nur Mahomed, who had been lazily watching him, stood still for a moment, then he came back whistling softly. He gathered up the rest of his dinner and carefully wrapped it up to carry away and bury somewhere ; and then he sent back the empty plates.

How furious the king was when, at the next morning's durbar, Nur Mahomed appeared before him fresh, alert, and smiling as usual. He was determined, however, to try once more, and bidding the young man come into his presence that evening, gave orders that he was to carry a secret despatch to the governor of a distant province.

' Make your preparations at once,' added he, ' and be ready to start in the morning. I myself will deliver you the papers at the last moment.'

Now this province was four or five days' journey from the palace, and the governor of it was the most faithful servant the king had. He could be silent as the grave, and prided himself on his obedience. Whilst he was an old and tried servant of the king's, his wife had been almost a mother to the young princess ever since the queen had died some years before. It happened that, a little before this time, the princess had been sent away for her health to another remote province ; and whilst she was there her old friend, the governor's wife, had begged her to come and stay with them as soon as she could.

The princess accepted gladly, and was actually staying in the governor's house at the very time when the king made up his mind to send Nur Mahomed there with the mysterious despatch.

According to orders Nur Mahomed presented himself early the next morning at the king's private apartments. His best horse was saddled, food placed in his saddle-bag, and with some money tied up in his waist-band, he was ready to start. The king handed over to him a sealed packet, desiring him to give it himself only into the hands of the governor, and to no one else. Nur Mahomed hid it carefully in his turban, swung himself into the saddle, and five minutes later rode out of the city gates, and set out on his long journey.

The weather was very hot ; but Nur Mahomed thought that the sooner his precious letter was delivered the better ; so that, by dint of riding most of each night and resting only in the hottest part of the day, he found himself, by noon on the third day, approaching the town which was his final destination.

Not a soul was to be seen anywhere ; and Nur Mahomed, stiff, dry, thirsty, and tired, looked longingly over the wall into the gardens, and marked the fountains, the green grass, the shady apricot orchards, and giant mulberry trees, and wished he were there.

At length he reached the castle gates, and was at once admitted, as he was in the uniform of the king's body-guard. The governor was resting, the soldier said, and could not see him until the evening. So Nur Mahomed handed over his horse to an attendant, and wandered down into the lovely gardens he had seen from the road, and sat down in the shade to rest himself. He flung himself on his back and watched the birds twittering and chattering in the trees above him. Through the branches he could see great patches of sky where the kites wheeled and circled incessantly, with shrill whistling cries. Bees buzzed over the flowers with a soothing sound, and in a few minutes Nur Mahomed was fast asleep.

Every day, through the heat of the afternoon, the governor, and his wife also, used to lie down for two or three hours in their own rooms, and so, for the matter of that, did most people in the palace. But the princess, like many other girls, was restless, and preferred to wander about the garden, rather than rest on a pile of soft cushions. What a torment her stout old attendants and servants sometimes thought her when she insisted on staying awake, and making them chatter or do something, when they could hardly keep their eyes open! Some-times, however, the princess would pretend to go to sleep, and then, after all her women had gladly followed her example, she would get up and go out by herself, her veil hanging loosely about her. If she was discovered her old hostess scolded her severely; but the princess only laughed, and did the same thing next time.

This very afternoon the princess had left all her women asleep, and, after trying in vain to amuse herself indoors, she had slipped out into the great garden, and rambled about in all her favourite nooks and corners, feeling quite safe as there was not a creature to be seen.

Suddenly, on turning a corner, she stopped in surprise, for before her lay a man fast asleep! In her hurry she

The Princess steals the King's letter.

had almost tripped over him. But there he was, a young man, tanned and dusty with travel, in the uniform of an officer of the king's guard. One of the few faults of this lovely princess was a devouring curiosity, and she lived such an idle life that she had plenty of time to be curious. Out of one of the folds of this young man's turban there peeped the corner of a letter! She wondered what the letter was—whom it was for! She drew her veil a little closer, and stole across on tip-toe and caught hold of the corner of the letter. Then she pulled it a little, and just a little more! A great big seal came into view, which she saw to be her father's, and at the sight of it she paused for a minute half ashamed of what she was doing. But the pleasure of taking a letter which was not meant for her was more than she could resist, and in another moment it was in her hand. All at once she remembered that it would be death to this poor officer if he lost the letter, and that at all hazards she must put it back again. But this was not so easy; and, more-over, the letter in her hand burnt her with longing to read it, and see what was inside. She examined the seal. It was sticky with being exposed to the hot sun, and with a very little effort it parted from the paper. The letter was open and she read it! And this was what was written :

'Behead the messenger who brings this letter secretly and at once. Ask no questions.'

The girl grew pale. What a shame! she thought. *She* would not let a handsome young fellow like that be beheaded ; but how to prevent it was not quite clear at the moment. Some plan must be invented, and she wished to lock herself in where no one could interrupt her, as might easily happen in the garden. So she crept softly to her room, and took a piece of paper and wrote upon it : 'Marry the messenger who brings this letter to the princess openly at once. Ask no questions.' And even contrived to work the seals off the original letter and to fix them to this, so that no one could tell, unless they examined it closely, that it had ever been opened. Then she slipped back, shaking with fear and excitement, to where the young officer still lay asleep, thrust the letter into the folds of his turban, and hurried back to her room. It was done!

Late in the afternoon Nur Mahomed woke, and, making sure that the precious despatch was still safe, went off to get ready for his audience with the governor. As soon as he was ushered into his presence he took the letter from his turban and placed it in the governor's hands according to orders. When he had read it the governor was certainly a little astonished; but he was told in the letter to 'ask no questions,' and he knew how to obey orders. He sent for his wife and told her to get the princess ready to be married at once.

'Nonsense!' said his wife, 'what in the world do you mean?'

'These are the king's commands,' he answered; 'go and do as I bid you. The letter says "at once," and "ask no questions." The marriage, therefore, must take place this evening.'

In vain did his wife urge every objection; the more she argued, the more determined was her husband. 'I know how to obey orders,' he said, 'and these are as plain as the nose on my face!' So the princess was summoned, and, somewhat to their surprise, she seemed to take the news very calmly; next Nur Mahomed was informed, and he was greatly startled, but of course he could but be delighted at the great and unexpected honour which he thought the king had done him. Then all the castle was turned upside down; and when the news spread in the town, *that* was turned upside down too. Everybody ran everywhere, and tried to do everything at once; and, in the middle of it all, the old governor went about with his hair standing on end, muttering something about 'obeying orders.'

And so the marriage was celebrated, and there was a great feast in the castle, and another in the soldiers' barracks, and illuminations all over the town and in the beautiful gardens. And all the people declared that such a wonderful sight had never been seen, and talked about it to the ends of their lives.

The next day the governor despatched the princess and her bridegroom to the king, with a troop of horsemen, splendidly dressed, and he sent a mounted messenger on before them, with a letter giving the account of the marriage to the king.

When the king got the governor's letter, he grew so red in the face that everyone thought he was going to have apoplexy. They were all very anxious to know what had happened, but he rushed off and locked himself into a room, where he ramped and raved until he was tired. Then, after awhile, he began to think he had better make the best of it, especially as the old governor had been clever enough to send him back his letter, and the king was pretty sure that this was in the princess's handwriting. He was fond of his daughter, and though she had behaved so badly, he did not wish to cut *her* head off, and he did not want people to know the truth because it would make him look foolish. In fact, the more he considered the matter, the more he felt that he would be wise to put a good face on it, and to let people suppose that he had really brought about the marriage of his own free will.

So, when the young couple arrived, the king received them with all state, and gave his son-in-law a province to govern. Nur Mahomed soon proved himself as able and honourable a governor as he was a brave soldier; and, when the old king died, he became king in his place, and reigned long and happily.

Nur Mahomed's old mother lived for a long time in her 'son's' palace, and died in peace. The princess, his wife, although she had got her husband by a trick, found that she could not trick *him*, and so she never tried, but busied herself in teaching her children and scolding her maids. As for the old hermit, no trace of him was ever discovered; but the cave is there, and the leaves lie thick in front of it unto this day.

[Told the writer by an Indian.]

STORY OF WALI DÂD THE SIMPLE-HEARTED

ONCE upon a time there lived a poor old man whose name was Wali Dâd Gunjay, or Wali Dâd the Bald. He had no relations, but lived all by himself in a little mud hut some distance from any town, and made his living by cutting grass in the jungle, and selling it as fodder for horses. He only earned by this five halfpence a day; but he was a simple old man, and needed so little out of it, that he saved up one halfpenny daily, and spent the rest upon such food and clothing as he required.

In this way he lived for many years until, one night, he thought that he would count the money he had hidden away in the great earthen pot under the floor of his hut. So he set to work, and with much trouble he pulled the bag out on to the floor, and sat gazing in astonishment at the heap of coins which tumbled out of it. What should he do with them all? he wondered. But he never thought of spending the money on himself, because he was content to pass the rest of his days as he had been doing for ever so long, and he really had no desire for any greater comfort or luxury.

At last he threw all the money into an old sack, which he pushed under his bed, and then, rolled in his ragged old blanket, he went off to sleep.

Early next morning he staggered off with his sack of money to the shop of a jeweller, whom he knew in the town, and bargained with him for a beautiful little gold bracelet. With this carefully wrapped up in his cotton waistband he went to the house of a rich friend, who was a travelling merchant, and used to wander about with his camels and merchandise through many countries. Wali Dâd was lucky enough to find him at home, so he sat down, and after a little talk he asked the merchant who was the most virtuous and beautiful lady he had ever met with. The merchant replied that the princess of Khaistân was renowned everywhere as well for the beauty of her person as for the kindness and generosity of her disposition.

'Then,' said Wali Dâd, 'next time you go that way, give her this little bracelet, with the respectful compliments of one who admires virtue far more than he desires wealth.'

With that he pulled the bracelet from his waistband, and handed it to his friend. The merchant was naturally much astonished, but said nothing, and made no objection to carrying out his friend's plan.

Time passed by, and at length the merchant arrived in the course of his travels at the capital of Khaistân. As soon as he had opportunity he presented himself at the palace, and sent in the bracelet, neatly packed in a little perfumed box provided by himself, giving at the same time the message entrusted to him by Wali Dâd.

The princess could not think who could have bestowed this present on her, but she bade her servant to tell the merchant that if he would return, after he had finished his business in the city, she would give him her reply. In a few days, therefore, the merchant came back, and received from the princess a return present in the shape of a camel-load of rich silks, besides a present of money for himself. With these he set out on his journey.

Some months later he got home again from his journeyings, and proceeded to take Wali Dâd the princess's present. Great was the perplexity of the good man to find a camel-load of silks tumbled at his door!

What was he to do with these costly things? But, presently, after much thought, he begged the merchant to consider whether he did not know of some young prince to whom such treasures might be useful.

'Of course,' cried the merchant, greatly amused; 'from Delhi to Baghdad, and from Constantinople to Lucknow, I know them all; and there lives none worthier than the gallant and wealthy young prince of Nekabad.'

'Very well, then, take the silks to him, with the blessing of an old man,' said Wali Dâd, much relieved to be rid of them.

So, the next time that the merchant journeyed that way he carried the silks with him, and in due course arrived at Nekabad, and sought an audience of the prince. When he was shown into his presence he produced the beautiful gift of silks that Wali Dâd had sent, and begged the young man to accept them as a humble tribute to his worth and greatness. The prince was much touched by the generosity of the giver, and ordered, as a return present, twelve of the finest breed of horses for which his country was famous to be delivered over to the merchant, to whom also, before he took his leave, he gave a munificent reward for his services.

As before, the merchant at last arrived at home; and next day, he set out for Wali Dâd's house with the twelve horses. When the old man saw them coming in the distance he said to himself: 'Here's luck! a troop of horses coming! They are sure to want quantities of grass, and I shall sell all I have without having to drag it to market.' Thereupon he rushed off and cut grass as fast as he could. When he got back, with as much grass as he could possibly carry, he was greatly discomfited to find that the horses were all for himself. At first he could not think what to do with them, but, after a little, a brilliant idea struck him! He gave two to the merchant, and begged him to take the rest to the princess of Khaistân, who was clearly the fittest person to possess such beautiful animals.

The merchant departed, laughing. But, true to his old friend's request, he took the horses with him on his next journey, and eventually presented them safely to the princess. This time the princess sent for the merchant, and questioned him about the giver. Now, the merchant was usually a most honest man, but he did not quite like to describe Wali Dâd in his true light as an old man whose income was five halfpence a day, and who had hardly clothes to cover him. So he told her that his friend had heard stories of her beauty and goodness, and had longed to lay the best he had at her feet. The princess then took her father into her confidence, and begged him to advise her what courtesy she might return to one who persisted in making her such presents.

' Well,' said the king, ' you cannot refuse them ; so the best thing you can do is to send this unknown friend at once a present so magnificent that he is not likely to be able to send you anything better, and so will be ashamed to send anything at all ! ' Then he ordered that, in place of each of the ten horses, two mules laden with silver should be returned by her.

Thus, in a few hours, the merchant found himself in charge of a splendid caravan ; and he had to hire a number of armed men to defend it on the road against the robbers, and he was glad indeed to find himself back again in Wali Dâd's hut.

' Well, now,' cried Wali Dâd, as he viewed all the wealth laid at his door, ' I can well repay that kind prince for his magnificent present of horses ; but to be sure you have been put to great expense ! Still, if you will accept six mules and their loads, and will take the rest straight to Nekabad, I shall thank you heartily.'

The merchant felt handsomely repaid for his trouble, and wondered greatly how the matter would turn out. So he made no difficulty about it ; and as soon as he could get things ready, he set out for Nekabad with this new and princely gift.

This time the prince, too, was embarrassed, and questioned the merchant closely. The merchant felt that his credit was at stake, and whilst inwardly determining that he would not carry the joke any further, could not help describing Wali Dâd in such glowing terms that the old man would never have known himself had he heard them. The prince, like the king of Khaistân, determined that he would send in return a gift that would be truly royal, and which would perhaps prevent the unknown giver sending him anything more. So he made up a caravan of twenty splendid horses caparisoned in gold embroidered cloths, with fine morocco saddles and silver bridles and stirrups, also twenty camels of the best breed, which had the speed of race-horses, and could swing along at a trot all day without getting tired ; and, lastly, twenty elephants, with magnificent silver howdahs and coverings of silk embroidered with pearls. To take care of these animals the merchant hired a little army of men ; and the troop made a great show as they travelled along.

When Wali Dâd from a distance saw the cloud of dust which the caravan made, and the glitter of its appointments, he said to himself : ' By Allah ! here's a grand crowd coming ! Elephants, too ! Grass will be selling well to-day ! ' And with that he hurried off to the jungle and cut grass as fast as he could. As soon as he got back he found the caravan had stopped at his door, and the merchant was waiting, a little anxiously, to tell him the news and to congratulate him upon his riches.

' Riches ! ' cried Wali Dâd, ' what has an old man like me with one foot in the grave to do with riches ? That beautiful young princess, now ! She'd be the one to enjoy all these fine things ! Do you take for yourself two horses, two camels, and two elephants, with all their trappings, and present the rest to her.'

The merchant at first objected to these remarks, and

pointed out to Wali Dâd that he was beginning to feel
these embassies a little awkward. Of course he was himself richly repaid, so far as expenses went ; but still he did
not like going so often, and he was getting nervous. At
length, however, he consented to go once more, but he
promised himself never to embark on another such enterprise.

So, after a few days' rest, the caravan started off once
more for Khaistân.

The moment the king of Khaistân saw the gorgeous
train of men and beasts entering his palace courtyard, he
was so amazed that he hurried down in person to inquire
about it, and became dumb when he heard that these also
were a present from the princely Wali Dâd, and were for
the princess, his daughter. He went hastily off to her
apartments, and said to her : ' I tell you what it is, my
dear, this man wants to marry you ; that is the meaning
of all these presents ! There is nothing for it but that we
go and pay him a visit in person. He must be a man of
immense wealth, and as he is so devoted to you, perhaps
you might do worse than marry him ! '

The princess agreed with all that her father said, and
orders were issued for vast numbers of elephants and
camels, and gorgeous tents and flags, and litters for the
ladies, and horses for the men, to be prepared without
delay, as the king and princess were going to pay a visit
to the great and munificent prince Wali Dâd. The
merchant, the king declared, was to guide the party.

The feelings of the poor merchant in this sore dilemma
can hardly be imagined. Willingly would he have run
away ; but he was treated with so much hospitality as
Wali Dâd's representative, that he hardly got an instant's
real peace, and never any opportunity of slipping away.
In fact, after a few days, despair possessed him to such a
degree that he made up his mind that all that happened
was fate, and that escape was impossible ; but he hoped
devoutly some turn of fortune would reveal to him a

way out of the difficulties which he had, with the best intentions, drawn upon himself.

On the seventh day they all started, amidst thunderous salutes from the ramparts of the city, and much dust, and cheering, and blaring of trumpets.

Day after day they moved on, and every day the poor merchant felt more ill and miserable. He wondered what kind of death the king would invent for him, and went through almost as much torture, as he lay awake nearly the whole of every night thinking over the situation, as he would have suffered if the king's executioners were already setting to work upon his neck.

At last they were only one day's march from Wali Dâd's little mud home. Here a great encampment was made, and the merchant was sent on to tell Wali Dâd that the King and Princess of Khaistân had arrived and were seeking an interview. When the merchant arrived he found the poor old man eating his evening meal of onions and dry bread, and when he told him of all that had happened he had not the heart to proceed to load him with the reproaches which rose to his tongue. For Wali Dâd was overwhelmed with grief and shame for himself, for his friend, and for the name and honour of the princess; and he wept and plucked at his beard, and groaned most piteously. With tears he begged the merchant to detain them for one day by any kind of excuse he could think of, and to come in the morning to discuss what they should do.

As soon as the merchant was gone Wali Dâd made up his mind that there was only one honourable way out of the shame and distress that he had created by his foolishness, and that was—to kill himself. So, without stopping to ask any one's advice, he went off in the middle of the night to a place where the river wound along at the base of steep rocky cliffs of great height, and determined to throw himself down and put an end to his life. When he got to the place he drew back a few paces, took a little run, and at the very edge of that dreadful black gulf he stopped short! He *could* not do it!

From below, unseen in the blackness of the deep night shadows, the water roared and boiled round the jagged rocks—he could picture the place as he knew it, only ten times more pitiless and forbidding in the visionless dark-ness ; the wind soughed through the gorge with fearsome sighs, and rustlings and whisperings, and the bushes and grasses that grew in the ledges of the cliffs seemed to him like living creatures that danced and beckoned, shadowy and indistinct. An owl laughed 'Hoo ! hoo !' almost in his face, as he peered over the edge of the gulf, and the old man threw himself back in a perspiration of horror. He was afraid ! He drew back shuddering, and covering his face in his hands he wept aloud.

Presently he was aware of a gentle radiance that shed itself before him.   Surely morning was not already coming to hasten and reveal his disgrace! He took his hands from before his face, and saw before him two lovely beings whom his instinct told him were not mortal, but were Peris from Paradise.

'Why do you weep, old man?' said one, in a voice as clear and musical as that of the bulbul.

'I weep for shame,' replied he.

'What do you here?' questioned the other.

'I came here to die,' said Wali Dâd. And as they questioned him, he confessed all his story.

Then the first stepped forward and laid a hand upon his shoulder, and Wali Dâd began to feel that something strange—what, he did not know—was happening to him. His old cotton rags of clothes were changed to beautiful linen and embroidered cloth ; on his hard, bare feet were warm, soft shoes, and on his head a great jewelled turban. Round his neck there lay a heavy golden chain, and the little old bent sickle, which he cut grass with, and which hung in his waistband, had turned into a gorgeous

WALI DAD AND THE PERIS

scimetar, whose ivory hilt gleamed in the pale light like snow in moonlight. As he stood wondering, like a man in a dream, the other peri waved her hand and bade him turn and see; and, lo! before him a noble gateway stood open. And up an avenue of giant plane trees the peris led him, dumb with amazement. At the end of the avenue, on the very spot where his hut had stood, a gorgeous palace appeared, ablaze with myriads of lights. Its great porticoes and verandahs were occupied by hurrying servants, and guards paced to and fro and saluted him respectfully as he drew near, along mossy walks and through sweeping grassy lawns where fountains were playing and flowers scented the air. Wali Dâd stood stunned and helpless.

'Fear not,' said one of the peris; 'go to your house, and learn that God rewards the simple-hearted.'

With these words they both disappeared and left him. He walked on, thinking still that he must be dreaming. Very soon he retired to rest in a splendid room, far grander than anything he had ever dreamed of.

When morning dawned he woke, and found that the palace, and himself, and his servants were all real, and that he was not dreaming after all!

If he was dumbfounded, the merchant, who was ushered into his presence soon after sunrise, was much more so. He told Wali Dâd that he had not slept all night, and by the first streak of daylight had started to seek out his friend. And what a search he had had! A great stretch of wild jungle country had, in the night, been changed into parks and gardens; and if it had not been for some of Wali Dâd's new servants, who found him and brought him to the palace, he would have fled away under the impression that his trouble had sent him crazy, and that all he saw was only imagination.

Then Wali Dâd told the merchant all that had happened. By his advice he sent an invitation to the king and princess of Khaistân to come and be his guests, together with all their retinue and servants, down to the very humblest in the camp.

For three nights and days a great feast was held in honour of the royal guests. Every evening the king and his nobles were served on golden plates and from golden cups ; and the smaller people on silver plates and from silver cups ; and each evening each guest was requested to keep the plates and cups that they had used as a remembrance of the occasion. Never had anything so splendid been seen. Besides the great dinners, there were sports and hunting, and dances, and amusements of all sorts.

On the fourth day the king of Khaistân took his host aside, and asked him whether it was true, as he had suspected, that he wished to marry his daughter. But Wali Dâd, after thanking him very much for the compliment, said that he had never dreamed of so great an honour, and that he was far too old and ugly for so fair a lady ; but he begged the king to stay with him until he could send for the Prince of Nekabad, who was a most excellent, brave, and honourable young man, and would surely be delighted to try to win the hand of the beautiful princess.

To this the king agreed, and Wali Dâd sent the merchant to Nekabad, with a number of attendants, and with such handsome presents that the prince came at once, fell head over ears in love with the princess, and married her at Wali Dâd's palace amidst a fresh outburst of rejoicings.

And now the King of Khaistân and the Prince and Princess of Nekabad, each went back to their own country; and Wali Dâd lived to a good old age, befriending all who were in trouble, and preserving, in his prosperity, the simple-hearted and generous nature that he had when he was only Wali Dâd Gunjay, the grass cutter.

[Told the author by an Indian.]

TALE OF A TORTOISE AND OF A
MISCHIEVOUS MONKEY

ONCE upon a time there was a country where the rivers were larger, and the forests deeper, than anywhere else. Hardly any men came there, and the wild creatures had it all to themselves, and used to play all sorts of strange games with each other. The great trees, chained one to the other by thick flowering plants with bright scarlet or yellow blossoms, were famous hiding-places for the monkeys, who could wait unseen, till a puma or an elephant passed by, and then jump on their backs and go for a ride, swinging themselves up by the creepers when they had had enough. Near the rivers huge tortoises were to be found, and though to our eyes a tortoise seems a dull, slow thing, it is wonderful to think how clever they were, and how often they outwitted many of their livelier friends.

There was one tortoise in particular that always managed to get the better of everybody, and many were the tales told in the forest of his great deeds. They began when he was quite young, and tired of staying at home with his father and mother. He left them one day, and walked off in search of adventures. In a wide open space surrounded by trees he met with an elephant, who was having his supper before taking his evening bath in the river which ran close by. 'Let us see which of us two is strongest,' said the young tortoise, marching up to the elephant. 'Very well,' replied the elephant, much amused at the impertinence of the little creature ; ' when would you like the trial to be ? '

' In an hour's time ; I have some business to do first,' answered the tortoise. And he hastened away as fast as his short legs would carry him.

In a pool of the river a whale was resting, blowing water into the air and making a lovely fountain. The tortoise, however, was too young and too busy to admire such things, and he called to the whale to stop, as he wanted to speak to him. ' Would you like to try which of us is the stronger ? ' said he. The whale looked at him, sent up another fountain, and answered : ' Oh, yes ; certainly. When do you wish to begin ? I am quite ready.'

' Then give me one of your longest bones, and I will fasten it to my leg. When I give the signal, you must pull, and we will see which can pull the hardest.'

' Very good,' replied the whale ; and he took out one of his bones and passed it to the tortoise.

The tortoise picked up the end of the bone in his mouth and went back to the elephant. ' I will fasten this to your leg,' said he, ' in the same way as it is fastened to mine, and we must both pull as hard as we can. We shall soon see which is the stronger.' So he wound it carefully round the elephant's leg, and tied it in a firm knot. ' Now ! ' cried he, plunging into a thick bush behind him.

The whale tugged at one end, and the elephant tugged at the other, and neither had any idea that he had not the tortoise for his foe. When the whale pulled hardest the elephant was dragged into the water ; and when the elephant pulled the hardest the whale was hauled on to the land. They were very evenly matched, and the battle was a hard one.

At last they were quite tired, and the tortoise, who was watching, saw that they could play no more. So he crept from his hiding-place, and dipping himself in the river, he went to the elephant and said : ' I see that you

really are stronger than I thought. Suppose we give it
up for to-day ? ' Then he dried himself on some moss and
went to the whale and said : ' I see that you really are
stronger than I thought. Suppose we give it up for to-
day ? '

The two adversaries were only too glad to be allowed
to rest, and believed to the end of their days that, after all,
the tortoise was stronger than either of them.

A day or two later the young tortoise was taking a
stroll, when he met a fox, and stopped to speak to him.
' Let us try,' said he in a careless manner, ' which of us
can lie buried in the ground during seven years.'

' I shall be delighted,' answered the fox, ' only I would
rather that you began.'

' It is all the same to me,' replied the tortoise ; ' if you
come round this way to-morrow you will see that I have
fulfilled my part of the bargain.'

So he looked about for a suitable place, and found a
convenient hole at the foot of an orange tree. He crept
into it, and the next morning the fox heaped up the earth
round him, and promised to feed him every day with fresh
fruit. The fox so far kept his word that each morning
when the sun rose he appeared to ask how the tortoise
was getting on. ' Oh, very well ; but I wish you would
give me some fruit,' replied he.

' Alas ! the fruit is not ripe enough yet for you to eat,'
answered the fox, who hoped that the tortoise would die
of hunger long before the seven years were over.

' Oh dear, oh dear ! I am so hungry ! ' cried the tortoise.

I am sure you must be ; but it will be all right to-
morrow,' said the fox, trotting off, not knowing that the
oranges dropped down the hollow trunk, straight into
the tortoise's hole, and that he had as many as he could
possibly eat.

So the seven years went by ; and when the tortoise
came out of his hole he was as fat as ever.

Now it was the fox's turn, and he chose his hole, and

the tortoise heaped the earth round, promising to return
every day or two with a nice young bird for his dinner.
' Well, how are you getting on ? ' he would ask cheerfully
when he paid his visits.

' Oh, all right; only I wish you had brought a bird with
you,' answered the fox.

' I have been so unlucky, I have never been able to
catch one,' replied the tortoise. ' However, I shall be
more fortunate to-morrow, I am sure.'

But not many to-morrows after, when the tortoise
arrived with his usual question : ' Well, how are you
getting on ? ' he received no answer, for the fox was lying
in his hole quite still, dead of hunger.

By this time the tortoise was grown up, and was
looked up to throughout the forest as a person to be
feared for his strength and wisdom. But he was not
considered a very swift runner, until an adventure with a
deer added to his fame.

One day, when he was basking in the sun, a stag
passed by, and stopped for a little conversation. ' Would
you care to see which of us can run fastest ? ' asked
the tortoise, after some talk. The stag thought the question so silly that he only shrugged his shoulders. ' Of
course, the victor would have the right to kill the other,'
went on the tortoise. ' Oh, on that condition I agree,'
answered the deer; 'but I am afraid you are a dead man.'

' It is no use trying to frighten me,' replied the tortoise. ' But I should like three days for training ; then I
shall be ready to start when the sun strikes on the big
tree at the edge of the great clearing.'

The first thing the tortoise did was to call his brothers
and his cousins together, and he posted them carefully
under ferns all along the line of the great clearing, making a sort of ladder which stretched for many miles.
This done to his satisfaction, he went back to the start-
ing place.

The stag was quite punctual, and as soon as the sun's

rays struck the trunk of the tree the stag started off, and was soon far out of the sight of the tortoise. Every now and then he would turn his head as he ran, and call out: ' How are you getting on? ' and the tortoise who happened to be nearest at that moment would answer: ' All right, I am close up to you.'

Full of astonishment, the stag would redouble his efforts, but it was no use. Each time he asked : ' Are you there? ' the answer would come : ' Yes, of course, where else should I be? ' And the stag ran, and ran, and ran, till he could run no more, and dropped down dead on the grass.

And the tortoise, when he thinks about it, laughs still.

But the tortoise was not the only creature of whose tricks stories were told in the forest. There was a famous monkey who was just as clever and more mischievous, because he was so much quicker on his feet and with his hands. It was quite impossible to catch him and give him the thrashing he so often deserved, for he just swung himself up into a tree and laughed at the angry victim who was sitting below. Sometimes, however, the inhabitants of the forest were so foolish as to provoke him, and then they got the worst of it. This was what happened to the barber, whom the monkey visited one morning, saying that he wished to be shaved. The barber bowed politely to his customer, and begging him to be seated, tied a large cloth round his neck, and rubbed his chin with soap ; but instead of cutting off his beard, the barber made a snip at the end of his tail. It was only a very little bit, and the monkey started up more in rage than in pain. ' Give me back the end of my tail,' he roared, ' or I will take one of your razors.' The barber refused to give back the missing piece, so the monkey caught up a razor from the table and ran away with it, and no one in the forest could be shaved for days, as there was not another to be got for miles and miles.

As he was making his way to his own particular palm-tree, where the cocoanuts grew, which were so useful for pelting passers-by, he met a woman who was scaling a fish with a bit of wood, for in this side of the forest a few people lived in huts near the river.

' That must be hard work,' said the monkey, stopping to look ; ' try my knife—you will get on quicker.' And he handed her the razor as he spoke. A few days later he came back and rapped at the door of the hut. ' I have called for my razor,' he said, when the woman appeared.

' I have lost it,' answered she.

' If you don't give it to me at once I will take your sardine,' replied the monkey, who did not believe her. The woman protested she had not got the knife, so he took the sardine and ran off.

A little further along he saw a baker who was standing at the door, eating one of his loaves. ' That must be rather dry,' said the monkey, ' try my fish ' ; and the man did not need twice telling. A few days later the monkey stopped again at the baker's hut. ' I've called for that fish,' he said.

' That fish ? But I have eaten it ! ' exclaimed the baker in dismay.

' If you have eaten it I shall take this barrel of meal in exchange,' replied the monkey ; and he walked off with the barrel under his arm.

As he went he saw a woman with a group of little girls round her, teaching them how to dress hair. ' Here is something to make cakes for the children,' he said, putting down his barrel, which by this time he found rather heavy. The children were delighted, and ran directly to find some flat stones to bake their cakes on, and when they had made and eaten them, they thought they had never tasted anything so nice. Indeed, when they saw the monkey approaching not long after, they rushed to meet him, hoping that he was bringing them some more presents. But he took no notice of their questions, he only said to their mother : ' I've called for my barrel of meal.'

' Why, you gave it to me to make cakes of ! ' cried the mother.

' If I can't get my barrel of meal, I shall take one of your children,' answered the monkey. ' I am in want of somebody who can bake me bread when I am tired of fruit, and who knows how to make cocoanut cakes.'

' Oh, leave me my child, and I will find you another barrel of meal,' wept the mother.

' I don't *want* another barrel, I want *that* one,' answered the monkey sternly. And as the woman stood wringing her hands, he caught up the little girl that he thought the prettiest and took her to his home in the palm tree.

She never went back to the hut, but on the whole she was not much to be pitied, for monkeys are nearly as good as children to play with, and they taught her how to swing, and to climb, and to fly from tree to tree, and everything else they knew, which was a great deal.

Now the monkey's tiresome tricks had made him many enemies in the forest, but no one hated him so much as the puma. The cause of their quarrel was known only to themselves, but everybody was aware of the fact, and took care to be out of the way when there was any chance of these two meeting. Often and often the puma had laid traps for the monkey, which he felt sure his foe could not escape ; and the monkey would pretend that he saw nothing, and rejoice the hidden puma's heart by seeming to walk straight into the snare, when, lo ! a loud laugh would be heard, and the monkey's grinning face would peer out of a mass of creepers and disappear before his foe could reach him.

This state of things had gone on for quite a long while, when at last there came a season such as the oldest parrot in the forest could never remember. Instead of two or three hundred inches of rain falling, which they were all accustomed to, month after month passed without a cloud, and the rivers and springs dried up, till there was only one small pool left for everyone to drink from. There was not an animal for miles round that did not grieve over this shocking condition of affairs, not one at least except the puma. His only thought for years had been how to get the monkey into his power, and this time he imagined his chance had really arrived. He would hide himself in a thicket, and when the monkey came down to drink—and come he must—the puma would spring out and seize him. Yes, on this occasion there could be no escape !

And no more there would have been if the puma had had greater patience; but in his excitement he moved a little too soon. The monkey, who was stooping to drink, heard a rustling, and turning caught the gleam of two yellow, murderous eyes. With a mighty spring he grasped a creeper which was hanging above him, and landed himself on the branch of a tree ; feeling the breath of the puma on his feet as the animal bounded from his cover. Never had the monkey been so near death, and it was some time before he recovered enough courage to venture on the ground again.

Up there in the shelter of the trees, he began to turn over in his head plans for escaping the snares of the puma. And at length chance helped him. Peeping down to the earth, he saw a man coming along the path carrying on his head a large gourd filled with honey.

He waited till the man was just underneath the tree, then he hung from a bough, and caught the gourd while the man looked up wondering, for he was no tree-climber. Then the monkey rubbed the honey all over him, and a quantity of leaves from a creeper that was hanging close by; he stuck them all close together into the honey, so that he looked like a walking bush. This finished, he ran to the pool to see the result, and, quite pleased with himself, set out in search of adventures.

Soon the report went through the forest that a new animal had appeared from no one knew where, and that when somebody had asked his name, the strange creature had answered that it was Jack-in-the-Green. Thanks to this, the monkey was allowed to drink at the pool as often as he liked, for neither beast nor bird had the faintest notion who he was. And if they made any inquiries the only answer they got was that the water of which he had drunk deeply had turned his hair into leaves, so that they all knew what would happen in case they became too greedy.

By-and-by the great rains began again. The rivers and streams filled up, and there was no need for him to go back to the pool, near the home of his enemy, the puma, as there was a large number of places for him to choose from. So one night, when everything was still and silent, and even the chattering parrots were asleep on one leg, the monkey stole down softly from his perch, and washed off the honey and the leaves, and came out from his bath in his own proper skin. On his way to breakfast he met a rabbit, and stopped for a little talk.

'I am feeling rather dull,' he remarked; 'I think it would do me good to hunt a while. What do you say?'

'Oh, I am quite willing,' answered the rabbit, proud of being spoken to by such a large creature. 'But the question is, what shall we hunt?'

'There is no credit in going after an elephant or a tiger,' replied the monkey stroking his chin, 'they are so big they could not possibly get out of your way. It shows much more skill to be able to catch a small thing that can hide itself in a moment behind a leaf. I'll tell you what! Suppose I hunt butterflies, and you, serpents.'

The rabbit, who was young and without experience, was delighted with this idea, and they both set out on their various ways.

The monkey quietly climbed up the nearest tree, and ate fruit most of the day, but the rabbit tired himself to death poking his nose into every heap of dried leaves he saw, hoping to find a serpent among them. Luckily for himself the serpents were all away for the afternoon, at a meeting of their own, for there is nothing a serpent likes so well for dinner as a nice plump rabbit. But, as it was, the dried leaves were all empty, and the rabbit at last fell asleep where he was. Then the monkey, who had been watching him, fell down and pulled his ears, to the rage of the rabbit, who vowed vengeance.

It was not easy to catch the monkey off his guard, and the rabbit waited long before an opportunity arrived. But one day Jack-in-the-Green was sitting on a stone, wondering what he should do next, when the rabbit crept softly behind him, and gave his tail a sharp pull. The monkey gave a shriek of pain, and darted up into a tree, but when he saw that it was only the rabbit who had dared to insult him so, he chattered so fast in his anger, and looked so fierce, that the rabbit fled into the nearest hole, and stayed there for several days, trembling with fright.

Soon after this adventure the monkey went away into another part of the country, right on the outskirts of the forest, where there was a beautiful garden full of oranges hanging ripe from the trees. This garden was a favourite place for birds of all kinds, each hoping to secure an orange for dinner, and in order to frighten the birds away and keep a little fruit for himself, the master had fastened a waxen figure on one of the boughs.

Now the monkey was as fond of oranges as any of the birds, and when he saw a man standing in the tree where the largest and sweetest oranges grew, he spoke to him at once. 'You man,' he said rudely, 'throw me down that big orange up there, or I will throw a stone at you.' The wax figure took no notice of this request, so the monkey, who was easily made angry, picked up a stone, and flung it with all his force. But instead of falling to the ground again, the stone stuck to the soft wax.

At this moment a breeze shook the tree, and the orange on which the monkey had set his heart dropped from the bough. He picked it up and ate it every bit, including the rind, and it was so good he thought he should like another. So he called again to the wax figure to throw him an orange, and as the figure did not move, he hurled another stone, which stuck to the wax as the first had done. Seeing that the man was quite indifferent to stones, the monkey grew more angry still, and climbing the tree hastily, gave the figure a violent kick. But like the two stones his leg remained stuck to the wax, and he was held fast. ' Let me go at once, or I will give you another kick,' he cried, suiting the action to the word, and this time also his foot remained in the grasp of the man. Not knowing what he did, the monkey hit out, first with one hand and then with the other, and when he found that he was literally bound hand and foot, he became so mad with anger and terror that in his struggles he fell to the ground, dragging the figure after him. This freed his hands and feet, but besides the shock of the fall, they had tumbled into a bed of thorns, and he limped away broken and bruised, and groaning loudly; for when monkeys *are* hurt, they take pains that every-body shall know it.

It was a long time before Jack was well enough to go about again ; but when he did, he had an encounter with his old enemy the puma. And this was how it came about.

One day the puma invited his friend the stag to go with him and see a comrade, who was famous for the good milk he got from his cows. The stag loved milk, and gladly accepted the invitation, and when the sun began to get a little low the two started on their walk. On the way they arrived on the banks of a river, and as there were no bridges in those days it was necessary to swim across it. The stag was not fond of swimming, and began to say that he was tired, and thought that after all it was not worth going so far to get milk, and that he would return home. But the puma easily saw through these excuses, and laughed at him.

'The river is not deep at all,' he said ; ' why, you will never be off your feet. Come, pluck up your courage and follow me.'

The stag was afraid of the river ; still, he was much more afraid of being laughed at, and he plunged in after the puma ; but in an instant the current had swept him away, and if it had not borne him by accident to a shallow place on the opposite side, where he managed to scramble up the bank, he would certainly have been drowned. As it was, he scrambled out, shaking with terror, and found the puma waiting for him. ' You had a narrow escape that time,' said the puma.

After resting for a few minutes, to let the stag recover from his fright, they went on their way till they came to a grove of bananas.

'They look very good,' observed the puma with a longing glance, ' and I am sure you must be hungry, friend stag ? Suppose you were to climb the tree and get some. You shall eat the green ones, they are the best and sweetest ; and you can throw the yellow ones down to me. I dare say they will do quite well ! ' The stag did as he was bid, though, not being used to climbing, it gave him a deal of trouble and sore knees, and, besides, his horns were continually getting entangled in the creepers. What was worse, when once he had tasted the bananas, he found them not at all to his liking, so he threw them all down, green and yellow alike, and let the puma take his choice. And what a dinner he made ! When he had *quite* done, they set forth once more.

The path lay through a field of maize, where several men were working. As they came up to them, the puma whispered : ' Go on in front, friend stag, and just say " Bad luck to all workers ! " ' The stag obeyed, but the men were hot and tired, and did not think this a good joke. So they set their dogs at him, and he was obliged to run away as fast as he could.

'I hope your industry will be rewarded as it deserves,' said the puma as he passed along; and the men were pleased, and offered him some of their maize to eat.

By-and-by the puma saw a small snake with a beautiful shining skin, lying coiled up at the foot of a tree. 'What a lovely bracelet that would make for your daughter, friend stag!' said he. The stag stooped and picked up the snake, which bit him, and he turned angrily to the puma. 'Why did you not tell me it would bite?' he asked.

'Is it my fault if you are an idiot?' replied the puma.

At last they reached their journey's end, but by this time it was late, and the puma's comrade was ready for bed, so they slung their hammocks in convenient places, and went to sleep. But in the middle of the night the puma rose softly and stole out of the door to the sheep-fold, where he killed and ate the fattest sheep he could find, and taking a bowl full of its blood, he sprinkled the sleeping stag with it. This done, he returned to bed.

In the morning the shepherd went as usual to let the sheep out of the fold, and found one of them missing. He thought directly of the puma, and ran to accuse him of having eaten the sheep. 'I, my good man? What has put it into your head to think of such a thing? Have *I* got any blood about me? If anyone has eaten a sheep it must be my friend the stag.' Then the shepherd went to examine the sleeping stag, and of course he saw the blood. 'Ah! I will teach you how to steal!' cried he, and he hit the stag such a blow on his skull that he died in a moment. The noise awakened the comrade above, and he came downstairs. The puma greeted him with joy, and begged he might have some of the famous milk as soon as possible, for he was very thirsty. A large bucket was set before the puma directly. He drank it to the last drop, and then took leave.

On his way home he met the monkey. 'Are you fond of milk?' asked he. 'I know a place where you get it very nice. I will show you it if you like.' The monkey knew that the puma was not so good-natured for nothing, but he felt quite able to take care of himself, so he said he should have much pleasure in accompanying his friend.

They soon reached the same river, and, as before, the puma remarked: 'Friend monkey, you will find it very shallow; there is no cause for fear. Jump in, and I will follow.'

'Do you think you have the stag to deal with?' asked the monkey, laughing. 'I should prefer to follow; if not I shall go no further.' The puma understood that it was useless trying to make the monkey do as he wished, so he chose a shallow place and began to swim across. The monkey waited till the puma had got to the middle, then he gave a great spring and jumped on his back, knowing quite well that the puma would be afraid to shake him off, lest he should be swept away into deep water. So in this manner they reached the bank.

The banana grove was not far distant, and here the puma thought he would pay the monkey out for forcing him to carry him over the river. 'Friend monkey, look what fine bananas,' cried he. 'You are fond of climbing; suppose you run up and throw me down a few. You can eat the green ones, which are the nicest, and I will be content with the yellow.'

'Very well,' answered the monkey, swinging himself up; but he ate all the yellow ones himself, and only threw down the green ones that were left. The puma was furious and cried out: 'I will punch your head for that.' But the monkey only answered: 'If you are going to talk such nonsense I won't walk with you.' And the puma was silent.

In a few minutes more they arrived at the field where

the men were reaping the maize, and the puma remarked as he had done before : 'Friend monkey, if you wish to please these men, just say as you go by : " Bad luck to all workers." '

'Very well,' replied the monkey; but, instead, he nodded and smiled, and said : ' I hope your industry may be rewarded as it deserves.' The men thanked him heartily, let him pass on, and the puma followed behind him.

Further along the path they saw the shining snake lying on the moss. 'What a lovely necklace for your daughter,' exclaimed the puma. 'Pick it up and take it with you.'

'You are very kind, but I will leave it for you,' answered the monkey, and nothing more was said about the snake.

Not long after this they reached the comrade's house, and found him just ready to go to bed. So, without stopping to talk, the guests slung their hammocks, the monkey taking care to place his so high that no one could get at him. Besides, he thought it would be more prudent not to fall asleep, so he only lay still and snored loudly. When it was quite dark and no sound was to be heard, the puma crept out to the sheep-fold, killed the sheep, and carried back a bowl full of its blood with which to sprinkle the monkey. But the monkey, who had been watching him out of the corner of his eye, waited until the puma drew near, and with a violent kick upset the bowl all over the puma himself.

When the puma saw what had happened, he turned in a great hurry to leave the house, but before he could do so, he saw the shepherd coming, and hastily lay down again.

'This is the second time I have lost a sheep,' the man said to the monkey ; 'it will be the worse for the thief when I catch him, I can tell you.' The monkey did not answer, but silently pointed to the puma who was pretending to be asleep. The shepherd stooped and saw the blood, and cried out : ' Ah ! so it is you, is it ? then take that ! ' and with his stick he gave the puma such a blow on the head that he died then and there.

Then the monkey got up and went to the dairy, and drank all the milk he could find. Afterwards he returned home and married, and that is the last we heard of him.

[*Adapted from Folk-lore Brésilien.*]

THE KNIGHTS OF THE FISH

ONCE upon a time there lived an old cobbler who worked hard at his trade from morning till night, and scarcely gave himself a moment to eat. But, industrious as he was, he could hardly buy bread and cheese for himself and his wife, and they grew thinner and thinner daily.

For a long while they pretended to each other that they had no appetite, and that a few blackberries from the hedges were a great deal nicer than a good strong bowl of soup. But at length there came a day when the cobbler could bear it no longer, and he threw away his last, and borrowing a rod from a neighbour he went out to fish.

Now the cobbler was as patient about fishing as he had been about cobbling. From dawn to dark he stood on the banks of the little stream, without hooking anything better than an eel, or a few old shoes, that even he, clever though he was, felt were not worth mending. At length his patience began to give way, and as he undressed one night he said to himself: 'Well, I will give it one more chance; and if I don't catch a fish to-morrow, I will go and hang myself.'

He had not cast his line for ten minutes the next morning before he drew from the river the most beautiful fish he had ever seen in his life. But he nearly fell into the water from surprise, when the fish began to speak to him, in a small, squeaky voice:

'Take me back to your hut and cook me; then cut me up, and sprinkle me over with pepper and salt. Give two of the pieces to your wife, and bury two more in the garden.'

The cobbler did not know what to make of these strange words ; but he was wiser than many people, and when he did not understand, he thought it was well to obey. His children wanted to eat all the fish themselves, and begged their father to tell them what to do with the pieces he had put aside ; but the cobbler only laughed, and told them it was no business of theirs. And when they were safe in bed he stole out and buried the two pieces in the garden.

By and by two babies, exactly alike, lay in a cradle, and in the garden were two tall plants, with two brilliant shields on the top.

Years passed away, and the babies were almost men. They were tired of living quietly at home, being mistaken for each other by everybody they saw, and determined to set off in different directions, to seek adventures.

So, one fine morning, the two brothers left the hut, and walked together to the place where the great road divided. There they embraced and parted, promising that if anything remarkable had happened to either, he would return to the cross roads and wait till his brother came.

The youth who took the path that ran eastwards arrived presently at a large city, where he found everybody standing at the doors, wringing their hands and weeping bitterly.

' What is the matter ? ' asked he, pausing and looking round. And a man replied, in a faltering voice, that each year a beautiful girl was chosen by lot to be offered up to a dreadful fiery dragon, who had a mother even worse than himself, and this year the lot had fallen on their peerless princess.

' But where *is* the princess ? ' said the young man once more, and again the man answered him : ' She is standing under a tree, a mile away, waiting for the dragon.'

This time the Knight of the Fish did not stop to hear more, but ran off as fast as he could, and found the princess bathed in tears, and trembling from head to foot.

She turned as she heard the sound of his sword, and removed her handkerchief from his eyes.

'Fly,' she cried; 'fly while you have yet time, before that monster sees you.'

She said it, and she meant it; yet, when he had turned his back, she felt more forsaken than before. But in reality it was not more than a few minutes before he came back, galloping furiously on a horse he had borrowed, and carrying a huge mirror across its neck.

'I am in time, then,' he cried, dismounting very carefully, and placing the mirror against the trunk of a tree.

'Give me your veil,' he said hastily to the princess. And when she had unwound it from her head he covered the mirror with it.

'The moment the dragon comes near you, you must tear off the veil,' cried he; 'and be sure you hide behind the mirror. Have no fear; I shall be at hand.'

He and his horse had scarcely found shelter amongst some rocks, when the flap of the dragon's wings could be plainly heard. He tossed his head with delight at the sight of her, and approached slowly to the place where she stood, a little in front of the mirror. Then, still looking the monster steadily in the face, she passed one hand behind her back and snatched off the veil, stepping swiftly behind the tree as she did so.

The princess had not known, when she obeyed the orders of the Knight of the Fish, what she expected to happen. Would the dragon with snaky locks be turned to stone, she wondered, like the dragon in an old story her nurse had told her; or would some fiery spark dart from the heart of the mirror, and strike him dead? Neither of these things occurred, but, instead, the dragon stopped short with surprise and rage when he saw a monster before him as big and strong as himself. He shook his mane with rage and fury; the enemy in front did exactly the same. He lashed his tail, and rolled his red eyes, and the dragon opposite was no whit behind him. Opening his mouth to its very widest, he gave an awful roar; but the other dragon only roared back. This was too much, and with another roar which made the princess shake in her shoes, he flung himself upon his foe. In an instant the mirror lay at his feet broken into a thousand pieces, but as every piece reflected part of himself, the dragon thought that he too had been smashed into atoms.

It was the moment for which the Knight of the Fish had watched and waited, and before the dragon could find out that he was not hurt at all, the young man's lance was down his throat, and he was rolling, dead, on the grass.

Oh! what shouts of joy rang through the great city, when the youth came riding back with the princess sitting behind him, and dragging the horrible monster by a cord. Everybody cried out that the king must give the victor the hand of the princess; and so he did, and no one had ever seen such balls and feasts and sports before. And when they were all over the young couple went to the palace prepared for them, which was so large that it was three miles round.

The first wet day after their marriage the bridegroom begged the bride to show him all the rooms in the palace, and it was so big and took so long that the sun was shining brightly again before they stepped on to the roof to see the view.

'What castle is that out there,' asked the knight; 'it seems to be made of black marble?'

'It is called the castle of Albatroz,' answered the princess. 'It is enchanted, and no one that has tried to enter it has ever come back.'

THE DRAGON AND THE MIRROR

[*This illustration is reproduced in color between pages 74 and 75.*]

Her husband said nothing, and began to talk of something else ; but the next morning he ordered his horse, took his spear, called his bloodhound, and set off for the castle.

It needed a brave man to approach it, for it made your hair stand on end merely to look at it ; it was as dark as the night of a storm, and as silent as the grave. But the Knight of the Fish knew no fear, and had never turned his back on an enemy ; so he drew out his horn, and blew a blast.

The sound awoke all the sleeping echoes in the castle, and was repeated now loudly, now softly ; now near, and now far. But nobody stirred for all that.

'Is there anyone inside ? ' cried the young man in his loudest voice ; 'anyone who will give a knight hospitality? Neither governor, nor squire, not even a page ? '

'Not even a page ! ' answered the echoes. But the young man did not heed them, and only struck a furious blow at the gate.

Then a small grating opened, and there appeared the tip of a huge nose, which belonged to the ugliest old woman that ever was seen.

'What do you want ? ' said she.

'To enter,' he answered shortly. 'Can I rest here this night ? Yes or No ? '

'No, No, No ! ' repeated the echoes.

Between the fierce sun and his anger at being kept waiting, the Knight of the Fish had grown so hot that he lifted his visor, and when the old woman saw how handsome he was, she began fumbling with the lock of the gate.

'Come in, come in,' said she, 'so fine a gentleman will do us no harm.'

'Harm ! ' repeated the echoes, but again the young man paid no heed.

'Let us go in, ancient dame,' but she interrupted him.

'You must call me the Lady Berberisca,' she answered,

sharply; 'and this is my castle, to which I bid you welcome. You shall live here with me and be my husband.' But at these words the knight let his spear fall, so surprised was he.

'I marry *you*? why you must be a hundred at least!' cried he. 'You are mad! All I desire is to inspect the castle and then go.' As he spoke he heard the voices give a mocking laugh; but the old woman took no notice, and only bade the knight follow her.

Old though she was, it seemed impossible to tire her. There was no room, however small, she did not lead him into, and each room was full of curious things he had never seen before.

At length they came to a stone staircase, which was so dark that you could not see your hand if you held it up before your face.

'I have kept my most precious treasure till the last,' said the old woman; 'but let me go first, for the stairs are steep, and you might easily break your leg.' So on she went, now and then calling back to the young man in the darkness. But he did not know that she had slipped aside into a recess, till suddenly he put his foot on a trap door which gave way under him, and he fell down, down, as many good knights had done before him, and his voice joined the echoes of theirs.

'So you would not marry me!' chuckled the old witch. 'Ha! ha! Ha! ha!'

Meanwhile his brother had wandered far and wide, and at last he wandered back to the same great city where the other young knight had met with so many adventures. He noticed, with amazement, that as he walked through the streets the guards drew themselves up in line, and saluted him, and the drummers played the royal march; but he was still more bewildered when several servants in livery ran up to him and told him that the princess was sure something terrible had befallen him, and had made herself ill with weeping. At last it occurred to him that once more he had been taken for his brother. 'I had better say nothing' thought he ; 'perhaps I shall be able to help him after all.'

So he suffered himself to be borne in triumph to the palace, where the princess threw herself into his arms.

'And so you did go to the castle ? ' she asked.

'Yes, of course I did,' answered he.

'And what did you see there ? '

'I am forbidden to tell you anything about it, until I have returned there once more,' replied he.

'Must you really go back to that dreadful place ? ' she asked wistfully. 'You are the only man who has ever come back from it.'

'I must,' was all he answered. And the princess, who was a wise woman, only said : 'Well, go to bed now, for I am sure you must be very tired.'

But the knight shook his head. 'I have sworn never to lie in a bed as long as my work in the castle remains standing.' And the princess again sighed, and was silent.

Early next day the young man started for the castle, feeling sure that some terrible thing must have happened to his brother.

At the blast of his horn the long nose of the old woman appeared at the grating, but the moment she caught sight of his face, she nearly fainted from fright, as she thought it was the ghost of the youth whose bones were lying in the dungeon of the castle.

'Lady of all the ages,' cried the new comer, 'did you not give hospitality to a young knight but a short time ago ? '

'A short time ago ! ' wailed the voices.

'And how have you ill-treated him ? ' he went on.

'Ill-treated him ! ' answered the voices. The woman did not stop to hear more ; she turned to fly ; but the knight's sword entered her body.

'Where is my brother, cruel hag ? ' asked he sternly.

'I will tell you,' said she; 'but as I feel that I am going to die I shall keep that piece of news to myself, till you have brought me to life again.'

The young man laughed scornfully. 'How do you propose that I should work that miracle?'

'Oh, it is quite easy. Go into the garden and gather the flowers of the everlasting plant and some of dragon's blood. Crush them together and boil them in a large tub of water, and then put me into it.'

The knight did as the old witch bade him, and, sure enough, she came out quite whole, but uglier than ever. She then told the young man what had become of his brother, and he went down into the dungeon, and brought up his body and the bodies of the other victims who lay there, and when they were all washed in the magic water their strength was restored to them.

And, besides these, he found in another cavern the bodies of the girls who had been sacrificed to the dragon, and brought them back to life also.

As to the old witch, in the end she died of rage at seeing her prey escape her; and at the moment she drew her last breath the castle of Albatroz fell into ruins with a great noise.

[From *Cuentos, Oraciones, Adivinas recogidos por Fernan Caballaro.*]